BLESSED ARE THE CRACKED

By

Delphine Richards

Published in the United Kingdom in 2013 by Cambria Books; Carmarthenshire, Wales, United Kingdom

THE STORIES

Prologue - Time to Think.   5

Donald's Cat.   9

What Would Delyth Do?   73

Brown Cow's Legacy.   117

The Llanefa Triangle.   153

The Perfect Wife.   183

The Family Man.   195

Heatwave.   205

Dedication

For Hedd. 'I could not have done it without you.'

Prologue - Time to Think.

Tegwyn Takes Stock.

He has read the paper from cover to cover; finished the crossword and the Sudoku.

Again his eyes are drawn to the engraved carriage clock; the one they gave him when he retired. He wonders why the minute hand moves so slowly.

'What are you going to do when you retire, boss?' they used to ask him at Headquarters.

'Play golf. Go to the gym. Travel. Go to the theatre.' He would give the same answers. Until Jamie Bowen, (who, in Tegwyn's opinion, will go far once he passes his sergeant's exam), said, 'But you do all that already, sir.'

'Don't worry about my welfare,' Tegwyn had said, 'You'll have enough to worry about when the new DCI takes over. He won't be a soft touch like me!'

DS Alun Lewis had rolled his eyes behind Tegwyn's back.

Then, eight months before he retired, Gwenda had died suddenly. An embolism, they said and tried to explain it to him at the hospital, but he had just held up his hand and nodded. Tegwyn had dealt with death in many forms during his career – and even before then. He was angry that some young doctor felt the need to spell it out for him.

His retirement party passed in usual fashion. Lower ranking colleagues made speeches in which over-embellished accounts of his mistakes made everyone laugh. Goodwill toasts were proposed and everyone was careful not to mention the word 'wife'.

He tried to keep busy: walking, going to the gym and getting involved with new charities. It was probably the extra walking that brought things to a head and, six weeks ago, he had undergone a hip replacement operation. Just as well he had kept up his private medical insurance after retirement, he thinks wryly.

The physical healing process is going well, but the mental agony of spending so much time in an empty house that has lost its hub, is harder to bear. He realises how ironic it is to think of all the years Gwenda spent alone in this house while he worked on some major enquiry or other. Divine retribution, some might say.

'You ought to write a book,' Owen Bell, the landlord of the Poacher's used to say to him before he retired, 'All the things you've seen and dealt with...'

Since then, Emma has also said it, 'You should write a book, dad.'

But he knows she is only saying it out of a desperate attempt to fill the empty space in his life - the empty space that he didn't fully appreciate when Gwenda had occupied that very void.

But, the boredom of recovering from a hip replacement had planted the seed in his mind. He had even contacted Hywel, (or Tim as he's known these days,) to ask his advice.

Hywel writes fiction, but Tegwyn had assumed the basics were the same. Thorough research was the first move, Hywel had said. Then, a careful assessment of what was likely to provoke litigation. Tegwyn knew about litigation. The word didn't scare him as it would have done someone who had not spent his working life dealing with the law.

With another quick glance at the carriage clock, he grabs the walking stick and gets to his feet. Then a careful manoeuvre up the stairs towards the spare bedroom that doubles as a storage room for all the paperwork he has brought home over the years. Best to do it now, he thinks, before Emma calls in to see him. She will worry if she knows he has gone upstairs on his own - though he is perfectly capable of doing so. She is afraid he might fall. She had been there when the doctor said that his bones were not as dense as they should be, and that he needed to eat more dairy products. The thought of it turns his stomach as he crosses the landing!

He sits in the spare bedroom and starts opening drawers and filing cabinets. Early cases give away their date by the old fashioned typewriter print, while more recent ones are slick and computer processed. He starts to read - so many minor details he had forgotten.

The hours fly by and his mind is whirring with possibilities.

Then, a thought occurs to him. How much of each story will never be known to him? All the cases are tightly bound in legality and correct procedure, but what about the facts that will never see the public light of day? Things that only the victim and the defendant would have known about. The dead victim cannot speak and the defendant, well, how often can we take his or her version of events as an accurate record, he thinks?

Unfortunately, real crimes don't end like a Sherlock Holmes or Miss Marple story, he reflects. People don't assemble in the drawing room to hear the detective running through all the possibilities before finally pointing to the guilty party!

He thinks back even further to events during his childhood – the stuff that filled the stomach of the Llanefa gossip-machine – what significant parts have been lost?

Hywel was right, he realises. It was going to take a lot of research. He doesn't even know if he will actually end up writing anything. He cannot see why anyone would want to read half a story when the most interesting and revealing parts will always be kept secret.

If only the people themselves could tell the story, he thinks, a 'warts and all' account of how it all came to be. Now, there would be a book worth buying!

He picks up another file and continues reading.

Donald's Cat.

It was completely dark and she knew she was dying. She was so sure of this fact, that she could feel the darkness pressing around her body, squeezing the life out of her with its unseen fingers.

It wasn't just dark. It was black.

She had once been to art classes in the community centre. The tutor had said that there were no such colours as black or white. Black was just an absence of colours, he had said, while white was a combination of all colours that reflected the light.

Yes, that was it! Black was an absence of colour due to there being no light reflected.

He had been partly right, she thought. Black may not be a colour, but it did exist. She could verify that right now. She was surrounded by it in this prison.

The reason there was no light was... she pushed the thought away before her heart began to increase its rate. She had been calm for a long time and needed to stay that way. Otherwise, an increased heart rate meant she would use up more air...

It was because of the cat...

She passed a hand over her face. The sticky clamminess of her skin felt like a new experience. That was no surprise - she had never been in a dying situation before! She wiped her battered hand down her top; she still had her Home Help tabard on. She could feel the woven Llanefa Social Services emblem protruding from the breast pocket. Above that, her ID badge ambushed her fingers with its sharp corners. She tilted it upwards towards her face, eager to see if a trace of light reflected off its plastic surface. The badge felt strange - dusty but slippery too. She realised that the slipperiness was coming from her sore fingers. This must be what it was like to be blind, she thought. She again traced her ID badge, trying to make out the words 'Kay Jones'. The indentations felt alien to her sore fingers. It reminded her of the time they had all gone to the Crystal Maze in Pembrokeshire. She'd had to put her hand into a darkened hole and describe through a radio link to the others what she could feel, while they, in the next room, tried to identify the object from a list they had on their computer screens. Trish had been there that day – it had been part of a Hen Party celebration. Not that you could call Carol, who was then 45 years old and embarking on her third marriage, a hen. Broilers, Trish had called them. Trish could always be relied on to provide the comedy. Or had been...

The darkness gave Kay another squeeze to remind her where she was. She wondered how long she had been there? It felt like several hours, though she had no great hunger or thirst... yet. Darkness had a way of distorting time and distance. She couldn't even tell how far away from the walls she was. The only thing she knew for certain was that her arms and fingers hurt from the effort of trying to open the door. There was also a vague message coming from her bladder. She ignored it. Needing a pee was low on the list of problems.

She again started the unanswerable questions. Why had she parked in such a stupid place? Why had she moved the cat? Why had she felt guilty enough to come here?

Because she felt she owed it to Donald – that was why she had come here. He was such a nice old gent and it was her fault that he was so upset.

A silly thought struck her - she didn't even know the cat's name. She had only ever heard Donald calling it 'Puss' or 'the cat'.

'Don't go near the cat!' he had said so many times, 'Leave it alone. It doesn't like strangers.'

She had felt like saying that she wasn't really a stranger. She had been Home Helping for Donald for eighteen months. She would have thought that the cat would have got used to her. And she should have got used to the cat. But that had not happened. At least she had not been overly allergic to it. Not if she didn't go too close.

It used to lie on the cushion of the rocking chair and pretend to be asleep, but whenever Kay had glanced quickly at it, she would see that its eyes were only partly closed and the green irises would glint like marbles as it watched her. Its white feet were usually tucked underneath its body, but occasionally it would stretch out a paw, yawn and flex its claws meaningfully.

Kay didn't think that it was the cat itself that made her wheeze, but its hair. The cushion had become so heavily covered in a layer of tabby hairs and dandruff that she could no longer tell what colour the material was. There had been a musty smell surrounding the chair. When she thought about it, she realised that the chair was a shrine to human senses – smell, sight (those green-marble eyes that followed her like the Mona Lisa's), hearing (it growled at her when she dusted the mantelpiece – growled more like a dog that a cat), touch (of its horrible fine hair levitating at knee level) and even taste, the way she got that peppery flavour in her mouth when she had been too close to it.

She had been certain that her wheezing would improve if she could wash the cushion cover. But to do that, the cat would have to be moved and Donald would not hear of it. Each morning, when she went to Donald's Sheltered Housing bungalow, she had checked the rocking chair, hoping to see an empty warm dent in the cushion, but every day, the green marbles had assessed her. She had tried to 'accidentally' nudge the chair with the Hoover, hoping it would jump off and go outside, but it had only opened its eyes wider and given a warning flick of its tail.

Kay had realised that she was actually scared of the cat. The blatant way it looked at her suggested that it would attack her if she crossed the boundary of its patience. She had even had a nightmare where the cat had leapt up and grown into the size of a German Shepherd and begun to eat her alive. From then on, she had stopped trying to get the cat to move, but she was sure that one day it would be outside, doing whatever disgusting things cats did, and she would be able to wash the cushion.

She had once confided in Trish about the cat. She had sympathised with her.

'The thing is with cats,' Trish had said while they warmed up in Zumba class, 'is that they are so bloody sly. If a dog gets caught short and shits on the floor, it does it *there*, in the middle of the room. It more or less accuses you, *I asked to go out. You left me too long. Deal with it!* But a cat, it goes *behind* things and *under* things. It leaves its shit fermenting in places you won't find for a few days – and when you do, it's likely to be somewhere you don't expect to find shit and you'll put your hand in it. Cherie Blair said they were unhygienic creatures – she was right! If I was you, babes, I'd spray some air freshener or something at it...'

Trish was what they called 'sassy'. And what Paul had called a 'Swansea Jack' - even though Trish had not lived in Swansea for over twenty years. After the first time Trish had spent an evening with them, Paul had later said 'She's a typical Jack, isn't she?' It was a phrase that could be used in a complimentary way – the original Swansea Jack being a large, brave dog that had saved great numbers of people from drowning after a shipwreck - but Kay guessed that he had meant it in the derogatory way that Llanefa people spoke of those who were more forward and open than they were. In Llanefa, people of Kay's generation and older were often stuck in a time warp when it came to social skills. The Stiff Upper Lip may have been the domain of the English, but the Stiff Mind was Llanefa's alone.

A fresh wave of panic came over Kay and, for the hundredth time, she worked her away around the inside of her prison and hammered on the walls. Nothing happened and her fists hurt in a way that suggested that she had broken the skin.

She couldn't see anything or hear anything - not even the sound of the traffic from the nearby by-pass. She hoped that meant that the road had been closed for some reason. But the part of her mind that screamed at her to find a way out, an air supply... anything – announced cruelly that the cabin was sealed. Airtight.

She continued to work her way around the walls, cautiously feeling with her feet in case she stood on the cat. Panic and hope blossomed together when she couldn't find it. Had the cat found a way out? Reality was like a sharp thrust from a knife. Of course the cat hadn't found a way out. The cat was dead! Hadn't she sat in her prison listening to its slow purring and shallow breathing until it had stopped? She had even put out her hand to *almost* stroke it as it neared the end, but the thought that it could see her while she couldn't see it had made her hand hover in mid air before returning to her side.

But, knowing it was dead didn't stop her imagining that she could still feel the green marble eyes watching her. They said that cats could see in the dark...

'Don't be so fucking stupid!' she whispered, surprising herself with the unfamiliar profanity. 'Dead cats can't see in the dark or anywhere else.'

Save your breath, babes. Trish's Zumba class advice came to her. Good advice here too.

She slid down the wall and stretched out her legs. Something *clingy* moved against her calf. Kay screamed and leapt to her feet. The thing stayed with her leg for a moment, then fell away.

Slowly, Kay inched back towards it. She crouched on the floor, making cautious sweeping movements with her hand. She subconsciously held her breath and tensed her leg muscles ready for flight to ... where?

Cobwebs, she told herself without conviction. She continued to sweep her left hand from side to side. She could feel nothing but the gritty, dusty floor of the cabin. She exhaled and rested her right hand beside her and screamed again as her palm came to rest on the dead cat.

It didn't move.

With some revulsion she felt it all over. It was definitely dead. She checked again, feeling the head, along the furry ridged ribs and down its tail. A sticky substance transferred itself to her hand. She pulled it away quickly and, for a second, the tail came with her before falling back on to the floor. Relief followed instantly as she realised that it had been the cat's tail that had stuck to her leg. She kept her fingers spread out and slowly brought her hand to her face (it was surprising how difficult it was to tell how close her hand *was* to her face) and sniffed cautiously. It smelled of some kind of motor fuel. She wiped her throbbing hand on the dusty floor and then on her tabard – wincing while she did so.

If she had been religious, she would have thought the situation was punishment for her actions.

Donald had been furious! His normally placid manner had been replaced by a raised voice and wide-open eyes.

'What did you do to it?' he had nearly shouted, his almost-lost Scottish accent becoming stronger.

'I just wanted to wash the cush...'

'I've told you to leave it alone! How many times have I said that?'

'I know. I'm sorry. I just...'

'It's not used to fast traffic. What if it tries to cross the by-pass? I just can't believe you made it go out...'

'I'm so sorry. I'm sure it will come back once I've gone.'

Kay had honestly believed that the cat would wait until she was out of sight before it slinked back.

Still crouched on the floor by the dead cat, she replayed it all in her mind. She had waited until Donald was on the toilet, then put on her Marigolds, covered her nose with her tabard and, before courage deserted her, quickly lifted the cat off the chair. It had been surprised for a millisecond. Then it had made a tortured sound while twisting its body and leaving a bloody scratch down Kay's arm before she dropped it. It had kept up the noise while it ran into the kitchen, up onto the worktop and out through the window. Kay realised that she had never seen it on its feet before.

The next morning, (a bad day for Kay even before she crossed the threshold of the Sheltered Housing bungalow), Donald's fury had been replaced by a quiet contempt in which he had asked her to leave his house. The cat had not come home.

Kay had been genuinely upset. She had always got on well with all her clients. She could understand that Donald was fond of the cat, but thought that the act of lifting the cat off a chair shouldn't have had such a dramatic result. (Not knowing at that point that far more trauma awaited her on this, The Worst Day of Her Life.) She had wished she could have spoken to Trish about it, but that kind of thinking was not going to help...

Instead, she had carried on with her work, visiting the other three regulars on her list. The last one, Ethel Davies, lived fairly close to the only big supermarket in Llanefa. When she had said she needed milk and bread, Kay had gone over to get them for her. Coming out of the CutCost store, she had glanced across at the by-pass which ran steeply above the side of the car park. Suppose the cat *had* crossed the by-pass and was lying dead or injured at the side of the road? Donald's house was not that far away from the road...

Taking the bread and milk back to Ethel, she had decided that she would drive along the by-pass in both directions.

She had driven at a cautious speed while apprehensively scanning the hard shoulder and grass bank for signs of a cat's body. The grass was fairly short following its late summer cut and she had been certain that it would be easy to spot without having to pull in or getting out to check.

Coming back on the eastbound carriageway, her attention had been taken by the cluster of houses on the other side of the road. The by-pass had effectively divided Llanefa by cutting off a corner of the small town. The residents had been opposed to the plan when it was first made public, but there were too few of them to alter what the Highways Authority had decreed. In a bid to appease the dissenters, a pedestrian underpass had been created and joined the car park of CutCost to the lane that approached Llwyncelyn Drive and its neighbouring roads.

Kay had driven back to CutCost's car park, locked her Renault Clio and set off towards the underpass. Although she had walked through it once before, she looked at it with new eyes – from a cat's perspective – and had been disappointed that its smooth walls and overhead lights did not provide a suitable bolthole for an offended cat.

Two boys of about fifteen had passed her in the opposite direction. Although it was only lunchtime they were not in school uniform and had a guilty look about them. She was suddenly glad that she had left her handbag stowed under the front seat of her car. To the best of her knowledge there had never been a mugging in Llanefa and she had no plans to change that statistic by becoming the first victim. The boys' hooded jackets and low-slung crotches of their jeans gave an impression that their bodies were too long for their legs. They had stared at her at intermittent one-second intervals as if wondering why someone f   rom Planet Adult would be walking alone through the tunnel.

'You haven't seen a cat through here, have you?' she had asked.

Their grunts had seemed to indicate that they had not seen a cat; that they were not absolutely certain what a cat was! They had loped away in the typical gait that teenage boys have.

Coming out on the other side, Kay had wondered where to look next. Llwyncelyn Drive had seemed an unlikely destination... She had turned around, about to give up the search, when her vision had rested on the grass bank running up towards the roof of the underpass. About a quarter of a mile further along and adjacent to the new road she had remembered that there was an old works service area that had been used when the by-pass was being built. Since the road had been finished, the service area lay abandoned with the remains of workmen's cabins, rusty machinery and unidentifiable metal that resembled a pile of chicken bones pushed to the side of the plate at the end of a meal. Apart from occasional teenagers on mountain bikes, it would be a haven for the cat. It could probably even find mice if it was hungry!

As she climbed down the other side of the grass bank and made her way towards the service area, she had realised that there were more hiding places than she had imagined. Although the contractors had cleared away much of the equipment, a lot of debris seemed to have been forgotten and bore the wounds of eighteen months of neglect. Two old Portakabins with broken windows and no doors sat side by side on the stony ground. She had stepped in and looked under the remaining worktops and inside drawers. There had been graffiti everywhere. The words 'Trish is Lush' had given her a little start until she re-read and saw that it said 'Tosh is Lush'. Kay had wondered how long she could expect to get negative feelings when she heard or saw the name Trish.

Some of the other equipment outside was small enough to check quickly – a cement mixer drum, an up-turned digger bucket, the remains of the outer fence stacked in a pile – and she soon exhausted her supply. The only other structure on the site was a windowless cabin about the size of a large walk-in wardrobe. It rested lopsidedly on the rocky ground and the door stood ajar by an inch or two. It looked like a very large safe or very small shipping container. She had suddenly remembered that the construction team had used explosives while building the by-pass. There had been opposition to that, too. This dark brown edifice must have been one of the secure explosives stores, she had thought. She had walked up close to it. The door had looked heavy and immobile. She had put her hand on the handle and pulled. To her surprise, it had swung easily towards her, the heaviness of it making her sway slightly as it creaked against her.

She had seen the cat straight away. Half curled at the back of the cabin, its leg at a strange angle. It had turned its head in her direction and growled weakly. It had tried to get up, but collapsed back on to its side with legs pedalling hopelessly in the air.

'Shit!'

She would have to take it to the vet, she had told herself. She had stepped into the cabin and felt a familiar wheezing developing as she walked slowly towards it.

'Puss, Puss. Come on, bach.'

As she had got nearer, the floor had given a sudden lurch and metallic bang. At the same time, everything went black as the door had slammed shut behind her.

Panic had overridden everything else and she had thrown herself at the door, pushing and kicking while her breath wheezed in her throat.

She would never have guessed that she contained such energy as she had pushed and kicked at the door. She had shouted too - loud, hysterical shrieks which were broken by bouts of wheezing and coughing. She had tried to calm herself and think logically, but these periods were short lived and she rapidly resumed her attack on the door – or where she had assumed the door to be.

Her mind had given her a cruel glimpse of her recent history and she had pictured herself leaving the car at CutCost, shoving her handbag under the seat and, before that, putting her mobile phone into the bag before going to get Ethel's shopping. Had put it in there because of the call she didn't want to have to answer. Nevertheless, in the darkness, she had checked her tabard pocket in case...

The wheezing had plateaued into a steady irritation that made her cough at regular intervals – the last cough of each bout becoming a retching sound. She had realised that the harder she breathed, the more likely she was to react to the cat's fur. She had tried to slow her breathing to a normal rate. I-i-in. O-o-u-t. Just like they did at the end of Zumba. Winding down, stretching slowly, waiting for their bodies to utilise the extra oxygen. That's what the leggy Zumba Instructor used to say.

'What extra oxygen?' Trish's voice piped up in her mind, 'You've worked me so hard, all my extra oxygen's been coming out of my arse!'

Kay remembered that comment which had resulted in the whole class dissolving into hysterical laughter. Even the Instructor, who tended to take herself quite seriously, had eventually giggled. Everyone had known what Trish was like. Who would have guessed that such a funny, likeable person...?

Extra oxygen! The thought had hit Kay as violently as if she had been knocked over.

She had put her hands in front of her and felt around the walls to check for draughts. She had even put her finger in her mouth to wet it, then held it near to the wall, the way her grandfather used to show her how to check for wind direction. Nothing. She had knelt down and done the same all around the bottom edge of the cabin. She knew she had gone all the way around when she had returned to the cat twice. It hadn't growled at her, but had purred loudly. Kay had felt a spike of hate in her mind. Was the cat *enjoying* the fact that they were trapped? Wasn't that why cats purred? Or did they purr when they were in great pain too?

But that had been ... how many hours ago? She never wore a watch and Kay's heart started to beat faster again as panic stifled reason. How long had it taken for the cat to die from its injuries? And, if no-one came to let her out, how long would it take her to die from thirst and starvation? Or from lack of air?

At least the wheezing had stopped. She guessed that the fact that the cat was dead had helped. If its skin was not constantly shedding cells, then she was not likely to breathe them in. She was suddenly overcome by a bout of sobbing - wet, snotty sounds that echoed back at her in the confines of the cabin.

'For they shall let in the light.'

The phrase popped into her mind as her crying slowed to a child-like hiccupping.

Where had that come from? If only she *had* some light. Her eyelids felt stretched to twice their normal size as she attempted to glean a molecule of light from the blackness.

Her breathing slowed as she calmed herself. If the cabin really *was* airtight, she needed to save her oxygen supply. Was the inside of a car airtight, she wondered? If so, how did people breathe when they went on long journeys? On a warm day, you might open a window, but in the winter, how was it that car drivers didn't run out of oxygen? She comforted herself with the memory of the previous year when she and Paul had driven to Edinburgh to take Llinos to the Veterinary College to start her course. They had made several stops on the way up, but most the return journey had been a non-stop affair through rain and darkness. (Hah, darkness! What had she known of darkness *then*?) But, and she felt a surge of hope at this, they had the windows closed and neither of them had suffered from oxygen starvation! The cabin felt just the same as the inside of a car, but bigger. *Was* it airtight? She tried to remember what she'd read in the Llanefa Guardian before the by-pass was built and the subject of explosives had come up. Didn't explosives need to 'breathe'? She knew that the contractors, Taylor, Payne and Rowe (TPR Construction) had been told they had to build an outer fence and an inner fence around the explosive store. She also had an idea that they were instructed to make an earth bank around it as well. Hadn't there been some directive that an earth mound would take the brunt of an explosion if an accident happened? The remains of the earth mound were still there, she realised. She had noticed it while looking for the cat. In her mind's eye, she relished that view again – the moments before she had been incarcerated. Why hadn't she taken more notice of the angle of the cabin on the rocks? It was obvious to her at this stage, with her Wise Woman's Hindsight, that it had been partially moved and was not stable – the reason that her weight had tilted it sufficiently to make the door slam shut. She could see it all now; like a cruel recurring nightmare that manages to terrify the sleeper each time it happens. Except that with a nightmare, you woke, covered in sweat, put the light on...

'For they shall let in the light.'

Why was that phrase going round in her head? She got to her feet and felt all round the walls again, looking for a microdot of light and feeling for a weakness or latch that she might have missed. Her hands were so sore that she wasn't certain that she would recognise a handle or catch if she touched it. She stumbled over the cat's body before falling to her knees and sobbing once more. She suddenly stopped her crying. Something had changed. She felt around the floor with her hands and soon found the cat's body again. The fur was soft but the body underneath was as hard as wood. Rigor mortis had set in.

Kay knew about rigor mortis. Over the years, she had found many of her clients dead in bed and knew it took several hours to happen. How long would it take for a cat, she wondered? It felt as though she had been trapped for more than a few hours, but, if she had a limited air supply, then it was *better* for her that the time she had spent in the cabin only *felt* longer than it really was. It meant she had many more hours of breathing time if there was no air coming in. (But that didn't apply as there *was* air coming in – just like the inside of a car, she reminded herself.)

When would Paul notice her absence? What time *was* it? She pictured him coming home from work and noting that her car was not there. How long would he sit indoors watching the six o'clock news and The One Show and Eastenders before he tried her mobile? When would he be hungry enough to try to find her? The thought of Paul being hungry made her stomach growl – never mind him, it seemed to say – what about me! And when he kept on ringing, would anyone hear her phone in the CutCost car park? Would anyone she knew be there to hear it and say, 'Isn't that Kay's car? Why doesn't she have her mobile with her? Do you think she's all right?'

But that was where the daydream became a nightmare. Even if that unlikely scenario took place, what would be the next step? What was the likelihood of that hero saying, 'She must be in trouble. Let's check the old TPR service area'? NFC, as Trish would have said – no fucking chance!

Her mind desperately created situations in which someone would put two and two together and make four hundred! She worked out the logistics. She was less than half a mile away from her car, locked in an old explosives store on an abandoned site; it would be at least the next day before Linda, her supervisor, noticed that she had not handed in her work sheet for the day. And maybe even the day after that, when clients or their relatives rang to complain that she had not made her allocated visits. A better chance was that Paul would try to find out where she was...

Oh yes! And he could do what, exactly? Her rational mind was giving her answers she didn't want to hear.

And if this thing was airtight, how much breathing time did she have? (It's not airtight – it's just like the inside of a car, she contradicted herself again.)

And if it wasn't airtight, how long could she survive without food or water before someone found her? Hadn't there been talk that this old site was going to be developed into a fast food outlet?

Would they only find her and Donald's cat as shrunken, dried out corpses when work started on that project?

Another panic attack took over and she hurled herself at the walls and door of her prison. Her too-full bladder bounced inside her but she kept on kicking and pushing at the unseen walls. In desperation, she even leapt up to try hitting the low roof in case there was a weakness there, some kind of split or crack.

'Blessed are the cracked.'

She slowed her efforts as the odd phrase filled her mind. A bizarre memory of where she had heard it before materialised in her head. It was one of the last emails she had received from Trish - an attempt to re-establish their friendship. It had been some cartoon images of people and animals doing funny, stupid things. Underneath it had read, 'A friend is someone who thinks you are a good egg. Even if you are a little cracked'

Then, under a picture of a cracked egg, was the phrase 'Blessed are the cracked. For they shall let in the light'

This memory overcame Kay and she slid to the floor, sobbing. She cried for herself, for Trish and for everything that had happened. As she sat against the wall, hugging her knees and with her hands throbbing, a great weariness came over her and her sobs faded away.

The dream came suddenly. She was hiding in the wardrobe in her bedroom – except it wasn't really her bedroom, her wardrobe was not big enough to hide inside – she was watching through the keyhole (why there was a keyhole was a mystery to her, even in her dream). She was waiting to catch Paul and Trish. She could hear their voices talking about mundane things – why this year's carrots were so poor, were they out of bread and milk – but she couldn't see them. At one point, Paul entered the bedroom to change his shoes. He didn't look at the wardrobe but he said, 'I know you're there and you won't catch me out' before leaving the room and switching off the light, leaving her in darkness.

Kay jumped awake and tried to push open the wardrobe door before comprehension kicked in. A new wave of panic gripped her and she threw herself at the walls of the cabin, her breath coming in great, ineffective whoops. The air was running out...

'*Stop it!*'

Trish's voice in her head, exactly as it had happened all those months ago.

Kay stood, panting against the wall. Yes, stop it - the air was *not* running out.

What had Trish said? 'Stop it! You are SO wrong. Me and Paul? NFC!'

It had been a shock – the way she had suddenly come out with that.

Kay folded up that unwelcome thought and tucked it away in the place that also held the before and after. Instead, she knelt down to feel all over the surface of the floor. The grit and dust formed small mounds in places and she scraped it away hoping to find a corroded part that was definitely letting in air. Every few inches she found a slightly raised metal band which had obviously been used to strengthen the floor when the cabin had been made. She tried plucking at the bands with her raw, battered fingers. Still she continued, inch by inch, on her knees like a crime scene investigator until she realised that her discomfort was becoming unbearable; her bladder was demanding attention. She realised at that moment how many hours must have passed while she was trapped. Everyone used to remark on her ability to go all day without needing a pee.

'You must have got a bladder like a camel, babes,' Trish used to say.

And that was the next dilemma in Kay's mind – should she pee in the corner of the cabin or try to save it – a small part of reason was suggesting that she needed to keep as much fluid as possible inside her. She told herself that it was a stupid theory – how could her urine be reabsorbed to stop her becoming dehydrated! Besides, her bladder was not just feeling uncomfortable, but in pain. Even the tops of her thighs ached with the need to urinate.

She felt around the walls until she found the 90 degree angle of one of the corners. She pulled down her underwear, squatted and let it go. The relief was unbelievable when it came. Her bladder had been full for so long that, for a second, nothing happened. As if her body had been denied for such a great length of time that it questioned whether she really was giving it permission to go ahead.

She felt the heat rise off the urine against her thighs and she realised how cold she was. Not freezing cold, but an uncomfortable coldness. For a second, she thought about trying to stop in mid flow – saving fluid and body heat – but her bladder was a like a racehorse after the tape goes up and there was to be no stopping it until there was nothing left to void. She could feel the urine running under one shoe, warming the side of her canvas loafer where the stitching was. She shuffled forward and pulled her tabard off over her head. Bunching it into a ball, she used a part of it to wipe herself before placing it to one side – where she thought the floor was clear of urine. She may have been running out of air or dying of thirst, but no way was she going to have a drippy fanny, she told herself, before realising how like Trish she sounded.

She pulled up her underwear and carefully moved over a few feet, away from the puddle. Once she had solved that discomfort, her hunger seemed to intensify and her stomach gurgled in protest at the injustice of having been relegated to less importance than the bladder.

Kay rubbed her arms briskly, but only managed to make her stomach rumble louder. Kay wondered if she really was hungry or whether it was thirst. What was it Trish used to say – *When you're hungry, drink some water. Your brain can't tell the difference. That's why we put on weight. We should be drinking instead.'*

That had been excellent advice, but not a lot of use to her here! And Trish's diet plan may have worked well in the past, but Kay's mind had taken on a cruel streak; I've just discovered the best diet in the world, she told herself. The Kay Jones Diet would be a runaway success – spend a week in a locked cabin and watch the weight fall off! This thought produced another sobbing episode and she sat down and drew her knees up again.

She hoped that Paul would now be making moves to try to find her. Maybe Llinos would phone home for a catch-up. At least she would spur him into taking some action if he adopted his usual laid-back approach to her disappearance as he did to most other things. But, would Llinos be able to come up with any ideas as to *where exactly* she was? The answer, sadly, was – no!

Kay tried to remember if she had told *anyone* about the thing with the cat.

The answer, again, was an instant 'No'. She had had had other things on her mind.

Except... what about the boys she had seen in the underpass? She had another daydream where the boys were sitting at home watching the local news. Her disappearance was the first item; one of the boys would see it, do a double take and ring his friend. She could visualise it – one of them ringing the other.

'Did you just see the news? That woman who's missing? Isn't that the woman we saw in the underpass looking for a cat when we were bunking off from school? Do you think we should ring the police?'

Then the police would decide that anyone searching for a cat near the underpass would go to the old service area.....

'Stop it! You are SO wrong.'

If her chances of survival depended on the boys, then she was toast, she realised. Apart from the fact that they had probably forgotten they had ever seen her, they were teenagers – nothing would force them to admit they were somewhere they shouldn't have been. Unless they phoned anonymously, her desperate mind suggested... Oh yes, and how many teenagers did she know who watched the news! And anyway, her disappearance probably wouldn't warrant a feature on the local news. (Well, maybe in a few days' time, her spiteful mind implied, when it's too late...)

She breathed in and out deliberately. Trying to keep calm, she told herself, but knowing she was also testing the air. Were there any signs that the air was thinning? Instantly, her heart leapt into action and her lungs drew huge amounts of air into her body. Her throat reacted by becoming constricted and she clawed at the clothes at her neck. Her breathing began to whoop uncontrollably and she turned around in stir-crazy circles, hitting her face against the unseen wall in an attempt to get out.

Stop it!

She stopped, her heart slowing a little and tears running down her face making tiny salty trickles into the corner of her mouth. She licked at them.

It was a panic attack. There was plenty of air.

She suddenly remembered starting to tell Paul about the cat the previous night, but he'd had a phone call from a friend who was looking for a second-hand car trailer so the story hadn't been told. Besides, Kay reasoned with herself, the cat had not been *officially* missing then. And anyway, the spiteful little voice in her mind piped up again, she'd had other things to think about that evening...

She wondered how long it would take before *she* was considered *officially* missing. Didn't the police adopt a wait-and-see attitude to missing non-vulnerable adults? Unless someone found her car...?

A further worrying thought was the idea that Paul would be taken in for questioning and valuable breathing time would be lost. (I can breathe, she told herself sternly).

She licked at her dry lips. The thought of water was torturing her. She pictured the bottle of Brecon Carreg she carried in her car and punished herself even further with the image of drinking it all in three or four gulps. The thought made her tongue feel as long as a dog's. She imagined that if she was rescued at that moment, she would be able to dunk her face into a bucket of water and lap it up in great pocketfuls, feeling it run down her throat and over her chin and neck. Or, better still, she could plunge her head into it and drink as deeply as a horse. The thought tortured her until the image of the dog returned to her mind...

Police dogs! Would they be able to track her? She could see them in her mind, following a scent from her car, through the tunnel, over the grass bank, the door being opened, the dog licking her face and wagging its tail; just like a scene from one of those films they put on at Christmas time. What were they called? She pictured a golden and white collie dog...

'It's not like Lassie Come Home, this canine scent recognition thing' Llinos's voice reminded her. They had been talking about her veterinary course when she was home over the summer. Llinos had been studying the difference in sensory abilities within several species.

'They follow crushed grasses, disturbed earth, that kind of stuff,' she had said, 'They can identify an individual's scent but not well enough to track a criminal through a full football stadium!'

Llinos had gone on to explain about scent receptors and how they worked, but it had all been too much for Kay to take in. She had just listened in fulfilled amazement at the amount of knowledge that had accumulated in her daughter's brain.

Kay was so proud of her. Llinos had wanted to be a vet since she was seven years old and Kay had caught her trying to put Sticking Plasters on their Jack Russell.

If only Llinos had still been home, Kay wished. But, although the course had not yet re-started she was back in Edinburgh doing some work experience with a zoo vet there. Kay had secret plans to throw a huge party when (there was no 'if' in her mind) Llinos qualified. This thought produced another episode of crying. How would her little girl cope with the death of her mother in such a terrible way? And what if there were questions asked about the other thing as there were bound to be now ... How unfair it was to leave Llinos with no answers. Llinos was very perceptive. She was the only one who had asked her if everything was all right after the time Kay had seen Trish and Paul...

In customary fashion, Kay had lied and said that all was fine, that she had a headache (she had a headache now, too) – the usual avoidance tactics.

Buttoning it all up had been the best way in Kay's mind. Of course, both Paul and Trish had been at great pains to explain, but it had sounded false and panicky to Kay. She had thought them both insensitive. If they were having an affair, they should have had the decency to make sure they did it well out of her sight; that had been her reaction at the time. She had only gone upstairs to change for the Zumba class while Trish waited with Paul downstairs. Over the months, Paul had accepted Trish as a friend – despite his initial assessment of her – and found her fun to have around, as did everyone else.

Kay had hardly reached upstairs when she realised that she had left her tracksuit bottoms downstairs in the utility room, having washed and dried them after the last class. She hurried downstairs in her bare feet, glancing quickly into the living room before she dashed across the hallway. The words, 'I'm just having a senior moment,' travelled from her mind to her throat and stayed there, as she saw Trish on the sofa with Paul almost astride her! Of course, they were both fully clothed and it looked more like horseplay than anything else, but it also seemed as though they had grabbed a moment of intimacy as soon as they had been left alone.

She must have made some noise – a gasp of horror maybe – when Paul looked up and sprang back from his position. Trish also looked across at her – a strange look, Kay had realised afterwards.

'She fell!'

'My knee...'

Both spoke at once with the urgent tones of the guilty.

'I need to take more water with it, babes,' Trish had said, her voice shaking as she looked across at Kay.

'OK now?' Paul had asked her.

'Yes, babes, don't fuss,' she had said before looking over at Kay, 'My knee just gave way - a good excuse to get out of the really difficult moves tonight!'

'Oh,' Kay had said, 'as long as you're ok...'

They had both been very quiet that evening. Kay had refused to even think of the incident in case thought caused a discussion. And that was not happening, she had told herself.

Throughout the Zumba class, she had noted Trish's ability to do everything the instructor had told them. A thought had entered her mind that someone who had lied about having fallen should have been more accurate in carrying it through. She had squashed that thought instantly.

When she had arrived home, Paul had been unusually alert. His normal TV-watching pose, with one calf resting on the thigh of the other leg, had been replaced with an upright sitting position.

'That was weird,' he had said with no preamble, 'she just went down like a ton of bricks. I thought she'd fainted. I practically had to lift her. Is she ok now?'

'Oh Trish?' she'd said, as if the whole incident had never registered on her mind (and lurked like a predator all through the Zumba class), 'Yes, seems fine now. I'm making some tea. Do you want one?'

And that had been it.

In her dark prison, Kay realised she was calming down, her breathing returning to normal as she stood next to the wall of the cabin. She could feel her breath creating a damp mist on the metallic wall. She felt a huge yawn developing. She gave in to it and followed it up with several others. There was a weariness seeping right through her.

'It must be late,' she whispered to herself. She had no idea why she was whispering, but she knew that if she heard her own normal speaking volume, it would compound the loneliness and desperation.

She turned with her back to the wall and leaned against it before sliding down into a sitting position once again. The yawning increased and she realised that she needed to sleep for a little while. The wall and floor were hard so she leaned across and patted her hand on the ground to try to find her rolled up tabard. Her palm landed in something wet and cold. With disgust she realised it was her urine. She wiped her palm back and forth on the dusty floor. The discovery set off another unpleasant possibility. Shouldn't the urine have evaporated if there was air circulating in the cabin? It was certainly obvious that the floor had no weakness in it or the urine would have drained out. Her tiredness disappeared instantly as the old concern revived itself in her mind – how much air did she have left?

She replayed the car interior scenario again to reassure herself that she would not suffocate, but, at the back of her brain, the cruel part was showing her a pie-chart with her air supply divided into portions of useable and toxic gases. Sections of something she had read recently flooded into her mind '...volume of oxygen to the lungs not equal to the content of oxygenated cells in the blood... respiratory failure...causing the heart to stop working...'

She even recalled an instance when one of their clients had died following a faulty chimney at his house. There had been an inquest, and it had been explained how the gases had built up over a timeframe of around twelve hours. Kay knew that her circumstances were different, but the question of how long a certain amount of air would last one person in a confined space still popped up in her mind like a sadistic Jack-in-the-box. Had she been in this prison for more than twelve hours? She believed that it had been much longer, but reason suggested that it only *felt* that way.

Her palm was sore and stinging from where she had put it in the puddle of urine. She again felt around for the tabard and this time managed to find it without mishap. She rubbed her hand on the material in an effort to rid her skin of any acidic residue from the urine. The pain took her breath away and she cradled one hand in the other and gently blew on the sore part.

Save your breath, babes.

She leaned back against the wall again. The whole situation with Trish had been so unpleasant! After the sofa incident, things had changed pretty quickly. Kay started to find excuses not to go to the Zumba class. The few times that Paul and Trish were in the same room together, she had imagined that she saw nervous glances passing between them. Kay had stopped popping in to see

Trish in the admin office when she dropped her work sheets off. Office gossip had offered several reasons for the obvious cooling in their friendship, but both women remained tight-lipped on the subject. They spoke to each other when it was necessary – usually in the company of other people (who tried to absorb any information with feigned indifference).

Occasionally, they bumped into each other with no-one else around. These had been the times that Kay had found the most difficult. She had kept the conversations at a neutral level – babbling at times to fill the space to stop Trish from raising the subject of Paul. Kay had not realised how obvious her feelings had been to Trish. Until the last time at the office.

Kay had been asked to sign an acceptance form for a new expenses system at work and she had gone to Trish's office to do so. Trish had gone to get the form for her and, on the way back to her desk, had tripped and fallen neatly in three stages – her knees, hip and finally upper body hitting the carpet in the wide space between desk and wall.

Kay had watched it happen as if in slow motion and had no doubt that Trish would have been unhurt. As she knelt down to help Trish up - her mind had been sounding a siren-like warning while she offered her hand. Anger built up in an instant. She had flashed back to the night of the Zumba class. Very convenient, she had thought, just a little more convincing needed to press home the fact that Trish had a dodgy knee. She must think I'm stupid, she had thought.

Trish had got to her knees, stared at her, then got to her feet.

'Stop it! You are SO wrong. Me and Paul? NFC!'

Kay had signed her form in silence and left the office without a word. It had been the last contact between them before things had taken on a new dimension.

Sitting in her prison on the abandoned work site, Kay felt her body winding down again. The tiredness was creeping back and her eyes felt heavy. She tilted her head back against the wall and let the sleep come to her. In what seemed like a short while, her head fell to one side and made her neck hurt. She felt around for the

31

tabard again, bunched it into a tight ball on the floor and lay down on her side with her head on it. Parts of the floor seemed to be digging into her side, so she sat up and swept away at the floor with her forearm before lying down again. This time, her anxious mind only put up a short fight before she drifted into another sleep.

She slept deeply, a result of exhaustion and mental trauma. When she woke suddenly, it took a few seconds to remember where she was. Panic brought her to her feet and stumbling on half-numb limbs to the nearest wall. She was already breathing rapidly, searching for a way out and the realisation that she had already covered this ground only made her hyperventilate. Hysterical sobbing took over and she sunk to her knees with the effort of breathing and crying.

Bad idea.

The awareness that she had had another dream while asleep on the floor drifted into her mind – the content becoming clearer as she calmed her breathing. She and Trish were standing in the toilets at work. Both were dressed for Zumba class in tracksuit bottoms and T-shirts and were putting on make-up in front of the mirrors.

The dream-Kay had turned to Trish and said, 'I'm sorry, Trish. Killing you was a bad idea.'

'Bad idea,' Trish had agreed, still applying mascara, 'I've got to go. I'm late for the zoo vet.'

The wide-awake Kay thought about her dream for a moment before whispering into the darkness, 'I really am sorry, Trish.'

She wondered what Trish would have done if she had been in here with her now. Probably, Trish would have entertained them both! She would have listed every man she had slept with – and graded him on technique! A fleeting image of Paul sneaked into her mind and she switched it off guiltily. Trish would have taken their minds off the awfulness of slowly suffocating (I am not suffocating, she told herself) by relating the five worse bikini waxes or smear tests she'd had. It was exactly what she'd done when four of them had broken down on the way home from the

National AGM (which had only been an excuse to call in the Designer Outlet off the M4 on the way home). Trish had been an endless source of funny stories – all allegedly true. Her account of a minor gynaecological procedure while they had waited for the RAC recovery van had rendered them all helpless with laughter.

There I was, girls, knees up in the air and fanny taking centre stage when the doctor looked over his mask at me and said, "Have you been eating lunch?". Well, that set me thinking, WHAT THE FUCK HAS HE SEEN DOWN THERE TO MAKE HIM THINK I'VE BEEN EATING LUNCH? A bit of salad or something? But I just said, "No but I had a bit of toast for breakfast".

Then he peeps over his mask again and says in a louder voice, "HAVE YOU BEEN BLEEDING MUCH?"

Kay felt the hint of a smile behind the corners of her lips – every sexually mature woman in Llanefa had heard about that one. Trish had been such a case!

Another little surge of hope came into Kay's mind. She felt that she had been asleep for hours - tried to convince herself that it had been hours - and the air felt just the same to her. (But when it's gone, it's gone, her rational self reminded her). Didn't that mean that there had to be air coming in *somewhere?* She put her hand out to touch the sides of the cabin. Her sore hands refused to tell her anything so she stood up and pressed the side of her face against the wall. It was damp with condensation. The air *was* running out. She knew it had to be. It was like the inside of a plastic bottle left out in the sun. She had no knowledge of how she felt that this was right, but no other explanation seemed possible to her. She felt another bout of sobbing developing, but as the tightness in her throat started, her eyes refused to shed any tears. Her mouth was so dry that she was sure she was becoming severely dehydrated. She had a sudden urge to lick the wall of the cabin, certain that it would give her some relief. She moved her jaws in a gum-chewing action. A small amount of saliva developed under her tongue and she swallowed it gratefully though her throat protested – her gullet felt as though it was breaking into tiny cracks. Her head was pounding in time to her heart. She could almost hear the beats and imagined that they sounded dry and laboured.

A nasty thought of how it would be like to die of thirst blossomed in her imagination. She pictured the tightening of her throat; her tongue swelling and blocking her airways. It made her think again of Trish. This time, tears did come, along with a weakness that sent her to her knees. Her shin landed across a raised metal band which scraped the skin. She fell sideways and landed on the dead cat. She heard her own crying voice 'Noooooh!' like a child that had been told she couldn't have an ice-cream. She tried to roll away from the cat's body when she became aware that something had changed again.

She came to her knees, breathing heavily through her mouth as her nostrils were too blocked with tears and mucus. Cautiously, she put out her throbbing hand and felt around on the floor. She found the cat's body again. Yes, it was different. It took a moment to work it out. The stiffness had all but gone! The last time she had touched the cat, it had been cold and hard. It was still cold, but there was some flexibility to it! She knew that it took longer for rigor to pass than it did to develop. Just *how* long had she been here? And how long had she slept?

Kay had never known thirst as intense as she was feeling then. So there *must* be air coming in, she reasoned with herself, you need air more than you need water so therefore you would run out of air before running out of fluid. In her confused mind she could not see the flaw in this theory. Her head pounded as she tried to work out how long a human could go without water. All kinds of irrelevant facts pushed into her mind and she began to feel overwhelmed.

Stop it!

It was getting her nowhere.

She comforted herself with the fact that the longer she had been there, the more likely that someone would be looking for her. A small feeling of elation inflated inside her. It wouldn't be long now! When she got out of here she was going to put things right, she would talk to Paul about the terrible thing she had done, she would even get Donald a new cat if he wanted one. She pictured herself carrying a tabby kitten with white feet – a replica of the corpse that lay somewhere near her – Donald's forgiveness, tears of joy. A lump formed in her throat as the happy picture developed.

NFC, babes.

God, what was she thinking! Get a grip, she told herself.

And what the *fuck* was Paul doing? He should have got people out looking for her by now!

He probably thinks I've left him, she realised with a start. What if he had just accepted her disappearance as something that had been on the cards since the thing with Trish and ... no, she was getting mixed up. That had all been and gone. But he would wonder if she had run away because of killing Trish – and who could blame him for thinking that. Maybe the police were already looking for her as a suspect rather than as a missing person. Her mind was flooded with possibilities. Why couldn't she think straight?

Another feeling of despair came over her as she remembered what they all called 'The Llanefa Triangle' following the disappearance of family pets. It had been in the paper. She remembered reading the accounts of two or three dogs that had gone missing and it wasn't long before everyone had a lost-pet story to tell. It had even made the local TV news at one point, with theories of alien abductions, witchcraft and a vivisection conspiracy. They couldn't just put her disappearance down to that nonsense – could they? They would surely have to make some serious attempts to find her? Her brain refused to allow her to make intelligent assumptions and she had the feeling of someone who has either been deprived of sleep or had far too much.

The everlasting question which brought on more tears resurrected itself in her mind - why hadn't she told someone where she was going?

She moved her jaws again. It resulted in a dry, sticky sound. The sound of someone dying, she thought. Instantly her thoughts switched to Trish.

Stop it! You are SO wrong!

Yes, she had been wrong – several times.

She remembered walking into the Admin office that day and seeing Clare where Trish was meant to be. A confused Clare, 'You'll have to bear with me. I'm just covering for Trish. She fell earlier. Knocked herself out. She's gone to hospital.'

Then later on, the chat among the other staff.

'Their keeping her in for tests. She's got a dropped foot.'

'What's a dropped foot?'

'I'm not sure, but my sister in law had it when she had a slipped disc. Squashed nerve or something?'

'Oh, they're probably only keeping her in because she lives on her own. Concussion and stuff...'

Kay had felt a coldness seeping through her – as if she had been dunked in a pool of icy water. So maybe Trish really had fallen that day she had seen her on the sofa with Paul. Maybe she had been wrong about their 'affair'...? She had decided that she would visit Trish when she was discharged the next day. But Trish hadn't been discharged the next day. Or the next. Instead, she had been subjected to an array of tests which had kept her in hospital for more than three weeks.

When Kay had gone to see her, she discovered a very different Trish – one who walked slowly with sticks. She had been walking down the ward with her back to Kay. Kay had not even recognised her.

'Hyia, babes,' she had said cheerfully as Kay had overtaken her 'What do you think of the 'old dear shuffle'? Think my Zumba days are over!'

And then, to Kay's horror, Trish had started laughing. A loud, from-the-gut laugh that would normally have had the power to infect others instantly. On and on she had laughed, while Kay veered from half joining in to sheer anger at her. In a few minutes, a nurse had come and helped her back to her chair.

'Got the giggles, Trish?' the nurse commented before settling her down, 'Just breathe in and out slowly for me.'

Kay had stood in perplexed silence until the laughing stopped and the nurse went away. She's lost her marbles, she had thought.

Trish had calmed down and her breathing had returned to normal.

'Oh fuck, do you think I've lost the plot?' she had mumbled.

'Don't be silly,' Kay had lied, 'you're probably still concussed or something. How are you feeling otherwise? I've brought you some chocolates. Belgian. The ones you like...'

Kay had realised she was babbling again. She had not been sure what she was trying to stop Trish from saying but, in Kay's experience, if something was best not said, then don't give the other person a chance to say it.

'They've done all kinds of tests but nobody will tell me anything,' she mumbled again.

Trish wondered if the hospital had given her some kind of sedative to calm her.

'Do you want me to ask them anything?' Kay had suggested.

'Would you, babes?' this time she had sounded almost like the old Trish.

Kay had found a member of staff, but as she was not listed as next-of-kin they had refused to say anything more than necessary. She should discuss anything else with Trish's brother, they had said. There had been a possibility of some kind of virus, they had added, but they were unable to say any more.

So Kay had returned to Trish's bedside and told her that it seemed likely she had a virus and that the staff were pleased with her progress.

Kay stared into the blackness of the cabin. A great sadness welled up inside her. Poor Trish. Poor her, too. They would have a ball, the two of them, once they got together behind the Pearly Gates.

'You must be joking, babes,' Trish's voice piped up in her mind, 'I'm going somewhere hot! If heaven doesn't have a beach, a bar and drop-dead-gorgeous waiters, then give me the place where all the bad boys go!'

Kay remembered that conversation – one of the last ones where Trish had almost been her normal self.

'I'm so sorry, Trish,' she whispered again, 'I didn't think it through.'

Her throat protested at her whispering and her brain gave her a vision of a tall glass of water with ice cubes stacked from top to bottom. It surely couldn't be long before someone found her, she thought. Then she could drink that long cool glass of water and feel the wet coldness of the glass on her hands, soothing the soreness where she had scrabbled like a rat in the darkness. She tortured herself even further with the image of bringing the edge of the glass to her lips.

It made her think of the Sippy-cup. She didn't want to think of the Sippy-cup and its cheerful blue cartoon penguin on the side. In an effort to dispel the penguin from her mind, she again went through every step that had brought her to this prison. Had she dropped anything on the way that would give her rescuers an idea where to look? She knew what the answer was, but that didn't stop her going over and over it all again.

What was it Trish used to say, 'When you're up to your neck in shit, the next stage is going under.'

Well, thanks a lot, Trish, she thought, I'll look forward to that next stage. The one that's even worse than this one!

'*You should have told someone,*' Trish's voice suggested in her mind.

'But you were the only one I would have told anyway,' she argued back, 'I wouldn't have told anyone else about all that crap with the cat.'

'Well, there you go,' she heard Trish in her mind, 'Life's a bitch and then you die!'

Dying, thought Kay. It all came back to dying.

Like the time she had gone to visit Trish in hospital just before she was sent home.

'I've got Motor Neurone Disease,' were the first words Trish had said to her.

Kay had hunted in her mind for a few seconds for an image. Then the familiar picture of Stephen Hawking had revealed itself in her thought processes.

'Oh God! Is that like...?'

'Yes. Him,' Trish had said, 'He's had it for years and years, but it doesn't normally happen like that.'

Kay had sunk into the chair beside her. She had felt the tears running over her eye rims but had not been able to stop herself.

Trish had responded in her usual manner, 'Stop it, babes. Only the good die young so I'll go on for years yet.'

Later on, when Trish was home and her brother had visited her, Kay had spoken to him about the prognosis.

'They usually say about two years,' he had said, 'But then, it doesn't normally develop until after fifty and she's not fifty till next year, so maybe... she'll have longer.'

'What about... who's going to...?' she couldn't formulate her sentences.

'She can come and live with us when she can't manage,' he had said, 'Caroline wants her to come now, but... you know how stubborn Trish is...'

The news had spread through Llanefa like water from a burst pipe. So many people knew and liked Trish. In a short time, The Llanefa MND Association had been formed. Fund raising events and raffles were run so that Trish would get all the equipment she needed as her body slowly failed to work. Karen, the secretary, had arranged to get a Light Touch Keyboard so that Trish could speak through the computer. They had a small get-together at Trish's house to try the Keyboard out. Trish had fiddled with it for a while before getting it to utter the immortal phrase 'HAVE YOU BEEN EATING LUNCH?' in a pseudo-American accent.

Everyone had laughed, including Kay, though inside she had wanted to cry again. She had found herself crying a lot. Unlike Trish, who was laughing a lot, though Kay was horrified to learn that inappropriate crying or laughing was an occasional symptom of the disease.

True to form, Trish's version of the disease had followed its own pattern and progressed rapidly. They had all taken turns looking after her so that she was hardly ever alone. Some of the older women had raised their eyebrows and suggested that the time was fast approaching when she should go to live with her brother and sister-in-law. A suggestion that Trish responded to with a loud-volume 'NFC' on the keyboard! She was still able to speak clearly if she was not too tired and those were the moments she saved until Kay was with her.

And, when they had been alone one day, she had said, as loudly and clearly as was possible, 'I want you to kill me.'

Kay had frozen in her tracks while her mind had raced around in circles trying to make sense of the phrase in every way except the obvious one. She had held her breath waiting for a Trish-style punch-line...

''snorra joke,' she had added.

Kay had given in to the support of the nearest chair. She had felt faint while a cruel mental picture of her with her hands squeezed around Trish's throat grew in her mind.

Trish tried to say more but had to resort to the Light Touch keyboard 'NOT IN A VIOLENT WAY,' it said 'I DO NOT WANT TO GO ON LIKE THIS AND GET WORSE. I WILL NOT EVEN BE ABLE TO SWALLOW MY OWN SPIT. MY TONGUE WILL SWELL AND I WILL CHOKE.'

This time, Kay's mind had flooded with images of her standing in a law court charged with murder; Llinos crying; Paul helpless and unable to cope. Then an image of boxes of paracetamol had replaced her first thoughts.

Trish had continued tapping the keyboard, 'I CAN NOT TAKE TABLETS. YOU KNOW I CAN NOT SWALLOW PROPERLY ALREADY.'

There was another pause while she tapped out more words, 'EVEN IF I CRUSH THEM THE GRITTY BITS STICK AND MAKE ME CHOKE. I TRIED ONE.'

Kay realised that she had not even spoken one word since Trish had made her bizarre request.

The thought prompted her first word, 'How?' while she had cursed herself for letting it go that far.

'MORPHINE,' she said via the keyboard before taking a deep breath and speaking 'Pashes.'

She typed out again, 'PATCHES.'

Kay had known exactly what she meant. She had plenty of clients who were on morphine, both slow-release patches and the oral form. In most of the cases, a nurse came to change the patches every three days, but some were able to do it themselves. Kay had even helped with some of them by cutting open the sachet with a scissors and disposing of the old one as it was peeled off the person's arm or chest.

'Have you got morphine?' she had asked Trish, while her mind had asked *Are you mad? Are you really going to help her with this?*'

'No, babes,' the effort to speak was huge '"swy I wanchu help.'

She turned to the Keyboard again, 'I AM NOT IN PAIN. I CAN NOT ASK DOCTOR FOR MORPHINE.'

The meaning of the words had begun to sink to the bottom of Kay's brain like a murky liquid clearing in a glass.

'I WANT YOU TO STAY WITH ME UNTIL IT KNOCKS ME OUT AND THEN PUT A PILLOW OVER MY FACE.'

'I can't do that!' she gasped out in a loud whisper, 'I just can't!'

'YOU ARE MY FRIEND. DO IT FOR ME. PLEASE.'

'There must be some other way.'

Kay had been traumatised by it all and for the second time in their friendship, she had found herself reducing the contact between them unless she knew there would be someone else present.

Shortly afterwards, she had received an email from Trish – a feat that would have taken her some time to achieve – with the cartoon pictures and the text that read 'A friend is someone who thinks you are a good egg, even if you are a little cracked. Blessed are the cracked for they shall let in the light.'

On the occasions that she found herself alone with Trish, the subject was raised simply by a look that passed between them and a shake of the head from Kay.

Kay had gone as far as attempting to plan it but she still believed that she would not be able to hold a pillow over Trish's face – a belief that lessened its grip as Trish had became less able to live normally.

Kay had discovered that stealing a morphine patch from one of her clients would be easy. Marion, who had a severe back problem that made her immobile, used them and was able to change them herself. All of her other clients had nurses who came in and changed the patch for them. Taking one patch would not be noticed until Marion stopped taking them – either because she was given a new drug or when she died, Kay realised. The next time Marion had to change her patch, Kay had helped her as usual, but before putting the box back in the bedside drawer, she had removed a new sachet and placed it in her tabard pocket. To buy some time, she had made sure that she did it at the start of a new box of five patches so that Marion would not realise that there was one missing until the following week. Kay hoped that Marion would blame her own disordered mind for miscounting.

She had searched on the Internet to see what strength would be fatal and found that Marion's patches were only half the fatal dosage to someone not used to using them. Enough to knock Trish out, but not enough to kill her...

She had spent evenings studying her laptop and tapping into her calculator while Paul sat transfixed to the TV screen and never once asked what she was doing.

That had been when she had bought the Sippy-cup. She had gone into the Co-op Chemist with no clear idea in her mind as to what she wanted to buy. Wandering around the two aisles that made up the shop, her eyes had come to rest on a row of cheerfully patterned Sippy-cups. The pictures on them were designed to encourage toddlers to drink from them. Kay had found herself in the bizarre position of looking for a more appropriate design. It had just seemed wrong somehow – giving a happy, funny cup to someone who was going to die. Her mind had accepted the stirrings of a plan that had been formulating in her subconscious. Not only was she giving a Sippy-cup to someone who was dying, but it was to be the means of killing her.

She had hurriedly made her purchase of the blue penguin patterned cup, convinced that the woman at the till would see into her mind and call the police.

From then on she had carried a plastic bottle in her bag when she went to visit clients. Whenever possible, she had taken some liquid morphine from the bottles of those who were prescribed oral morphine and poured it into the plastic bottle. When she had sufficient quantity, she had spoken to Trish about it.

'When you're ready, I can put the patch on your arm. I'll fill the Sippy Cup with liquid morphine and you can drink it slowly over the space of a few hours. Not too quickly – it might make you sick.'

As soon as the words had come out of her mouth she realised how cruel it sounded. Trish could no more drink something quickly than... Than she, Kay, could put a pillow over her friend's face. She had thought for a second before re-phrasing her reluctance to, no more than she could run a four minute mile. It was then that Kay had wondered if she really could help Trish in the way she wanted.

'Afterwards,' she had said, avoiding the words that meant 'dying', 'I'll come back and take the patch off and no-one will know about it.'

'WANT YOU TO STAY,' Trish had said, 'I NEED THE PILLOW. GOT TO BE CERTAIN.'

'It will take hours. By the time I come back, I'll ... do whatever.'

'LOVE YOU, BABES.'

That had started Kay crying again, but Trish had slowly tapped her Key Board.

'WANT TO LIVE OR DIE. NOT IN BETWEEN.'

That had been the last time the subject had been discussed until the eve of Trish's suicide. Kay had slept badly after Trish had decided that the next day was when she wanted to end her life. She kept wondering what it was like for Trish to know that it was her last night alive. Kay had wanted to stay overnight with her, but they both agreed that it would look suspicious if the routine was changed. They had all drawn up rotas weeks before and it wasn't Kay's turn to stay. Trish had wanted it that way so that Kay would not be the one who had been alone with her all night. Kay had pictured Trish lying in the dark, savouring her final night and wondering if there was anything else beyond...

In her dark prison, Kay realised that she was in the same position as Trish had been that night. All she could do was to keep breathing calmly – save the air (there must be air coming in, she told herself, I wouldn't have lasted this long.) Her arms and legs ached, her throat felt as if it was crumbling away. She could picture her gullet, peeling and flaking in dried out pieces. Her panic was pressing against her mind – just waiting for an opportunity to break in and cause chaos in her lungs and heart. Kay tried to occupy her mind by remembering the dates of birth of her nephews and nieces, but no sooner than she had started thinking' Sion and Cerwyn, fourteenth of April 2000...' than her mind would lead her off elsewhere, '...seventh of August, Trish. She won't be fifty until next year, so maybe she'll have longer than two years...'

Kay sat with her face pressed into her hands, hysteria creeping through her body. Maybe, if she pressed her hands hard enough against her eyes for a few minutes, when she took them away again, there would be a bit more light. She tried it. The darkness bounced back around her as soon as the dark red blobs faded from her retinas. She did it again, drawing some comfort from the dark, multicoloured shapes that swam over her eyeballs. They looked like shirts waving on a clothes line or the green top that Llinos had to wear for her course. This time, hysteria won and she broke into screaming cries, hitting her head against her knees before getting to her feet and throwing herself at the walls. The screaming lasted for only a minute before she was aware of the sound of the sea; waves crashing on a beach and a tight feeling inside her head.

'I'm dying,' she thought as the sound became louder in her head and her forehead pounded.

She felt the floor tilting forward and she toppled down into a faint. She was not aware of the mental blackness that had engulfed her before she hit the ground.

She had no idea how long she had been unconscious for, but she was suddenly aware of being awake and lying on the hard floor of the cabin. There was no moment of wondering where she was – the memory was cruelly clear as soon as she had opened her eyes and registered the blackness of her surroundings. Her right hand throbbed from its position under her side and she rolled on to her front and released it gently. She rolled back on to her side and used her elbow to help herself up. As soon as she had got to the sitting position, her head started to pound again and the same feeling of an expanding emptiness filled her skull. She quickly leaned forward until the pulsating sound became stronger. She was going again. She rolled on to her back and felt around with her feet until they were up against the wall. Slowly, the faintness started to subside and her other pains came back into focus.

I couldn't have been out of it for long, she told herself, a faint never lasts long in normal circumstances. That proved that there had to be air coming in, she told herself triumphantly, otherwise she would not have even come round.

In stages, she started to sit up again, checking each small movement against the floating emptiness inside her head. She got to her knees when a watery feeling came over her tongue and she felt a retch develop. She breathed partway in before the retch came again and brought with it some small amounts of food. Another, more powerful bout of retching followed but she brought up no more than a little watery fluid. The nausea was passing but the expanding balloon inside her head was still there. Kay lay down on her side again and tried to breathe deeply.

She lay there for a long time, motionless apart from the shivering that vibrated through her body at intervals.

In her mind, the passages she had read, came back to haunt her, 'volume of oxygen in the lungs... oxygenated cells in the blood... blessed are the cracked, for they shall let in the light.'

'Stop it!'

Trish's voice in her mind again. The only place she would ever hear it now.

Make yourself a list. Think of something else, she told herself. Like... the cars they had ever owned from the first one that Paul had when they had started going out together – a multi-coloured Ford Escort bound together by filler and red oxide paint, then a Fiat, then a Peugeot – no there was something else in between – a Renault? She pictured her own Renault in the CutCost car park. *Why* hadn't anyone found her yet? How long had it been? How long could she last like this? She felt her heart rate speeding up again. Think of the cars, she told herself. The Fiat, then another Fiat before the Peugeot! That was the thing with Paul working in a garage – there had always been a steady array of different cars on their drive. She steered her mind away from images of Renaults. She tried to remember other lists. Pupils in Llinos's primary school – a happy time. There was Anwen, Bethany, Zoe... what was the name of the one who had to wear glasses? Sian? Sharon? Karen? The name association immediately gave her a mental image of Karen who had taken on the role of Secretary of the Llanefa MNDA. She had been marvellous, arranging the Light Touch Keyboard and even roping in a well known Llanefa-born author to highlight the Association when he came back to the town for another charitable event. Kay's stomach rumbled.

'HAVE YOU BEEN EATING LUNCH?' she thought the words in the American accent of the Key Board Voice Activator. The thought of food made her feel a little nauseous again, but the need for water grew until her mind could think of nothing else.

'Ok, time to move from here, you lazy cow,' she whispered to herself, 'things to do, people to see.'

She tilted herself on to her elbow and waited to see if the faint feeling came back. Her head pounded but the expanding balloon had gone from inside her skull. Her hips and knees ached with the effort of moving after being held in such an unnatural position for a while. The stiffness had penetrated deep into her muscles – like the dead cat, she thought. Like Trish too. She wondered at what point Trish had died while she was imprisoned in here.

'I'm so sorry, Trish,' she whispered again 'I should have stayed with you and did what you wanted. I just didn't think I could do it...'

Stop it!

Kay tried to swallow as her protesting throat crackled drily. Yes, stop it. No need to torture herself either by thinking of what had happened or by whispering and aggravating her gullet.

She had been a coward. She had deliberately kept her mobile phone in her bag so that she could avoid the call that she would almost certainly have had from Maggie, who was Trish's carer for the day, to say that Trish was falling into a coma. She had so wanted it to be all over by the time she got the call. She had planned to rush to Trish's house, saying that her phone had had no network service and asking to spend a moment alone with Trish before secretly removing the morphine patch and taking the empty Sippy Cup with her. She knew that both would have been discovered by now. The doctor attending to certify death would have examined Trish and would almost certainly have found the morphine patch on her arm. If not, then it would be found at a later stage – either at a post mortem (there was a strong likelihood of there being one) or by mortuary staff. How long would it take for people to work out that her co-incidental disappearance was likely to be connected to Trish's death?

It was natural justice, she thought, that they should both die at the same time – and both due to her actions.

The thought of Llinos's despair spurred her into action. She slowly came to her knees, testing for the faint feeling in case she fell over. Scrabbling in the dark, she found some gritty stones. She picked up a small handful then got to her feet. Instantly, the faintness hit her again and she quickly lay down and put her feet up against the wall until it passed. Getting back on to her knees, she decided she could do what she needed to without standing. Shuffling over to the wall, she felt a momentary touch of cat fur which raised her pulse rate for a few seconds.

Stop it!

She waited until her heart rate came down again, checked for the inflating balloon and shuffled forward once more. She reached the wall and sat back on her heels. She felt around in her sore hand for the stones with the most obviously pointed ends and picked one up, letting the others fall to the ground. Her right hand refused to hold it like a pencil; the pain flashed through up to her wrist and she dropped it on the floor.

'Fuck!' she whispered and tried to find another one on the floor by her knees.

Eventually, she picked up another stone and, this time, held it in her left hand. She tried to scrape away at the wall, not knowing whether or not she was leaving legible marks. Her confused mind gave her shortened messages to try to write. 'WANTED TO DIE' was one. Having finished it, Kay realised that message could be misinterpreted, so she shuffled around and tried to write 'TRISH WANTED TO DIE' on another part of the wall. After another period of confused thinking, she again moved and scraped, 'SHE ASKED ME TO HELP'. Her left hand was throbbing as badly as the right by now and she didn't think she had the energy to write anything else. She still had no idea as to whether she had left a legible message or not. She yawned and ended it with a shiver through her body. Perhaps she should lie down for a moment. She moved around again, hunting for her tabard in robotic, clumsy movements when her knee thudded down on to the cat's body and an unpleasant wet sound followed instantly. A faint smell of raw chicken rose to meet her. It was enough to make her heave again. This time, nothing came up but she put her arm over her face and buried her nose deep into the bend of her elbow. She waited for the watery feeling on the back of her tongue to subside. Just as she was thinking she had it under control, a mental image of the cat's intestines bursting forth from its anus flooded her mind and the heaving resumed more strongly until she had brought up another small amount of food. She knelt on all fours, strings of fibrous saliva sticking to her chin and cheek. She didn't attempt to wipe them away, but concentrated instead on breathing carefully to try to control the nausea. The balloon was back in her head and she could feel the pressure pushing all her senses out of her body. She again quickly lay down and raised her feet against the wall. The cat's body was too near to her face and another bout of heaving developed. The effort was too much and she felt herself going into another faint.

This time she knew that it didn't last long. No sooner than the sound of the waves had built up to their maximum inside her head and she had slipped momentarily away from it, than the feeling of coming to was already in progress.

Get away from the guts, she told herself, while her stomach gave a token lurch. She shuffled to one side and on to her knees, hoping that she was going in the right direction and holding her left hand out (trying to keep it at least a few inches from the ground so that she was more likely to put her hand on fur than intestines – her mind had convinced her that it *was* intestines she had heard.) She felt her knee touch something wet and she pulled away with horror before consoling herself with the memory of the pool of her urine that lay somewhere in the dark. She tested the air for odour. The sweet hamburger and onion aroma of her armpits was the only smell, she realised gratefully.

She pushed herself back against the wall and sat there with her legs drawn up. Her wrist touched a wet part of the wall where the condensation had collected. She pulled it away quickly, but not before her mind could get another dig at her.

Air's running out, it said.

Kay tried to sob, but nothing happened apart from a pressure inside her nose and the beginnings of the balloon in her skull.

You are my friend, said the voice in her mind, *do it for me*.

Her head ached and she rubbed her temple on her forearm.

Everything ok? Llinos asking her after the time she had seen Trish and Paul on the sofa.

Bit of a headache, she had replied. Now she *really* knew what a headache was!

Come on, Paul. Hurry up. The air's running out.

Not long to go now, Trish's voice in her head. Why was everything unpleasant pushing into her mind. Think of something else, she ordered herself. Bet I can't remember who used to be in my class at school...

Try to go through in alphabetical order – Catherine Boyd – always the first one named during registration, Helen Davies, Meinir Davies, Menna Evans ... Aled Thomas (hadn't he died quite young? I've got to stop thinking of death, she thought.)

She stopped the pattern of her breathing for a moment, when had Trish said that? Not long to go now? Was it the night before? Or after she had put the morphine patch on the underside of her arm?

I can't do any more, babes. Blessed are the cracked, for they shall let in air.

I'm losing it, she thought. Lack of oxygen. Volume of oxygen in the lungs not equal to the blah-di-fucking-blah!

Stop it, babes! Not long to go now.

It must have been that evening – hours after she had picked the cat off the chair. She had called in to see Trish. *Why* hadn't she said anything to her? Or to Leah who had been there for most of the day? A mocking laugh sounded in her mind. Because, in case you had forgotten, Leah was bringing clean washing in from the line when you arrived. And, let's just run through it one more time, what happened when you got into the house?

Tomorrow.

There had been no need for Trish to say any more. Everything else, trivia about a stroppy cat and its annoyed owner, had melted away from her mind. As soon as Leah had left, they had planned the final details. Kay had said that she would bring the morphine patch and the bottle of oral morphine with her the following morning before starting her calls.   She often called in on her way to work if it was not her turn to stay the night with Trish. She would apply the patch and give her the Sippy Cup (which had been used for more innocent purposes by Trish since Kay had bought it) with its lethal contents. Then it was a waiting game for both of them as Kay went about her work, having signed Trish's death warrant then; (and her own later on when she had found the cat, she thought now.) The only last word Trish had said to her was 'Pillow', as if she could have forgotten what she had promised to do when she would undoubtedly be summoned back to Trish's house later that day.

I've done it. Not long to go now, babes.

Kay's mind buzzed with strange conversations and phrases. She realised that she had no idea where she remembered them from. Blessed are the cracked, she thought, that's me. I've definitely cracked. I don't care anymore, she told herself. If I die, I die. I'm not so young that I haven't lived my life. The philosophical part of her brain was putting her affairs in order.

'Mam! I've got in!'

The memory of Llinos, holding the letter from Edinburgh Vet School, broke into her previous ordered thoughts and she leaned forward and sobbed weak sounds into her arms. What was she thinking of! She couldn't just give up! Oh no, she was going to... the futility of her situation glowed like a comet in her mind. She was going to sit here until someone found her; that's what she was going to do! (It was all she *could* do, but tried not to let her mind voice those thoughts.) She got to her feet and kicked at the walls a few times until the expanding balloon came back into her head, forcing her to lie down once more.

She tried lying down on her side, then wriggled on to her back. Everything seemed to hurt when it touched the hard, rough floor. The gritty surface dug into the back of her head and she had to move again. She realised that the balloon was leaving her and she was able to sit up and minimise the pain by having less of her body area on the floor. She sat completely still for a few seconds to check if the faintness would come back. When it didn't, she relaxed her breathing once more. Low blood pressure, she told herself, always had it. Plus lack of food and water. Even less food than usual after Trish had made her intention clear the previous evening, Kay had hardly touched her evening meal. *Was* it the previous evening, she wondered? How long ago had that happened?

Won't be long, babes.

And what was all this crap her mind was giving her? Wasn't it bad enough to be dying from lack of air and water without her mind counting down the last few hours or minutes? (There probably *is* air coming in, the thought formed in her mind. No, it fucking isn't - accept it, she contradicted herself.)

In a brief flash of lucidity, she realised that she needed a pee again. And why not, she asked herself? Why not fill the cabin with pee and sick and cat guts? At least her bowel had not joined the party, she thought gratefully.

This time, she shuffled into a corner and repeated her earlier action, though the volume was considerably less and the smell held the strange tang of dehydration. She shivered miserably and crawled away from the puddle. She sat down against the wall and ran through it all yet again. There was nothing she could think of that might provide a clue to those looking for her. Nothing that would make them look in the old TPR service area anyway, she amended. The fact that Trish's death was probably being investigated at this moment was more of a reason why anyone would try to find her. The police would go through her work sheets and check where she had been at any given time.

A faint glimmer of hope ignited in her mind when she thought of Donald. Surely, he would tell them about the cat (too far back in the sequence, the bitchy little voice in her brain said, you went back the next day, remember?). But they *would* call with him, wouldn't they?

And what about Ethel? Would she have been able to add anything? No, said her rational brain, you went to the supermarket - you parked the car there. End of!

Kay stifled another sob. Whichever way she worked it out, it ended the same way.

Not long now, babes.

And these fucking voices in my mind are going to kill me long before I run out of air, she thought bitterly.(Before adding to her thoughts, but there *is* air coming in; I wasn't thinking straight before.)

She felt a strange hiccup developing. At the end of the sound, she felt as though she had swallowed something the wrong way. She coughed to try to clear it, but the more effort she made, the more it seemed to stick. She swallowed a few times instead; fighting with her throat as the dryness scratched her gullet. The feeling was getting more uncomfortable and she leaned forward and spat onto the floor. She again tried to clear her throat, each expectoration followed up with a sharp inward gasp of air that brought with it the smell of the cat's insides. That set off another bout of heaving and she tried to turn away from the direction of the smell. She felt a thud as her head hit the side of the cabin, but her panic overrode any pain she might have felt. The heaving was still happening – a 'graaaaagh-urk' noise outwards which ended with a dry whooping noise as she tried to breath in afterwards.

Calm down, she told herself, you're hyperventilating. Calm breaths. Lie down. Relax.

She fell forward on to her front and folded her arms at face level so that she could rest her head on them. Part of her arm was resting in urine, but she ignored it. Breathing was much more important than a little pee on her arm. Taking shallow breaths seemed to work best. She couldn't feel the balloon coming back so she kept the pattern going. Every ten or so breaths, she wanted to inhale deeply. Finally, she gave in to it and tried to fill her lungs with air. It felt as though she had a plastic bag stuck in her throat which was stopping the air going through. Panic broke in and she scrambled to her feet with wide open mouth and her hands trying to rub at the outside of her throat. Something was wrong with her throat! Her heart was thumping so hard she could feel her entire top half vibrating with each beat. The sound of her breathing was all around her – swift, snoring sounds that broke through the sound of her heart and the thudding of her feet as she spun round in terrified circles.

The balloon was coming back, but it felt different. It pressed inwards instead of out. She fell to her knees and leaned against the wall while her breathing continued its kraaaagh-kraaaagh rasping sounds.

The panic was fading away and she felt a happiness flooding through her. It's just an allergy, she thought. No need to panic.

Kraaaagh-kraagh.

Just relax. Sleep for a moment.

Kraaaagh-kraaaagh.

Not long now, babes.

Shut up! Shut up!

Kraaaagh-kraaagh.

I've wet myself, she thought. The knowledge amused her.

Kraaaagh-kraaagh.

The noises were overwhelming – her breathing, the thump of her heart and a scratching sound as her knees thrashed through the gravel on the floor.

The cat is coming to get me! It's the cat!

Stop it!

It's a rat. It's got in. Through the air holes! I'll be fine!

Kraaaagh-kraaagh.

Then there was nothing.

At some point, she saw a blinding white light that contained the image of Paul and Llinos before blackness fell again.

The Llanefa Guardian. 16th September 2011

Page 2.

Horror Chamber Left at By-Pass Site.

A Llanefa woman was rescued from an abandoned explosives store earlier this week after being trapped for 48 hours.

It is believed that Kay Jones, 47, became accidentally locked in the airtight store at the former site of TPR Construction (Exeter). Rescuers and family members found her unconscious and she was taken to West Wales General Hospital where she remains in a critical condition.

A public outcry followed as to why the entire service area was not cleared by TPR Construction after completion of the by-pass. Nearby resident of Llwyncelyn Drive, Sarah Klebowski said 'It's not right. There are lots of children living in this road. Any one of them could have gone in there. The council should have done something about it. We were never happy about the explosives and stuff they had there.'

A full investigation into the incident will be carried out by Health and Safety Executives alongside other public bodies.

No-one at TPR Construction (Exeter) was available for comment.

Death of Llanefa MNDA Founder.

A woman found dead in suspicious circumstances at her Llethr Road home last Friday has been named as 49 year old Patricia Connolly. Following a diagnosis of Motor Neurone Disease, Patricia became a founder member of Llanefa MND Association together with a number of local women who raised money and public awareness of the disease.

Police attended at her home after a visiting doctor raised the alarm.

Investigating officer DCI Tegwyn Prydderch said that a local woman would be questioned as soon as medically possible and that they were not looking for anyone else in connection with the death.

A full obituary will follow next week.

PART TRANSCRIPT OF WITNESS INTERVIEW AT LLANEFA POLICE STATION.

Witness name – Leah James. Date – 10th September 2011.

Interviewing Officer – DS Alun Lewis.

AL: So, moving on to later that day, how would you describe Trish's mood?

LJ: Ok, really. We had a bit of a laugh when we saw someone outside on the pavement. It was Bara. You know, he's not quite right. He was trying to tie his shoelace but it got caught up with the lace on the other shoe...

AL: Did Trish tell you at any time that she wanted to end her own life?

LJ: No, never. Trish was always a happy person. Well, before the Motor Neurone... but she never really lost her sense of humour. She just couldn't always make herself understood and I think that frustrated her. There were times that she was... sort of... but never... depressed or anything.

AL: You're sure that there were no other visitors to Trish's house apart from the ones you've mentioned.

LJ: Certain. I took over from Gail that morning. Sometimes we get a Tesco delivery from Carmarthen on a Friday, but not last week. We only do it once a month. Most of the time we shop in Llanefa for her. Used to. Hard to get used to saying that...

(Sobbing sound from the witness)

AL: When Kay Jones called that afternoon, would you describe her mood as normal?

LJ: I suppose she seemed a bit quiet. Her and Trish were the closest of all of us. When they got together lately, they just seemed... a bit sad. We all knew what was going to happen, didn't we? It was probably just harder on them. Being such close friends and that...

AL: How much of their conversation did you hear?

LJ: Well... most of it I suppose. I was in and out of the room so I could have heard most of what they said. Oh, apart from when Kay arrived. I was bringing washing in from the line then. And, of course, I left before Kay did.

AL: And was there anything they said that led you to believe then – or later after you'd had a time to think about it – that Trish was going to end her own life the next day.

LJ: Absolutely nothing. That's God's honest truth.

PART TRANSCRIPT OF WITNESS INTERVIEW AT LLANEFA POLICE STATION.

Name of Witness – Julie Carr. Date – 10th September 2011.

Interviewing officer – DS Alun Lewis.

AL: Let me just run through quickly what you've told me. Stop me if you need to change anything. You got to Trish's house at about 6pm. Kay was just leaving. You stayed with Trish until 8am yesterday morning. There were no other visitors apart from Kay. Trish didn't say anything to you about wanting to end her own life.

JC: That's right.

AL: Did Trish ask you for any pain relief?

JC: No. She wasn't ever in pain. Not that I was aware of anyway.

AL: And you definitely stayed there all night? You didn't need to pop home at any time?

JC: No. My husband works away on the rigs. The kids are grown up. I was happy to stay overnight with Trish.

AL: Did you know if Trish had any painkilling drugs in the house?

JC: There were some paracetamols in the bathroom cabinet, but those were probably bought for one of us, being as we spend... spent... so much time there.

AL: And when you left her house yesterday morning, your replacement... (SOUND OF PAPERS MOVING) ...Maggie Evans, hadn't arrived?

JC: No. I knew she wouldn't be long. We didn't feel we had to be with Trish twenty-four-seven. Just enough of the time to make sure she was ok. We normally text each other to say that we've arrived or left....

WRITTEN WITNESS STATEMENT OF

Margaret Jane Evans dob 19-9-58.

19, Tanycoed, Llanefa, Carms. Occupation – Part-time care assistant.

My name is Margaret Jane Evans and I live at the above address with my husband, Robert Evans.

For about the past eight months, my friend, Patricia Connolly, known as Trish, has been suffering from Motor Neurone Disease. As a result, together with a number of other friends, I have been helping to look after her. Every month, we drew up a rota to work out who was going to be with her at any given time of the day or night. We knew that she would need professional medical care at some point, but wanted to keep her at home for as long as possible.

At around 8.45am on Friday 9th September 2011, I went to Trish's house, at 10 Llethr Road, Llanefa, with the intention of spending the whole day and evening there. When I arrived, another friend, Kay Jones, was with Trish in the downstairs room that has been used as a bedroom since the Motor Neurone diagnosis. Kay often calls in on her way to work as a Home Help, so I thought nothing of it.

As Kay was leaving she told me that she had given Trish a drink and that she was comfortable. Kay seemed a little upset but was not crying or anything.

After Kay had gone, I went in to see Trish. She seemed a little quiet but didn't indicate that she needed anything. Her Light Touch Keyboard was beside her and she was quite good at operating it when she wanted to tell us anything. She was sitting in her chair with a pull-across tray on wheels in front of her. On the tray was a Sippy Cup with a blue penguin pattern on it. Trish had been using it for a few weeks as it made it easier for her to drink without choking. She was able to hold the cup herself as it is designed for toddlers to use.

I put the television on as usual and I started tidying up generally. I talked to Trish as I was working and I commented on one of the Big Brother stars who was being interviewed on TVAM. Trish responded by using the Keyboard. I noticed that she was taking frequent sips from the Sippy Cup, so I asked her if she needed any more to drink. She said 'No' so I carried on tidying up.

About two hours later, I was wondering what Trish would want for lunch. The normal practice was to liquidise foods for her because she had a fear of choking so we needed to make sure it was cooked thoroughly before putting it in the blender and we tended to plan ahead a bit on mealtimes. I went to ask her what she wanted and I saw that she was sleeping in the chair. I went to see if she was ok as that was quite unusual. She opened her eyes, but she looked really worn out. She was still holding the Sippy Cup so I tried to take it from her, but she seemed to wake up more and didn't want to let it go. I propped her up a bit in the chair and asked her if she wanted to go to bed but she shook her head.

I asked her if she would like some lunch but she sort of whispered 'No'. I asked her if she was feeling ok and she said 'Yes'.

I decided to let her rest and I did some of Trish's ironing. I'd brought my own laundry with me too so it took a bit of time.

I popped my head round the door a few times and she was still sleeping. At some time in the afternoon, she got very agitated - moving her arms all the time, though she couldn't move them very far. And she looked as if she was trying to get up. I went to her and held her arms and asked her if she was all right. She had her eyes open, but she looked as if she was drunk. She kept whispering something like CPR, CPR. I assumed she meant the resuscitation thing, so I asked her if she could breathe ok. She just kept trying to say CPR again until she just tired herself out and her eyes closed. I was a bit worried but I thought that it was better for her to rest. I rolled the chair over to the bed and lifted her on to the bed. The way it's designed makes it easier for us to move her. As I got her into bed, she opened her eyes again and tried to grab at my cardigan and her hand locked on to the material. She fell into a sleep again almost straight away and I just pulled the light throw over her.

I waited with her for about half an hour but she slept quietly. Then I went to the bathroom. On the way back to Trish's room, the phone rang and I answered it. It was one of these sales calls about solar panels so it took a few minutes to get him off the phone. While he was talking, I thought I could hear sounds coming from Trish's room and I tried to tell the man that I had to go. I put the phone down and went into the room but Trish was fast asleep, although her position in bed had changed. That was unusual too. She had become quite immobile over the past six weeks or so. She was lying slightly on her left hand side and when I went to check on her I saw that she had a biro by her right hand. I know that it was my biro because it had my husband's company name on it. Trish must have caught hold of it when I was trying to get her into bed. When I looked closer, I saw that she had written something on the back of her left hand. It was hard to make out. It looked like KIPA or KTPA. I didn't know what that meant and it must have been a huge effort for her to do it. But she was sleeping so peacefully, that I left her alone and just checked every half hour or so.

Then, at about six o'clock, when I checked her, I just thought she seemed a bit too still. I put my hand on her and she felt quite cold. It was then that I felt for her pulse and I couldn't feel it. I just panicked and phoned the doctor at his home – he lives in the same road as we do. He came to the house straight away and after he had examined her, he told me that she had passed away. I was really upset and crying, but he started asking me over and over what I had given her. I just kept on crying and I didn't know what he meant. He was holding the Sippy Cup while he was asking me. Then he asked if I had put the morphine patch on her. I still didn't know what he meant and he said that the police would have to be informed. He phoned the police then but he made me stay in the room with him. When I said I wanted to phone Kay, he got really loud and said that I was not to phone anyone until the police had been.

When the police came, I was asked to go with them to Llanefa Police Station to speak to DCI Prydderch. He and another officer asked me lots of questions for hours. I said the same as I am now recording in this statement. I said I knew nothing about a morphine patch or assisted suicide. I've known Tegwyn Prydderch for years and I told him that he should know me better than to suggest I had been involved in anything like that. They also asked me what the letters KTPR meant. I said that I didn't know. Then I realised that they were talking about the biro marks on Trish's hand and I said I thought they spelt KIPA but that I still didn't know what they meant.

When I left the police station, I wanted to speak to Kay, but when I rang her home and her mobile there was no reply. I later found out that Kay had gone missing.

By the next day, Kay still hadn't been found and her daughter, Llinos, had been contacted and was on her way home from Edinburgh. It was obvious to me by then that the police were also looking for Kay as they wanted to question her too. An officer called at my home on three occasions to see if I had heard from Kay. They said that she had left her car at the CutCost car park. Again I told them that I didn't know anything about Kay's disappearance.

I was very worried about Kay and still upset about Trish. The second night I hardly slept at all and I kept having nightmares about Trish when I did.

On the afternoon of the 11th September I was just thinking about it all and it suddenly became clear in my mind that the letters on Trish's hand *were* KTPR and that she meant KAY TPR. The only TPR I knew of was the building site of the by-pass crew so I phoned Kay's husband, Paul, to ask if anyone had looked there.

I did not go to the TPR site with them and I have not had any contact with Kay while she has been in hospital. Furthermore, I have no knowledge of any arrangements made between Kay and Trish prior to her death.

This statement is true. I have made it of my own free will.

Signed – M J Evans.

* * *

Copy of Email from Llinos Jones to Ellie Barnard.

23-11-2011   10:38am.

From: animadllin@googlemail.co.uk

To: ellie@dignityforthedying.co.uk

Subject: CPS Result.

Dear Ellie,

Just a quick email to thank you for all your help during the enquiry into Trish Connolly's death.

We have, today, received confirmation that the Crown Prosecution Service is not going ahead with the case of assisted suicide in relation to my mother's part in the incident. It seems that the email that was found on Trish's computer (from herself, to herself – to save you going through your records on this) has added strength to the belief that Trish was going to end her own life with or without help. The mis-spellings are apparently proof that a person with a neurological condition such as MND would have written them as certain letters have the # and] characters immediately after them and is consistent with the kind of palsy that affects the hands.

Of course, my mother will still be prosecuted for the theft of a Class A drug and will certainly lose her job as a Home Help. Her current suspension has made that certainty a little easier for her to deal with. We are hoping that the sentence will be fairly lenient and the defence team are also very positive.

I may have told you that Edinburgh Vet School have kindly suggested that I take a year off and re-join them next September/October. However, after all that has happened, the thought of spending my life vaccinating dogs and cattle seems like worse decision I could have made. And I certainly NEVER want to see another cat of any description!

Instead, I am looking into the possibility of a career in law – though, who knows, I may change my mind again!

So once again, many, many thanks for your support. My mother will be in touch once she has more news.

Kind regards

Llinos Jones.

Radio Chatter Studio, Bristol.   21st January 2013.

There Are Many More Things, Horatio.

Presenter – Dan Cavill.

Dan: Welcome to another wet Monday night on There Are Many More Things, Horatio, where we talk about those topics that you won't hear on most other radio stations. Tonight, our guest is Kay Jones from Lan-eepha in Wales who, you may remember, made the headlines when she was trapped inside an old explosives store while she was looking for a lost cat. Good evening, Kay, we are delighted you could join us today.

Kay: Hello, Dan. I'm pleased to be here.

Dan: Now, before we go ahead with our discussion and calls regarding the sixth sense that humans can develop under extreme circumstances, let us remind listeners that your experience of this phenomenon is connected mainly to that incident when you became locked in the explosive store.

Kay: Yes, that's right. My friend had Motor Neurone Disease and as she lost some of her other abilities, she developed an ability to communicate through her mind.

Dan: So, Kay, when did you first notice this non-verbal communication between your friend and yourself?

Kay: Just before she was diagnosed, there were a few things she did that annoyed or irritated me – like all friends do – and I would just think some uncharitable thought about her. But, on several occasions, she replied verbally to what I was thinking. At first I thought that she had just read my expression, but as time went on there seemed to be more to it. When she first said that she wanted to end her own life, I just pictured a box of paracetamol and she told me that she couldn't swallow tablets, for example.

Dan: That might be considered to be a very standard thing for someone in her position to say...

Kay: I thought so too, but later on when I was trapped inside the old store, I could hear her voice telling me things.

Dan: Cynics would probably suggest that the trauma of being trapped in an airtight container for two days was a reasonable justification for hearing voices in your head.

Kay: I agree, but the way it happened and the way that she was able to communicate with another person, *even after her death*, to lead someone to find me, is beyond any rational explanation.

Dan: Just remind us – your friend was actually... passing away... at the time you became trapped?

Kay: Yes.

Dan: One thing – and I promise this is the only time I'll bring this up, Kay – you had helped her to end her life by supplying her with an overdose of morphine and you were subsequently charged and convicted of this?

Kay: No, I was charged and convicted of theft of prescription drugs – the morphine – as it was the only form of drug she said she could take. Because she wasn't on any morphine herself, I stupidly took small amounts from sources that I thought wouldn't be missed. Trish sent herself an email to say that she intended to end her suffering even if no-one was able to help her. I wasn't charged with assisted suicide. Only the theft. I had a suspended sentence and community service. And I lost my job. The charity Dignity For The Dying were a big help to me and supported me throughout the case.

Dan: We'll be giving listeners more details on that at the end of the programme. Meanwhile, Kay, tell us the sort of things that happened during the alleged communication between you and your friend while you were trapped.

Kay: I was panicking, as you can imagine and I was worried about whether or not there was air coming in. That made me worse and I was hyperventilating and hitting and kicking the walls, trying to get out. Almost each time I did it, I heard her voice saying 'Save your breath, babes'. And when I started imagining that I was running out of air, she kept saying 'stop it'. At first I thought I was just remembering things she'd said but then the voice said things that had not been said before. Although the voice was in my mind, I've got no doubt she was communicating with me. Then, when things got really bad, she kept saying 'Not long now' and I thought it was because I was close to running out of air and... dying. But now, I believe that she was reassuring me that help was not far off.

Dan: Do you know how long it took from hearing that to actually being rescued?

Kay: I had no idea of time. It was just black in there and I never wear a watch. I was unconscious when I was found. I just remember a bright light and seeing the face of my daughter and my husband for a second. That must have been when they opened the door.

Dan: Just tell us how they knew where to find you.

Kay: That was all down to Trish. Remember that she had very little mobility and she was close to death. She managed to write on her hand, the letter K and the initials of the construction company that had used the abandoned site – I'm obviously not allowed to mention the name of the company until the enquiry is over. The person who was with Trish when she died didn't think it was anything significant, but the night after her death, this person – who I'm also not allowed to name as she doesn't want any publicity – had a nightmare about Trish, where she was sitting in her chair and holding her hand out to her and showing her the letters written on it. She thought about it the next day and put two and two together and suggested to my husband and daughter that they should look on the old service area.

Dan: I bet they will both be grateful to that person's grasp on the facts!

Kay: Well, yes. Though my marriage has since broken down, but, at the time, they just couldn't believe that I was still alive.

Dan: Kay, we have a lot of callers who want to speak to you. First on Line One is Cathy from Weston Super Mare. Good evening, Cathy, what would you like to ask Kay?

Cathy: Yes... hello. I'm just... well... I just had to call and say 'bless you' to Kay and to tell her that this is something that happens all the time. My husband, since his passing, communicates with me all the time. When I'm doing everyday things, I can hear his voice coming from the cupboard – always from the hall cupboard – 'Put the kettle on, love' he says or 'Weather's too bad for gardening today'. Always the same sort of thing. I leave the cupboard open now because my hearing's not so good and I don't want to miss what he says. You'll find that you'll keep on hearing your friend, my love, it's quite normal.

Kay: Um... thank you, Cathy.

Dan: Well, time for our second caller. Hello on Line Two, to Tom from Bristol. Good evening, Tom.

Tom: Good evening, Dan and to you too Kay.

Dan: What would you like to ask Kay, Tom?

Tom: I don't mean to sound rude, but I think this is all a load of ... excuse my language.. codswallop...

Dan: Phew, Tom, I wondered what you were going to say...

Tom: ... because, no offence, Kay, you had a dreadful experience, but my father was in the war and these terrible scenes do things to your mind...

Kay: But this was...

Tom: ... I've no doubt that you really *believed* that your friend could communicate with you but scientific tests could probably prove that lack of oxygen and light contributed to what you thought you heard...

Kay: Not thought. It was as clear as you on the...

Tom: ...and hoped you could hear...

Dan: A reminder to our listeners that, this evening we are talking about the sixth sense – not the film, but whether or not humans do develop a telepathic ability in certain circumstances. Kay Jones from Lan-eepha is here to take your calls...

Tom: I hadn't finished, Dan...

70

Dan: ... on 0700 111 222...

Tom: I just wanted to give Kay a word of advice...

Dan: Ok, go ahead, Tom.

Tom: You've had a very bad experience, my dear. You have to try to get over it now. Whatever you thought you heard has got to stay in your mind only. If it helps you to get over it, then that's a good thing. But, if you keep dragging it out for others to ridicule, it will destroy your mind and you'll just end up cracking.

Kay: Thank you for your concern, Tom, but if I end up cracked... I'll just tell you what my friend would have said, 'Blessed are the cracked, for they shall let in the light'.

Dan: Kay? Kay, are you leaving us? Wait a moment! Kay?

Sound of door closing.

Dan: Keep listening while we play some music before returning to this interesting topic.

* * *

Kay stood in the rain in the car park of Radio Chatter. She took out her keys and unlocked her car. Somewhere in the background she could hear someone calling her to come back. Tom had been right, she thought. This was *her* business alone now. Her friendship with Trish had been a once-in-a-lifetime bond; not something she should share with others.

She got into the car and started the engine. She switched on the radio – a pleasant music channel – to dispel the misgivings going around in her head.

The familiar jingle of a snack food advert caught her attention.

'Have you been eating lunch?' began the male voice in the advert.

Kay smiled to herself and pointed the car in the direction of the place she now called home.

What Would Delyth Do?

Tegwyn finds a letter.

The date is painfully close to the time of Gwenda's funeral. He had only opened it in the belief that it was a card of condolence. He had instantly dismissed it and put it away. It had been a deliberate act at the time.

He opens it again, peeling the letter itself away from the photocopied documents that accompany it.

It is from Alison Wood who lives in Shropshire. He feels a twinge of embarrassment at his bad manners in not replying to her.

She begins by apologising for troubling him. She has heard he is retiring soon and asks for his help in finding her half-sister, Elin, who has gone missing. She lists the attached documents containing useful information. She leaves her email address and phone number.

Tegwyn puts the letter to one side. He does not believe he can help her, but he makes the decision to contact her soon, if only to apologise for his delayed response.

At the end of the Swinging Sixties, when the masses had heard all there was to hear about 'free love', a few places still held the Eleven Plus exam in high esteem. Llanefa, with its outlying farming district, was such an area.

As she squirmed into rigid new school uniform in the changing rooms of Siop y Graig, Elin James was reminded of the value of the Eleven Plus as the conversation unfolded between her mother and Miss Davies, the niece of the original owner of Siop y Graig. Though known as 'Young Miss Davies' the proprietor was herself in her late sixties and held firm views on the attire of Grammar School pupils.

Box after box of tissue-wrapped items came out for Elin to try. Engulfed in an overlong pinafore tunic, Elin felt overwhelmed by her mother's determination to mould her into the Perfect Pupil.

'Here's the beret,' said Young Miss Davies, handing the strange looking item to Elin's mother who immediately placed it on Elin's head with a corkscrew action.

'Not too far back,' advised Young Miss Davies 'Every year we see young girls starting the term with correctly positioned berets. By the Easter term, they've been pushed to the back of the head and by the summer term they've disappeared altogether.'

With resignation, Elin could see that her mother was taking it all to heart.

'And here's the sash,' said Young Miss Davies, getting into full swing.

'Thank you, but we won't need that,' said Elin's mother 'We've already got one after my sister's daughter. She left school last year. Off to college to train to be a teacher.'

Young Miss Davies looked impressed.

'And what does she want to do?' asked Young Miss Davies nodding her head in Elin's direction.

'Either a doctor or a barrister,' said her mother, though Elin had never dared offer an opinion on the subject.

'Very good,' praised Young Miss Davies, taking another look at the scruffy child 'Very bright, is she?'

'Oh yes. She could read before she even started school,' boasted her mother 'She was the only one who passed the Eleven Plus from Pwll y Coed Primary this year. The other three failed.'

'She just needs to stick at it now, then,' said Young Miss Davies in an exact imitation of the preachings of Elin's mother.

After leaving Siop y Graig, laden with almost every item on the Parents' List, it was obvious that Elin's mother had been further enthused by Young Miss Davies. Walking back to her father's juddering car and all the way home to their run-down farm, Elin's mother was in full flow.

'You heard what she said!' she repeated 'I've told you the same myself. All this money we've spent on your school things. I wish I'd had your chance. Don't let me down like Delyth did.'

Elin sighed very quietly. For as long as she could remember, her sister, Delyth, had been used as a template of how not to behave. Elin had only ever met her once - she was sixteen years older than her. That had been a strained Christmas visit when Elin had been about four years old. Within a very short time her mother had sent Delyth on her way with a command not to come to her door again.

The gospel according to Elin's mother was that Delyth had passed her Eleven Plus, but had not worked hard enough and was 'sent back' to the Secondary Modern at the age of thirteen. The only thing Delyth had been interested in, Elin's mother had snorted in disgust, had been painting her nails, wearing fashionable clothes and chasing boys.

'I won't have you wasting our money and bringing trouble to the house,' had always been her final few words on the subject.

Elin was so in-awe of her mother that she could not imagine how Delyth had been bold enough to defy her. However, she could see that it had resulted in her sister being disowned by the family and Elin was terrified of how she would cope with such a situation. Molly James was a strict woman who did not believe in 'sparing the rod' but it was her strong will that made Elin the cowed child she was.

All too soon, the end of the summer holidays came and the fruits of Siop y Graig were laid out for Elin's first day. The most hated items in her eyes were the grey gymslip, the beret and a misshapen, home made sports kit-bag that had been donated by an elderly relative. The kit-bag was as unlike the Siop y Graig versions as ice is to fire, but her mother had insisted that it had been good enough for the great uncle it had come from. The beret was an unknown concept to her and, though she avidly read her weekly Mandy comic to see if any of the girls in those stories wore a beret and in what fashion, she saw no evidence of any. The gymslip was probably the biggest curse to her as it was several inches too long and swirled around below her knees. Despite it being the age of the mini-skirt, Molly refused to shorten it as it was only 'bad girls' who wore short dresses and chased boys.

'You'll grow into it!' had been her conclusion to the subject.

The first morning arrived and Elin stood at the end of the farm driveway waiting for the school bus. She had been used to seeing it pass by occasionally while she walked to Pwll y Coed Primary School, though the passengers had then been an alien species hidden behind the steamed up windows.

The bus stopped and she climbed the steps, trying to disregard her trembling knees. On looking around she could see no empty seats so she walked along and stood next to two boys who were standing and holding on to a seat handle. One of the boys said something to the other and a minor, but good-natured fight broke out between them until the bus driver yelled a warning.

Further down the road, two older girls got on, chatting happily to each other. One of them gave the beret a puzzled glance and, to her horror, Elin noticed that no-one else was wearing one.

At Llanefa Grammar School, after hanging her coat where others did the same, she was herded into a classroom with a flock of first-year's, some of whom looked as lost as she did. A form teacher walked into the classroom and beckoned silence.

'That's Mr Winston,' whispered a girl in front of her to her companion 'He was my sister's form teacher the first year. She said he's horrible!'

'Quiet!' barked Mr Winston before calling out the pupils' names from a list he held.

Elin's desk neighbour was a girl called Menna Davies and Elin hoped they would become friends. However, Menna was obviously from the same Primary School as the two girls in front of them and they consulted each other in hushed tones at regular intervals.

By break-time, Elin realised that she knew no-one from her own age group and that the few older girls she recognised from neighbouring farms were unwilling to acknowledge a pupil from a lower year.

She stood around, hovering on the outskirts of a cluster of girls from her form, beaming broadly whenever any of them teased each other or said anything faintly amusing. One of them, Carol, was clearly the leader and Elin was gratified when she occasionally said something which seemed to include her too.

'What's the matter with your sash?' she eventually asked Elin.

Elin glanced down at her waist and noticed for the first time that her sash looked stretched and faded compared to the bright maroon and grey of Carol's.

'It's just... I had it... It was my cossen's,' she said, mixing up her words and blushing.

The four girls burst out laughing.

'I've got a cossen!' one of them repeated and they giggled again.

'Are you foreign?' Carol asked 'Me Carol.'

That set them all off again.

'That's why her tunic is so long,' spluttered another before hysterical laughing took over.

Elin pinned her smile to her face and felt the blush burn throughout her body.

The girls soon lost interest in her and chatted amongst themselves while Elin stood nearby, rolling and unrolling the long fringed ends of her sash.

At dinner time, she found herself on the table of a different set of girls from her class. Sporadic chatting and eating eased Elin into a safe zone. Although it was clear that she was the outsider, she felt less luminous while sitting at the table.

Later she wandered along near the group she had eaten with. The most verbose of them was a tall, thin girl called Janet, but whose bright ginger hair had earned her the nickname 'Coch'. Elin again stood like the herd outcast and yearned to be part of a group. Unlike Carol and her friends, Coch was kinder, but ran up and down at irregular intervals with an imaginary hockey stick or tennis racquet, such was her love of sports. Pleased to be included, Elin bore this strange behaviour with great puzzlement.

Going home on the bus brought more anguish as she donned the beret and ignored the stares and obvious whispers of her travelling companions.

Molly was anxious to hear about Elin's first day, but quickly dismissed her attempt to describe her classmates. Molly wanted to know what subjects she would be doing, how many pupils in the class and what position she expected her daughter to be ranked after the end of term exams. Elin was too embarrassed to tell her mother about Carol's comments, but hesitantly mentioned that no-one seemed to wear a beret and that her tunic was 'a bit too long'. As expected, Molly ranted at length about her favourite subject – bad girls. Elin sat at the tea table with a dutiful expression and eventually felt convinced that maybe her tunic was not as long as she had imagined. As regards the beret, Molly was delighted, she said, that Elin was the only one wearing the correct uniform. She would be an example to the other girls and would probably be commended by the headmaster for it.

And so began a routine of traumatic schooldays for the lonely child. Friday afternoons lifted her spirits while Sunday evenings loomed over her like a terminal illness. She had inherited the nickname 'Maxi' after Carol had offered advice on how to hitch her tunic up shorter by pulling it up and tightening the sash to stop it slipping down again.

'That's more like a maxi dress than a mini skirt!' she had commented while her friends giggled.

Coch and her sports-mad friends often had hockey practice in the lunch break so Elin, who had no talent in that direction, saw little of them. Elin's mother had decreed that playing sports was a waste of time and, in any case, she should not expect her father to drive her to and from weekend venues to play against other schools. Socialising, Molly had declared, was for bad girls.

'You can help me here at the weekends,' she had added 'Life is not all play, you know.'

It seemed to Elin that 'bad girls' had far more fun than she did.

During the Easter term, she sat in an English class while they discussed the current book they were studying. Every so often, Miss Jones, the English teacher would stop a pupil reading so that she could explain a particular word that they didn't understand.

'Does anyone know what that word 'sibling' means?' she asked.

Everyone was quiet.

'Does anyone here have a brother or sister?' she prompted.

Several hands went up – including Elin's.

'Elin?' she said 'Do you have brothers and sisters?'

'Just a sister, Miss.'

'And what is her name?'

'Delyth, Miss.'

'And you, Meirion,' she pointed to a boy at the back 'what are the names of your brothers or sisters?'

'Owen and Sion, Miss,' he said.

'Owen and Sion are your siblings,' she said 'And Delyth is your sibling, Elin'.

Later, during break, Elin heard Carol's voice calling, 'Maxi!'

She turned around hopefully. It was the first time she remembered Carol seeking her out.

'You know what you said about your sister?'

Elin looked at her in confusion.

'My mother said that your sister isn't really your sister. She's your mother.'

Elin half laughed

'No. Delyth is my sister,' she corrected.

'Don't you know?' said Carol incredulously 'My Auntie Val said that your mother - *your real mother* - was in her class. She got pregnant in the fifth form. She had to leave school and afterwards, she went away, and your grandmother looked after you and brought you up'.

Elin felt a blush lighting up her face.

'You must have known that!' Carol insisted.

'I ... She said... I don't think...' Elin spluttered.

'You ask your *grandmother* tonight,' Carol finished 'What I'm telling you is right!'

She turned away and Elin caught a murmur from one of Carol's followers 'I don't think she really knew...'

'*Everyone* else knows. She must have!'

Elin felt as if her heart was beating its way out through her tunic. She realised that she hated Carol and would try to stay out of her way.

Unfortunately, Carol and her friends, Bethan, Lowri and Julie, often sought out Elin to offer advice about clothes and hair. With the confidence of youth, Carol would ask Elin why she had not shortened her tunic or why she wore her beret to school. Elin was too embarrassed to say that her mother insisted so ended up spluttering and failing to answer the question. Due to her mother discouraging any social contact between her and any other children, Elin was a shy child who had no idea how to interact with others.

One evening at home, Elin hung around the cowshed doorway while her father finished the milking.

With her mother safely out of earshot, she chatted to her father about nothing in particular while he responded with an occasional 'Hmm.'

'Carol said something really funny in school,' she said, nervously giggling with false amusement.

'Hmm.'

'She said that Delyth wasn't really my sister…'

Her father hissed loudly.

She waited for a continued response before realising that his reaction had been to the examination of a heifer's udder.

'I'll have to get the vet for this,' he tutted, 'It's much worse than it was.'

The holidays were the saving of Elin's sanity. Each week stretched out with a promise of infinity. Occasionally, she lapsed into daydreams where she was told that the school had burned down and she would never have to return.

During the Easter holidays of her second year, Elin was delighted to notice that she had grown several inches and that the reviled tunic had become an acceptable length – for her, at least. Carol still looked at it and shook her head in disbelief.

'You'll never get a boyfriend with your dress that long,' she told Elin (who blushed up to her side-parting at the brutal truth).

By then, the beret travelled to and from school inside her satchel and was donned exclusively while she was getting on the bus and within sight of the farmhouse.

Elin had begun to develop a sixth sense when she knew Carol was going to speak to her and would quickly walk away before some unpleasant question or opinion was directed at her. Elin had tried to be liked by Carol and her crowd of friends, but their treatment of her (which they never saw as unkind) always resulted in agonies of self-questioning when she was alone. She often replayed entire conversations in her mind – usually when she was feeding the calves before going to school - in preparation of the day ahead. In those imagined conversations she gave Carol the right answers and even asked Carol some clever searching questions that reversed the relationship between them.

Sometimes, Carol would ask her if she ever saw her mother – her real mother – and Elin would just shrug her shoulders.

Shopping with Molly at the weekend was a nightmare for her as she scanned the shops and Llanefa streets in case Carol appeared. It was not the possible sight of Carol that Elin feared, but the worry that she would say something indiscreet in Molly's hearing and, in doing so, release her mother's anger and Elin's subsequent punishment when they arrived home. Her heart thumped loudly with fear until they were safely back in the old car and on the way out of the town.

There were times in school when Elin bumped into Carol when her three friends were not with her. On those occasions, when she scrutinised Elin's face and said 'You need to use some lotion on those spots,' Elin simply made some kind of accepting gesture before hurrying away.

However, when her friends were with her, it was much worse as they cackled their laughter in response to Carol's comments.

One afternoon, just before the double games lesson as they all donned their shorts in the girls changing rooms attached to the gym, Lowri came in and asked Carol if she could borrow her maths book. Carol dug it out of her satchel and gave it to her.

'I'll be in the library,' she told Carol.

Elin looked on in puzzlement as to why Lowri was not joining them for double games.

Bethan noticed and said 'Lowri's got the curse and a bad tummy. She's got a note to miss games. You haven't started your periods yet, have you?'

'Don't be silly!' said Carol 'She doesn't even wear a bra yet!'

Elin stood in her knickers and vest in the changing room while all the others turned to look at her skinny underdeveloped body with no signs of impending adulthood. She blushed so hard that she could feel tears seeping into the rims of her eyes. She bent down to pull on shorts and was horrified to feel the tears increase with gravity. She burst into a volley of artificial coughing with dramatic rubbing of the bottom of her throat to try to provide a reason for her reddened, watering eyes.

'I've swallowed a fly,' she explained, though no-one took any notice and the attention of the girls had moved on to another topic.

Shortly after their return to school following the Whitsun break, Elin's class were scheduled to go on a school trip to Aberystwyth. They were to visit the Theological College in the morning; there was to be an exhibition of religious paintings that were temporarily on loan to the College. The afternoon was to be a more relaxed affair with a chance to take the funicular railway journey to the top of Constitution Hill (though an essay of the experience was expected sometime later).

Molly James had made known her opinion of school trips to Elin in the run up to the day out. It was the knowledge of the resulting essay to be submitted that stopped her from sending a note to prevent Elin from attending.

'This is a chance to study, mind!' she warned Elin, while giving her a few coins to cover the day's expense, 'It's not a holiday trip. If I hear that you've been wasting time and enjoying yourself, there'll be trouble!'

She followed up this warning with a glance to where she kept her cane. Despite Elin being a teenager, Molly James was still apt to use the small cane across the girl's legs in a practised and swift correction when she felt that it was deserved.

Elin caught the bus to school with her beret perched on her head as usual. Once they were on their way, she whipped it off and stuffed it into her satchel.

In the school cloakroom, it became evident that the others had brought coats or jackets that were not part of the school uniform. Hairstyles had been modified and Carol had brought two bottles of nail varnish with her.

After Assembly, Class 2E made their way down to the bus bay where their transport was waiting. The bus was a superior model to the one they travelled to school on and its new smell gave everyone an air of excitement and anticipation. The boys rushed to the back seats where they fought each other for the best places. The less swift sat on one side of the bus as near as possible to the rear. One of them flicked the beret out of Elin's hand as she rummaged in her satchel for the money her mother had given her. She got up and walked back to retrieve it from the floor.

One of the boys said 'Moo!' loudly and another stuck out his foot as she went back to her seat. She fell heavily in the gangway and hit her knee. She felt tears coming so she kept her face down and slid into the nearest seat and pressed herself up against the window. No-one else sat beside her. Coch and her friends sat near the front as one of them was not a good traveller.

Miss Bowen, the form teacher for the Second Years, and Mr Winston, the geography teacher, carried out a quick head count before they set off.

At regular intervals, she heard the yells of the boys as they teased each other and, more regularly, the seagull-like laughter of Carol and her friends as they chatted to each other. When they went quiet, the distinctive pear-drop smell of nail varnish filled the air.

Elin felt herself dozing off as the bus rocked smoothly on its way to Aberystwyth.

She was woken by the word 'Maxi!' being said quite loudly.

It was Carol's voice. Instinct told Elin to keep her eyes closed and hope that she would be left alone.

The voices continued in a normal tone.

'Is she really asleep?' Lowri said.

'Think so.'

'She's weird, she is!'

'Funny how her mother was a real case at school, my Auntie Val said. You couldn't call Maxi a case – never in Europe!'

The others squawked their amusement.

'She just doesn't seem to understand how we try to help her. I've said and said about making that dress shorter. And that beret is a bloody scream! Apparently her mother – grandmother – makes her wear it.'

'I wouldn't let my mother do that - never in Europe!'

'The thing is her mother, grandmother I mean, is scared that she'll get pregnant like her real mother did. So she tries to make her look as awful as possible so that no boy will ever like her. That's what my Auntie Val said.'

'That's terrible!'

Then Carol's voice came in a lower tone, 'And she smells of cows! Have noticed when you're really close to her? Has your nail varnish dried, Bethan?'

Elin's heart raced at an alarming rate. She kept her eyes closed and waited for the heat of her blush to fade away. She was afraid to open her eyes in case the action let the tears out and she would not be able to stop until she had sobbed out the entire tear content of her body. She inhaled deeply to check for the smell of cows. The action brought a shaky exhale that threatened to turn into a bout of crying. Instead, she turned her embarrassment into rage against Carol, Molly and Delyth (though she would not recognise her if she saw her). Her hands shook and her legs felt too weak to move. She wished she had been asleep and not heard what Carol had said. Or, if only she had responded when they had spoken to her – they would not have dared say anything as insulting if she had only spoken back to them. The whole incident was replaying itself in her mind and she knew that it would stay there for a long time and leave a scar as real as if her skin had been sliced open.

Several decades later, an office junior at Cambridge University knocked on a door marked 'Professor E Roberts. English and Applied Linguistics.'

'Come in,' Elin's voice called out.

The junior went in, trying not to stare at Elin's designer clothes and handmade Italian shoes.

'This letter has been forwarded from one of the other colleges. It was sent to the wrong one by mistake,' said the junior.

'Thank you,' said Elin dismissing her and opening the envelope.

Inside nestled a folded dark red card and a handwritten note. The red card bore the large letters 'Charitable Auction. Llanefa Action Group for Lost Children and their Families'. Below it were the details of an evening to be held at The Poacher's Rest, Llanefa to raise money for the charity that offered help to parents who had lost children or who had children who needed special medical care. The auction was to be timed to the anniversary of the death of Carol Jenkins during her time at Llanefa Grammar School. The Poacher's Rest, Elin read, were installing a hand carved bench in their restaurant in memory of Carol. RSVPs, Elin saw, were to be returned to Mrs Janet Morris.

Opening the note, she saw familiar handwriting.

'Dear Elin,' it read 'I do hope you will be able to make this auction (and chance for a bit of a re-union with me, Lowri and Bethan — we all still live in Llanefa). I'm sorry this is a bit short notice, but I almost couldn't trace you at all — it gives your name as Eleanor Roberts on the site I looked on. Thank goodness for Google and Bethan's patience in tracking you down!

If you are able to come, I wonder if you would like to stay overnight with us as it will be a bit far for you to travel back to Cambridge. It will also give us a chance to have a good chat and catch up generally. (And, of course, have a giggle about the 'good old days'!)

Hope to hear from you soon,

Janet (Coch) xx.

PS I've been remembering all the silly nicknames we used to call each other and I seem to recall that you were 'Maxi', though I've no idea why! What wouldn't I give to be that age again!'

Elin put down the letter and started up the computer. She felt a coldness seep through her. Llanefa and its associated unpleasantness still had the power to taint her life. Her dominated childhood, the search for Delyth after Molly died (and the disappointment when she was again rejected), her failed marriage to a man who turned her into a victim of violence and her resulting change of name to discourage him from contacting her again — all were linked in her mind to her upbringing.

But the memory of the day in Aberystwyth bloomed biggest in her mind.

The bus pulled up outside the Theological College in Aberystwyth. There was an instant rush of pupils in the gangway while Mr Winston bellowed for restrained behaviour. Elin leaned her head against the glass of the window and wished she could stay there while Class 2E went about their designated visits. The thud of feet as they went past her matched the thumping of her heart. For a moment, she considered pretending to be asleep and missing the day's activities, but Miss Bowen's voice brought her back to reality.

'Come on, Elin! Are you in a dream again?'

She got shakily to her feet and pulled her satchel and coat towards her.

'Everyone line up here!' Mr Winston's voice yelled from outside.

She walked slowly to the bus door and descended the steps as miserably as a condemned prisoner.

'Moo!' shouted one of the boys.

'I know you really are animals, but there's no need to show everyone,' scolded Mr Winston 'Now, get in line and start behaving if you don't want detention for the rest of next week.'

There was a token laugh from some of the boys and a seagull sound from nearby that made Elin think of Carol and her friends.

'Oooh, look! That seagull came really close,' a girl's voice said.

The group set off along the pavement and into the Theological College, where they were all made to wait while Mr Winston went to find the person who would take them on a tour of the paintings.

'Is that nail varnish you're wearing, Carol Jenkins?' asked Miss Bowen in some horror, 'I hope that will all be removed by next Monday.'

'Yes, miss,' she replied sedately before turning her head and rolling her eyes at the other girls.

'Let me see your hands, girls,' Miss Bowen commanded.

They obediently put their hands out so that she could make a note of who needed to be checked the following week.

When she got to Elin, she stopped and peered 'What *have* you got under your nails? I hope you don't go to cookery class with grubby nails like that!'

Elin looked in horror. Feeding the calves just before she left for school sometimes left a dark line under some of her nails. She had attempted to have a wash before going to catch the bus, but her mother had reacted in a suspicious way and demanded to know what she would be doing that would need her to smell of soap.

'If you've started chasing boys, there'll be trouble!' was her parting shot.

Inside the quiet college galleries, Elin was relieved that they were all told to say nothing unless they were asked a question. There was some covert whispering from time to time but Miss Bowen curtailed it with a sharp 'Shhh!'

As the temperature warmed in the building, Elin became convinced that she could smell cows and she discreetly checked her wrists by pretending to rub at her cheek. It was definitely there! She was mortified! How could she have not noticed it before?

The morning wore on and they were eventually ready to be released on to the streets of Aberystwyth again.

'Right, you can go and eat your sandwiches or get something in a cafe now,' said Mr Winston, 'We'll meet up at the bottom of Constitution Hill in an hour. Keep away from the Amusements Arcade – you are not allowed in there. And stay away from the pier – it's dangerous and part of it has been blocked off.'

Non-school regulation coats were immediately put on and pony-tails were hurriedly untied. Girls with loosened pigtails had their hair whipped around their faces as the cold May wind defied the approaching summer. It was clear that some of the girls were intent on treating the day out as a social event rather than an educational one.

Elin looked about her in dismay. Where could she go to eat her sandwiches? The obvious answer was to sit at one of the benches on the seafront. Several were occupied with elderly people doing the same thing.

She made her way towards the seafront.

A shout behind her made her turn round. Coch was running towards her.

'Are you coming to the cafe with us?' she asked.

'Er... I've got sandwiches. I'll eat them here,' she said, too embarrassed to reveal that, at thirteen years old, she had no idea of the price of a snack as she had never been allowed to visit a cafe without her mother.

'Ok, see you later on then,' said Coch as they swung past. Elin thought she could detect relief in her answer. One of Coch's friends threw a chewing-gum paper into the air and, despite the wind, carried out a tennis serve on it so that it landed in a nearby bin.

Elin moved discreetly away from them, conscious of the smell of cows that she had discovered on her wrists.

She found a bench with an elderly woman sitting at one end of it. She strategically placed herself on the opposite end and dug in her satchel for her sandwich pack.

'Day out with the school, bach?' asked the woman.

Elin nodded and made a low 'Hmm' sound. She hoped that the woman would not come closer and begin talking to her. The woman appeared to take the hint and there was no further conversation between them.

She swallowed her sandwich with effort while her throat felt constricted with the effort of not crying. In the distance she could hear the gulls squawking their mocking sounds before swooping in closer to check for left-over bread. Their cries made Elin look over her shoulder for the presence of Carol and her friends.

Eventually, Elin finished her sandwich, stood up and looked towards the bottom of Constitution Hill where they were all to meet up. She walked slowly in that direction, her satchel swinging loosely from one shoulder. The day had warmed slightly and she imagined herself at home, cycling down the lane while birds chirped in the hedge. Or, sitting in the sun on the back step while she shelled peas and listened to her mother's wireless in the background. The thought brought the prickle of tears to her eyes again and she tried to dispel them by remembering a rude poem she had heard one of the boys reciting.

'Good morning, Mr Murphy,

God Bless your heart and soul.

Last night I tried to do your daughter,

But could not find the hole...'

Elin thought for a moment – the words were not quite right. She tried again and got further.

'And when at last I found it

All shining like a pin.

Good gracious, Mr Murphy,

I could not get it in.

And when at last I got it out

Something, something sore

Good gracious, Mr Murphy,

The bugger asked for more'

She knew that was not right either, so she went over it several times in her mind – the rhythm of the poem matching her stride. She made up words for the parts she didn't know and felt a giggle work its way to her mouth. She found herself at the foot of the hill where some people stood near the handrail. She realised that the

90

silly poem had taken her mind off the unpleasantness of the morning.

Again she went through the poem, finding the correct words occasionally while looking out at the sea. She could see a boat moving slowly on the horizon and could smell the seaweed scent from the beach. The gulls continued to swoop and call out. Elin barely heard them as she repeated the poem in her mind – a few words still escaping her. It took several minutes for the sound of the gulls to penetrate her mind as the laughter of her class mates and she turned around in dismay to see Carol and her three friends coming towards her. It was too late to move away.

'There you are, Maxi,' she said 'you should have come with us. We found a chemist that had something you could have put on those nasty spots.'

As they walked closer, they all hopped up and kicked the handrail.

'Have you kicked the bar?' asked Carol.

Elin had no idea what she was talking about.

'Er.... um...er,' she said, while she felt her face glowing with the warmth of a blush.

'You've got to kick the bar,' she continued 'for luck. Otherwise you'll get bad luck the rest of the year. Go on, kick it'

Elin half snorted a false amused sound.

'Aren't you going to do it?' asked Julie.

'Er.. well... er.. I've already done it,' she mumbled.

'Don't believe you,' said Bethan 'Do it again, then.'

'Oh, leave her alone!' said Carol in despair.

'That smell is foul!' said Julie.

Elin jumped and her heart raced away in panic. She pulled back slightly.

'I know,' said Julie 'It's seaweed – ych!'

'I quite like it,' said Carol 'It's a bit like runner beans!'

The other three laughed their seagull sounds while Elin tried to pull away from them a little further.

Once everyone had assembled at the foot of the hill, the whole class boarded the train that took them to the top. In order to fit the whole class in, they squashed together on the hard seats. Elin was unhappy to have to sit beside Menna on the way to the top. She drew herself together in an attempt to minimise the smell of cows. Mr Winston reminded them that they needed to take notice of the landscape in order to discuss it at a future geography lesson and Miss Bowen added that they were also required to write an essay of their experience for the English class. Elin tried to look about her so that no-one would ask her any searching questions, but also checked furtively to see if Menna was showing signs of having smelled the cow odour.

At the top of the hill, they disembarked to find many other visitors taking photographs and admiring the view.

The wind was stronger at that height and Mr Winston raised his voice to make himself heard as they stood in front of the small cafe on top of the hill.

'I want you to remember what we said about different types of rock formation,' he said 'You need to look around for as many types as you can see – and write it down. There will also be different plant types growing depending on the kind of soil and rock underneath. Make some drawings of the plants while you're here and you can write an essay ready for next week.'

Some of the boys made faces when they thought he could not see them. Lowri half giggled until a sharp look from Miss Bowen put a stop to it.

'And when you've finished your geography essay, you can write an English one too,' Miss Bowen added 'You should know the history of Constitution Hill if you've been paying attention, so include that in the essay as well as the history of the paintings we saw earlier.'

Carol puffed her cheeks out and raised an eyebrow at the other girls.

'And you obviously want to write an extra essay on good manners, Carol Jenkins!' she said, tartly.

Carol lowered her face.

'Right, let's get cracking,' said Mr Winston when a few seconds' silence had followed Carol's admonishment, 'Off you go and get started. Keep away from the cliff edges and stay on the paths. We'll be coming round to see how you're getting on'

They wandered off in unenthusiastic clusters, muttering about the task ahead. Mr Winston and Miss Bowen went in different directions to monitor the ones most likely to be wasting time.

Elin looked around to see where she was least likely to be bothered by anyone else. A couple dressed in casual clothes and wearing backpacks appeared from the path that went towards Clarach Bay. Once they had walked past her, she headed in that direction. She gratefully noticed that there was no-one else in sight, but she constantly checked if anyone appeared from either direction.

The grass bank at the side of the path continued for several yards before starting to slope downwards towards the sea; she walked towards the edge so that she would be further away from anyone who passed that way. She peered cautiously over the side; part of the drop was a gradual grassy slope while the rest was much steeper with rocks that jutted out like teeth. She stopped looking before the sight made her dizzy.

She could still see the ship on the horizon, but it had gone further away. Elin felt a pull inside her. How she wished she was on a journey to a place away from her troubles. Another pang reminded her that she would miss her parents if she ran away. But Delyth had survived, her mind suggested. Though, had Delyth run away or been *forced* away? Elin realised how little she knew about her sister – if she really *was* her sister. She sighed. It was no use wishing. She was too young to run away. She would be brought home and then..... her heart stepped up its rate as she imagined the punishment she would receive from Molly on her return.

In a brief moment, her mind turned to the only other option. She gazed down at the cliff and the rough sea. How long would it take for her journey to the bottom? And would she feel much pain? She remembered falling down the stairs at home and knocking herself out. A sharp bump of pain then nothing for seconds... or was it minutes? She had never found out how long it had been because when she came round, her mother had been leaning over her, dragging her by the arm and shouting at her.

'Why do you have to be so clumsy? Are you deliberately trying to give me more work? I haven't got time to nurse you or visit you in hospital!'

Elin thought about this. Would a *real* mother be that cruel?

She looked again at the sea – a decision forming in her mind. The fall downstairs reconstructed itself in her mind. Once the sharp pain had happened, she would feel nothing...

The sound of the waves seemed to increase and call to her. It had a hypnotic effect and she gazed down dreamily. She took a step or two forward. The wind felt as if it was taking her off her feet. She experienced a rush of pleasant adrenalin; she felt as though she could fly and swoop before reaching the sea. Her mind gave her a vision of hovering just above the water before flying in the direction of the ship while the coastline whizzed by and faded away.

Later she would wonder if Aled and Gareth had saved her life.

'We can copy it off Matthew later. This is facking boring.'

Elin jumped around and saw the two boys on the bank above her. They obviously had not noticed her, but their voices carried over her head.

'Haydn won forty quid on the one-arm bandit the other week!'

Aled let out a long whistle.

'If no-one has won much in the Amusements here this week, we could be lucky! Twenty quid each!' Gareth said.

'Why don't we...' said Aled triumphantly, '... tell Matthew that we're going down to see the pier. That'll make him shit bricks! He'll be too chicken to tell anyone!'

Gareth made a half low, half high chuckle as his voice-box battled the choice between man and boy.

Elin stood motionless, willing them to turn away and not see her. Her fear of humiliating attention had blown away all thoughts of jumping from the cliff top.

Aled gave Gareth a playful punch on the arm, followed up by some fake karate kicks. He jumped away as Gareth leapt after him and they both disappeared from Elin's sight.

She let out her breath and relaxed her shoulders. She could still hear faint sounds from the two boys as they got further away from her. She walked along the path until the high sides of the hill rose sharply above it. Spotting a few large rocks, she sat down where an overhanging grass bank gave her cover, and took out her schoolbook. She glanced around and spotted a plant that she could draw. She looked out at the sea one more time, but the call of the waves had gone.

Elin drew the plant in her school book before moving on a few yards to draw another one.

'There you are, Elin,' Miss Bowen's voice broke into her thoughts. Elin jumped.

Miss Bowen stopped a few feet away.

'Have you nearly finished?' she asked.

'Yes, miss,' Elin said, pointing to the plant she was drawing.

'All right. Don't forget the other side of the hill. There are lots of different plants and rock types there.'

Miss Bowen turned and walked away. There was something *unappealing* about the girl, though she had to concede that she was a diligent, if not particularly bright, pupil. A late developer, Miss Bowen thought. She hoped that puberty would not turn her into another Carol Jenkins - a thought that returned to her guilty mind much later.

Once Miss Bowen had gone, Elin finished her drawing and moved further towards the Clarach Bay path. She gazed half-heartedly at the ground for rock types, but soon her mind had wandered off and she re-lived the previous week when she had walked along the roadside hedge at her home while a grey squirrel had leapt from tree to tree in front of her. Elin's fertile imagination had suggested that the animal was trying to lead her somewhere - rather than the reality of it trying to escape the human who followed it. Her mind had created all sorts of fantasy scenarios where she had followed the squirrel into a hollow tree and had emerged the other side into a new life where she existed amongst forest creatures that spoke to her. It was a childish dream that she often returned to; despite being a teenager, her emotions were that of a child as she attempted to cling to happier times when the 'sin' of growing up was not constantly stunted by Molly.

She had come to a halt on the cliff-top and was living the scene inside her head. (Molly had caught her doing it on many occasions and had told Elin that she looked vacant and that her mouth hung open.)

'What's the matter with you?' Carol's voice broke into her reverie.

Elin started like a nervous horse and clamped her mouth shut. She saw that Carol was alone.

'I was just looking,' she said, while her eyes scanned hastily for some item she could claim to be looking at.

'You looked as if you weren't all there!' said Carol.

Elin said nothing in the hope that she would go away. Instead, Carol walked towards her. Elin glanced about her for a means of distancing herself.

Then, without any preamble, Carol suddenly announced 'They're sly cows, those three!'

Elin had no idea what she was talking about.

She did not have to wait long.

'Honestly, you'd think they could keep a secret! They just want to snitch on Aled and Gareth! I told them they're just pathetic!'

Elin began to make sense of the words.

'Have they gone down to the Amusements?' she asked Carol.

Carol looked sharply at her 'How do you know?'

'I thought I heard them say...' Elin's voice tailed off.

'Anyway, they've gone down to the pier first. I wish I'd gone with them. I can't believe that Julie and Bethan would tell on them. Do you know what Lowri said? That it might be dangerous and that we should stop them!' Carol huffed out her breath in disgust, 'She was on her way to tell Miss Bow-wow and I just walked off and left them. Silly cows! I could see Bow-wow and Wincy running around and telling everyone to wait in the cafe with that caretaker bloke while they went down in the train.' Carol examined her varnished nails as she said this.

'I'm never going to speak to Julie or Bethan – and especially Lowri – ever again!' she stated eventually - a prediction that came true later that day.

Elin half turned and took a few steps away from Carol. She hoped that their conversation was over. To her dismay, Carol followed her.

'Have you done any of these stupid drawings?' she asked.

Elin nodded.

'Let me see them,' she said. It was not a request but an automatic assumption that Elin would comply.

'They're not very....' she began, but Carol was already undoing the buckle on Elin's satchel.

'I'll copy them,' Carol said 'Let me have your book and I'll do them over the weekend. I can't find any stupid plants!'

As she tried to open the satchel, she spotted the beret nestled in its sanctuary inside.

Elin held her breath in the hope that it would be overlooked.

'Why do you wear that awful beret?' Carol said 'No-one else does. I can really help you smarten yourself up a bit if you'll only do I say.'

Elin could feel herself getting flustered and all the smart answers she imagined herself giving Carol faded away like the ship she had seen on the horizon.

'Er... er... It's just the... I don't always...' she tripped over her words.

'For goodness sake, give it here!' Carol snapped and snatched the satchel away from her.

'No!' Elin felt her eyes threatening tears again 'Leave it...'

But Carol had swung away from her and opened the satchel fully.

She triumphantly pulled the offending garment from its hiding-place and dropped the satchel on the floor.

'Please don't...' Elin said.

Carol looked fiercely at her.

'I'm trying to help you! It will stop people thinking you're weird.'

Elin launched at her but Carol jumped back.

'This is going where it should have gone a long time ago!' Carol stated.

She turned around and threw the beret in the direction of the sea. The wind caught it and whirled it halfway back to her. It landed on a rocky piece of ground at the edge of the hill.

Elin's battle with tears had been lost and she sobbed unselfconsciously, the sound losing its impetus in the buffeting whoosh of the wind.

She lunged forward to rescue the beret, but Carol was too quick for her.

'Let it go!' she shouted at Elin and leapt at the beret. She bent down to pick it up and the wind whipped up under her clothes and hair, temporarily blinding and unbalancing her.

She let out a shriek before tumbling over the edge.

Elin jumped backwards in shock. She heard Carol shrieking again.

'Help me!'

Elin stepped forward carefully while trying to keep her balance as the wind came in pulsing gusts.

Carol was clinging to the cliff face. One leg rested on a small rocky ledge while the other swung from the knee in an effort to find purchase.

'Quick! Help me!' she screamed up at Elin.

Elin had a brief feeling of satisfaction as she saw the tears on Carol's face, but it was soon replaced by horror. She looked around to see if there was anyone who could help, but the lonely spot she had chosen to get away from the others had worked – there was no-one in sight.

'Don't go!' Carol shouted in between sobs 'Don't leave me!'

Elin leaned forward. The view made her dizzy and she closed her eyes for a second.

'I'll get someone,' she tried to shout, but shock and the noise of the wind reduced it to little more than a stage whisper.

She again pulled back and looked about her – where *was* everyone?

'Nooooo!' shouted Carol 'Maxi! Don't go!'

A small sensation of hate made itself felt. She began to turn away and took a step further from the cliff edge.

'Noo –oo – oo..!' Carol sobbed 'I'M FALLING...'

The last two words came out as a shriek and Elin turned back towards her. She saw that Carol had slipped further down and that there were fragments of rock bouncing down the cliff underneath her. She lay down on her tummy and looked down at Carol.

'Help me. My hand...' she said and tried to reach up to Elin.

Below them, the sea rolled up against the rocks, sending foam and water up the side of the cliff. To Elin it looked as if it was trying to get at Carol. The entire motion made her feel dizzy and she closed her eyes again.

'Here! Here!' Carol shrieked 'LOOK!'

Elin opened her eyes and looked down into Carol's fierce face.

'You've got to pull me!' she said 'My hand.'

Elin reached her arm down, but a gap of about six inches remained between them.

'Lean forward,' Carol commanded 'Further.'

Elin wriggled a little closer while the dizziness played tricks with her head.

She touched the tips of Carol's fingers.

'Further. Come down more!' Carol shrieked the command at her.

Suddenly, she grabbed Elin's hand and pulled against it. Elin felt herself slide forward dangerously and clung on to the grass and stone with her other hand.

'Pull!' Carol ordered.

Elin pulled but her thin, underdeveloped body was outweighed by Carol's.

'Pull, for God's sake!' she screamed.

Elin began to feel panic as she continued to slide towards the cliff edge. She tried to let Carol's hand go but the other girl clung on in desperation.

'Don't you let go! Don't you bloody DARE!' she shouted.

Elin panicked even more and struggled backwards.

Carol's face was bright red.

'Pull!' she shouted again.

Elin's grip loosened and she again tried to let go of Carol's hand.

'Pull! Pull me up! What's wrong with you, you *smelly cow*?' she sobbed in frustration.

The squawk of a nearby seagull added the final straw in Elin's mind and she flicked her arm side to side and let go of Carol's hand. The sudden movement upset what little balance Carol had and she seemed to lean backwards away from Elin. Her face had become a series of circles – her eyes, mouth and face formed different sized 'O's. A scream came out of one of the 'O's and she fell backwards. Elin turned her eyes away, but not soon enough and she saw Carol hit an outcrop of rocks before continuing downwards towards the sea.

Elin scrambled to her knees and turned back towards the safety of the path. Her beret had become lodged against a rock and she automatically picked it up and forced her shaking legs back into less dangerous territory.

There was still no-one in sight and she stood with a wildly beating heart on the windy bank. What could she do?

The sound of a seagull shrieked behind her and she spun round, half- expecting to see Carol standing there. All she saw was the flat horizon of the sea.

She ran towards the back of the building that housed the cafe. As she rounded the corner of the wall, she slowed to what she thought was a nonchalant walk. (Her upbringing of physical punishment had taught her to do everything necessary to avoid getting into trouble.) The unrealistic thought that Carol had probably landed in the sea and had managed to swim to shore made its presence in her head.

You smelly cow!

The words went around in constant circles in between other thoughts.

She leaned against the wall and sat down on the floor. She could feel her heart thumping against her back as she pressed against the hard wall. She could hear some shouts coming from the other side of the building as some of the boys play-fought. Mr Winston and Miss Bowen were obviously still not back because she heard the man who was in charge of the building shouting at them to stop it.

She opened her satchel and rolled the beret up and tucked it away inside. Lowri came into view and looked around, taking in the sight of Elin, but disregarding her.

'I don't know where she is,' she said over her shoulder to one of the others before going back out of sight 'Maxi's sitting down round there. I didn't ask her...'

A second later, Julie came around the corner 'Have you seen Carol?' she asked.

Elin shrugged.

Lowri appeared beside her.

'I wonder if she's gone down to see what the boys were doing?' she said in a lower voice.

Julie's eyes widened 'She'll cop it with Bow-wow if she has!'

Some other girls appeared.

'We think Carol's gone down to the pier with the boys,' Julie said conspiratorially.

The others looked both horrified and impressed before turning around to see who else they could tell.

'She'll bloody get it!' someone murmured.

Coch's face joined them.

'Is it true Carol's gone down to the pier?'

'Sssh!'

'Shit! She hasn't, has she?'

'No-one's seen her for ages.'

'We'll say she felt ill and went down. OK?'

Heads nodded and murmured assents were given.

The man in charge of the building came round the corner.

'Right, you lot, back in here where I can keep an eye on you,' he said.

Elin got up and they all drifted back towards the seating area. She sat as far away from the others as she could. Her silence was nothing unusual and no-one took any notice of her.

Later on, only Miss Bowen came back up Constitution Hill. They later found out that Mr Winston had stayed down with the two errant boys – telling them exactly how much detention they had earned and how much he hated them.

Miss Bowen was tight-lipped and refused to be led into answering questions.

'Did you find them, Miss?'

'Are they ok, Miss?'

All those asking, received sharp glances and Miss Bowen tapped her nose as an answer.

Lowri was more interested to know if Carol had been with them, but was afraid to ask and show knowledge of any wrongdoing or to get Carol into trouble if she had not been discovered with the boys.

Class 2E were eventually herded on to the train to take them down to the town. Miss Bowen counted them all on; then counted again before asking the question.

'Where is Carol Jenkins?'

Lowri, Julie and some others swapped quick glances but said nothing.

'Lowri! Where is she?' Miss Bowen sounded angrier than anyone had ever heard her – a result of the stress she had suffered while unsuccessfully looking for the boys on the pier.

'I don't know, Miss,' said Lowri, her face reddening as she said it.

'Don't you lie to me, miss!' Miss Bowen snarled 'Where is she?'

'We really don't know, Miss,' Julie piped up, 'We haven't seen her for ages. I think she was feeling ill. I think she said something about going down to the town'.

Miss Bowen sighed, the bloody trip was turning into a nightmare – three children running wild in Aberystwyth. Alun Morris, the headmaster, would have plenty to say about it when they got back. He had been against the idea of the trip from the beginning. It seemed that he had been right all along.

Resigning herself to the fact that Carol Jenkins - a handful at the best of times – was almost certainly with Mr Winston or hiding near to the Amusements Arcade where they had found the boys, Miss Bowen decided to take all the children down on the train and deal with Carol when they reached the town.

They made a quiet descent to the bottom of the hill. Miss Bowen's fierce expression deterred even the highest of schoolboy spirits and there was hardly a sound until their footsteps clattered off the platform. The woman who had been selling the train tickets waved a cheery goodbye to them but had little response as Class 2E filed past with serious faces.

On Miss Bowen's instruction, they walked in a long line along the pier and up to the Theological College where they assembled on the pavement.

Mr Winston came out to meet them and Miss Bowen had a few quiet, hurried words with him. He frowned and went back into the college. After a few minutes, he came out and spoke quietly to Miss Bowen before she went indoors while he cast a disapproving eye over the, by then, restless teenagers.

'Just stand quietly until the bus arrives,' he said in distracted tones. He even seemed to turn a blind eye when David James snapped the back of Coch's bra strap.

Eventually, Miss Bowen came out of the college with Aled and Gareth who looked slightly smug at the commotion they had caused. Miss Bowen again consulted Mr Winston in hushed tones and he nodded his head in agreement. Some of the pupils thought they had heard words like 'Police' and 'Phone Mr Morris' but none of them were certain of the content of their teachers' conversation. When they had finished their whispered consultation, Miss Bowen turned and walked back into the college without speaking to the children.

Very shortly, the bus arrived and they climbed the steps with less enthusiasm than on the outward journey. The doors hissed shut.

'Sir, Sir!' said Lowri urgently 'Miss Bowen isn't here!'

Mr Winston looked at her with the expression of one examining a dung beetle.

'Miss Bowen is staying here to deal with your missing friend,' he said 'If you know where she is, you can save yourself a lot of trouble by telling me now. Otherwise, you can think about it every lunchtime when you have detention in the library until the end of term.'

He glanced at the others in an attempt to force a blurted confession.

Lowri's eyes became small hard brown spots surrounded by large white eyeballs.

'But I don't know where she is, sir!' Her voice was slightly tearful.

Mr Winston's expression hardened further before he turned away in disgust.

The bus began its way home and whispered debates took place between various groups of children. Aled and Gareth were made to sit near the front where Mr Winston was able to prevent any contact between them and the other children, though it was clear that most of Class 2E wanted to ask them for their account of the afternoon.

Elin sat alone as usual. She tried to close her eyes, but sleep refused her that refuge and all she saw behind her closed eyelids was Carol's round, screaming face as it fell away from her. She told herself that she had only tried to get a better grip on Carol's hand; the longer she thought about it, the more she convinced herself that it was the truth. The image of Carol's face flicked on and off in her mind like the failing strip-lighting in her father's barn. She re-played the scene and again imagined Carol landing in the water and swimming to safety, but her memory cruelly brought the image of the jutting out rocks that had temporarily interrupted her journey down to the water. She began to feel nauseous.

She closed her eyes again and tried to remember the squirrel leaping from tree to tree in front of her. When that failed to work, she pictured herself emerging from the hollow tree with the woodland creatures waiting for her.

Eventually she began to relax and her body gave in to drowsiness. The bus moved with a comforting sway and she nestled down into her seat. The woodland image returned to her mind and she immersed herself into the fantasy.

She did not think she had been asleep when the slowing down motion of the bus and a collective 'Uuugh!' from some of her classmates claimed her attention. She opened her eyes and looked out through the window. The bus had swerved wide to avoid something on the road. On getting closer, she could see it was a dead badger that had obviously come down to the road from the high hedgerow and been run over by a car. It was a common sight on the rural roads.

'Guts all over the road!' said a boy's voice in fascination.

Elin tried to look away but her eyes defied her and swivelled back to the sticky mess on the road. Loops of intestine and patches of red covered the tarry surface of the road. The badger's head was still intact but its abdomen was torn open. The wetness took on a gloss from the sunlight.

The bus swerved back onto the correct side of the road and accelerated smoothly.

The image of the badger stayed in Elin's mind. Seeing injured or dead animals did not normally bother her – it was a fact of farming life – but the intestinal loops were making her think of Carol and how she had hit some jutting-out rocks as she had fallen down the cliff-side. Elin tried to dispel the image but it continuously returned to her mind, playing over and over and becoming more graphic with each minute.

Her mental image showed her Carol's descent, the way her body had hit the rocks: her imagination added the sudden splitting of her abdomen and the terrible picture of her intestines bursting out like thick wires and flailing around her as she fell.

Elin felt a lurch in her stomach and tried to scramble to her feet. Her beret was already in her hands. She had been holding it like some kind of comfort blanket since leaving Aberystwyth.

As she got to her feet, her stomach let go and, in desperation, she vomited into the beret.

'Stop the bus!' someone yelled.

Elin felt another lurch but managed to hold it until the bus had stopped. She raced down the steps and knelt over the grass verge. She heaved several times, but nothing came up. Her meagre lunch sandwich had all but gone.

She sat back on her heels, feeling light-headed, but slightly better. She was aware of her beret still in her hands and she hit it against the ground to get rid of any vomit.

'Are you ok?' Coch's voice came behind her.

Elin glanced round to nod her head and saw that Rhian, one of Coch's sports-mad friends, was also standing outside the bus and leaning against it.

'Rhian gets travel sick too,' said Coch, gesturing with her head 'I think you set her off!'

Elin looked away as she heard Rhian's cough followed by a retch.

She tested herself by thinking of Carol falling. Thankfully, she realised that the terrible images had gone from her mind.

Tentatively, she thought about the dead badger too and was relieved that it did not cause any further nausea.

Coch had turned away and was checking on Rhian. Elin slowly got to her feet and went back into the bus where a lively discussion was taking place.

'It was definitely the sausage roll from that cafe. I said it tasted funny.'

'Mine was fine.'

'But you could smell it. You said!'

Mr Winston quieted them with a sharp look.

'Sit at the front,' he ordered Elin, 'in case you're sick again.'

He leaned out of the bus door and called out, 'Is she ready to get back on?'

Coch came back up the steps with a white-faced Rhian.

'Sit there,' Mr Winston said, pointing next to Elin's seat.

Elin tried to roll her beret up as tightly as possible to disguise the smell of vomit.

Both girls sat in silence until the bus arrived back at Llanefa Grammar School.

Due to their delay while looking for Carol, the school buses had left and Mr Winston tried to make hurried arrangements to ferry the children to their homes. All of Class 2E were from the eastern side of Llanefa which meant that none were within comfortable walking distance. Mr Winston went into the school to make some phone calls while the others debated as to the whereabouts of Carol. Aled and Gareth were adamant that she had not been with them and the rest of the girls began speculating wildly. Elin began to feel nauseous again and decided to walk home. She told Coch that she was going to walk and left the school before anyone could stop her.

On the outskirts of Llanefa, near the petrol station, there was a minor road that led to a shortcut over an earth track and she chose this route for her homeward journey.

It was a quiet road and, as expected, she saw no-one. It gave her time to think about the day's events and convince herself that she had not deliberately made Carol fall.

It was a long walk and Elin had to stop and sit down twice. She felt weak due to hunger and stress. As soon as she sat in the long grass, her mind leapt into action by replaying Carol's fall – each time giving her a different version. Eventually her brain settled on the most comfortable scenario. As she began to remember, the part of her mind that tried to keep her sane offered her the vision of trying to get a better grip of Carol's hand. She recalled the feeling of sliding forward as Carol's weight pulled her down. She'd *had* to do something. She had gripped the grass with one hand but she knew that she, too, would also fall over the side. She had tried to let go so that she could grasp Carol's wrist. It all became clear to her; she had not *deliberately* made Carol fall. She had been trying to save her. She would tell them what had happened. She would be a hero!

Her brief feeling of elation suddenly burst as she remembered the frantic search for Carol and the way Mr Winston had tried to force them into giving him information.

She instantly burst into tears and covered her face with her hands. She couldn't tell anyone. There had been nothing she could have done.

'No use crying over spilt milk! What's done is done. Let it be a lesson to you,' her mother's voice piped up in her memory. Her mother was right. It was what Molly said every time Elin did something wrong.

She sniffed and wiped her eyes and nose with her sleeve. Her grubby nails came briefly into view - grubby from feeding the calves.

'You smelly cow!' Carol's shriek replayed in her mind.

And still I tried to save her, Elin thought.

If I had saved her, she would have *had* to have been nice to me, she thought, before remembering the times that Carol had copied some of her school work and shown, not gratitude, but a taking for granted that it was Elin's duty to help her.

She shuddered as she remembered the moments where she had considered jumping over the side of the cliff. The brutal way that Carol's body had bounced against the rocks made her grateful that she had not given in to her despair.

She got to her feet before another bout of crying could take hold. She swung her satchel over her shoulder and held the cheesy-smelling beret by hooking one finger into its rim.

She came out on to the tarred Pwll y Coed road and turned towards her parents' farm. She concentrated on putting one foot in front of the other. The pattern of her footfalls beat a poetic rhythm and she was reminded of the rude poem that had distracted her earlier that day; though it felt like months away by then. She deliberately changed the pattern of her steps so that the poem could not match them and give her memories she wanted to be rid of. Every four of five steps, she hopped twice on the same foot so that there was no convenient timing of her feet to her tortured mind.

A squirrel appeared in the hedge beside her. She briefly acknowledged its presence, but she had no use for childish stories in her head. On she went - one, two, three, four, hop; one, two, three, four, hop. Her vision swam and her throat felt dry.

Her exhaustion wore the hop down to a shuffle; she pictured her parents' house and longed for somewhere to sit down.

The sound of a car alerted her. The vehicle was coming towards her. She could hear it, but it remained out of sight behind tall hedges. She wiped at her face self-consciously, not wanting to display the obvious signs of tears. She considered hiding over the hedge, but a quick glance round showed her no means of access. Realising that it was too late, she bent her head forward and kept walking. A few seconds later, her father's car came into view. Molly sat in the passenger seat, her face locked into disapproval. Elin's heart began to accelerate.

The car stopped beside her.

She opened the back door. Immediately, Molly began shouting at her, 'Where have you been? Didn't I say that this trip was a chance to learn something not run around enjoying yourself...?'

She was still shouting as Elin began to get into the car, but the rest of her words seemed to be coming from far away. A sharp slap on her face brought her mind back into focus.

'Don't ignore me when I'm talking to you!'

Her mother had twisted around in her seat and had her hand raised for a second blow.

Elin burst into tears again. Molly James dropped her hand.

'Where have you been?'

'I'm sorry... the bus was late back... I've been sick...there was... some of the boys...' Elin could say no more.

'Boys!' Molly shrieked 'Why do you always have to make me worry! As if I hadn't had enough to cope with when Delyth was your age! Now you're getting just as bad!'

Elin sobbed into her hands.

'It's no use crying!' Molly continued 'You need to think before doing these things!'

It was her usual punishment speech and Elin played the script in her mind as Molly launched into it. The familiarity of the scene was almost a comfort to Elin. She listened dutifully and wore a contrite expression, though she had no idea that she was doing it.

Once they arrived home, Molly's anger seemed to have subsided and Elin was sent to change from her school uniform. Elin showed her the soiled beret and Molly reacted in horror.

'I won't be able to wash that!' she said 'It will shrink and lose its shape. I'll have to try and get another one!'

Nevertheless, Elin tried to soak it in cold water, but it was clear that the hated garment had had its day.

Throughout the evening, she lapsed into quiet crying at intervals; making efforts not to alert her mother and earn further punishment.

At bedtime she gave in to her despair and lay on her back in the darkened room while her tears ran down into her ears. She eventually fell asleep where her dreams were filled with strange images of mermaids who had Carol's face. She jumped awake every few hours; each bout of wakefulness gave her a few seconds' false impression that all her trauma had been a dream. Then her true memory took over the story and provided a vivid representation of Carol's accident.

At some point, Elin fell into an exhausted, dreamless sleep until her mother's voice woke her.

'Are you going to stay in bed all day? There's work to be done! When I was your age I'd had to finish school!'

Elin swung her body out of bed. Her legs protested at holding her up. Molly James was still halfway through her 'when I was your age' speech.

Elin began to ask what time it was, but her throat tightened in a painful spasm followed by a volley of chesty coughing. She attempted to swallow a few times, but the pain was too sharp.

Molly looked at her in disgust, 'Just because you've got a cold doesn't mean the calves don't get fed!'

Elin stood in bemused silence. She had no idea why her mother was in such a bad mood. Some part of her guilty mind suggested that Molly knew what had happened to Carol, but Elin stayed silent. It was to be many years later that Elin discovered Molly's fear of having to take the girl to a doctor or hospital where knowledge of her birth mother may have been accidentally revealed.

She went through the motions of washing and getting dressed while her legs protested at every move and her head pounded in pain. She did no more than glance at her cup of tea before nausea gave her a warning. A cautious sip of water made her throat explode into pain and she rubbed ineffectually at it.

Once outside she went through the automatic motions of mixing the calves' powdered milk, though each movement was followed by a few seconds' rest. She took each bucket of milk and leaned over into every calf pen to feed the inhabitant. Some of the bigger calves head-butted the bucket in their eagerness to drink and Elin cringed in pain as the effect of the thump resonated throughout her aching body.

By the time she had fed the last calf, Elin gave in and slid down into a sitting position against the wooden slats of the pen.

'Just for a minute...' she told herself.

She remembered very little after that. Images of her parents, with her mother's voice raised and her father tutting quietly, came and went.

Her next clear memory was of being in bed and trying to get out of it.

Another recollection was of sitting up in bed and trying to say, 'The calves will eat Carol!' though she gratefully realised later that her inflamed throat had prevented Molly from understanding what she was trying to say.

Her coughing came from a progressively deeper location within her chest and she was vaguely aware that the local doctor had appeared in the room with her mother. The cool stethoscope on her chest was a relief, though she failed to sit up to have her back listened to and became irritated by his attempts to lift her.

Conversations came to her in fragmented sections; she could remember some sections clearly while other parts of the remaining days became absorbed in her mental fog.

'No! There's no need!' her mother's piercing voice brought the present into sharp focus.

'If she doesn't improve, she'll *have* to be admitted...' came the doctor's voice in response.

Eventually, Elin began to get better though it took several weeks. By the time she was up and about, Molly told her that Carol Jenkins had drowned in the sea at Aberystwyth. Her body had been found the day after their school trip. Molly's tone was so uncharacteristically gentle that it was her voice, rather than the news, that made Elin cry.

The shock, the funeral, the constant questioning and debating were all over by the time Elin went back to school. With no close friend to provide her with up-to-date news, Elin's return to the classroom went almost unnoticed. The resilience of youth had resulted in the whole class moving on and putting the tragic incident behind them. The only one who glanced every day at the empty space where Carol's desk had stood, was Elin. It was a gesture she kept to herself. Even during her subsequent years at Llanefa Grammar school, she was always aware of one missing desk.

Without even checking her diary, she started a letter document on the screen.

'Dear Janet,' she began *'Thank you for your kind invitation. Unfortunately, on that date...'*

Elin paused for a few moments to think of a convincing lie to complete the sentence.

'... I will be abroad and will be unable to attend.'

She glanced down at her desk drawer, the one that contained the boxes of Paracetamol tablets. These were her present day comfort blanket. Once again, she was tempted by the chance to escape. She thought of Aled and Gareth who had saved her once; and of the ship that had beckoned her. The image of the sea lingered in her mind. She thought about the fantasy of flying over it. Her childhood imaginings had never fully left her. The more she thought about it, the clearer her mind became.

She glanced back at her screen before printing out Janet's letter ready for posting. Then she activated her internet provider to search for South American countries. Photographs and maps appeared along with general information. Elin held her breath. How difficult would it be to vanish? Buy a return ticket, get a travel visa, but disappear into an anonymous society instead of flying home. She would make the news for a short time, but eventually she would just become a name that was mentioned in social gatherings, 'Did they ever find that woman who went missing in Chile or Peru or wherever it was..?'

Outside her window, the sound of urban gulls reminded her of the cruel teenage laughter from her childhood and her hands shook slightly as she switched off the computer.

Brown Cow's Legacy.

Tegwyn picks up a pale yellow certificate.

Last year's date and the title 'Llanefa Charitable Auction' are printed along the top.

Underneath, it reads 'Receipt – the under-named has successfully bid to have his/her name included in a new novel by author Tim Howe.'

Below that, someone has carefully written 'Tegwyn Prydderch' in Old English script.

The auction had been a great success, Tegwyn recalls. Tim, though a year or two older, had been at Llanefa Grammar School with him.

Tegwyn looks forward to reading about his eventual role in the new novel.

He puts the certificate back in its envelope.

The cornfield of Llwyncelyn Farm was the nearest we got to an adventure playground in non-politically correct 1968. It was a huge ten acre field that sat behind a small row of council houses at the edge of Llanefa.

Llwyncelyn Farm was apparently the biggest farm in the area at that time and the field we played in was far enough away from the farmhouse to give us the freedom to avoid adult interference. It was also far enough away from our homes and the problems we escaped when we went outdoors to play.

When I say 'we', I can see now that it was those of us who would probably be best described as misfits. We had dwindled down to just three fairly soon - Barbara, Noel and me. During the first fortnight of the summer holidays the field had been highly populated by children, but they soon became bored with it after every game had been tried and played, and each leafy hiding place had been explored. I was happy with that situation. I was an anxious, ingratiating child and an easy target for the bullish behaviour of some of the other boys.

I wasn't known as Tim Howe in those days. That came many years later as a suggestion from my publisher. In earlier days, I went by the name that appeared on my birth certificate – Timothy Hywel Jones. Everyone called me Hywel then.

The appeal of the cornfield for me was the seclusion it gave once the plants started to grow. It wasn't even corn as I would think of it now. Everyone called it Indian Corn back then. Today, I think it might be better known as maize.

The plants grew to a huge height that towered above us. From mid July onwards, we were able to play without being spotted amongst the plant stems. We had the whole summer holiday to use it as the crop was not normally harvested until October.

In 1968, it was the summer before we went on to secondary school – Llanefa Grammar for me and the Secondary Modern out on the Carmarthen road for the other two.

The farm was owned by Mr Brown; a stocky little man who always wore a flat cap and carried a thick stick (which Noel swore was really a gun if you got close enough to see it). He also wore a tweed jacket and a collar and tie, regardless of the weather. I imagine he saw himself as a gentleman farmer, though, in truth, he had few casual workers and seemed to do most of the work himself, (it was well known that the young men he hired never lasted long because he was far too mean to pay much). In 1960s Llanefa, Mr Brown was a novelty - he was English. I heard later that he was from Shropshire, but his accent made him difficult to understand and we children lived in fear of being questioned by him and not being able to answer! There was a Mrs Brown, too, but we rarely saw her. During my last visit back to Llanefa, I saw a woman driving a huge tractor with some kind of sophisticated harvesting machine behind it, but in the Sixties, Llanefa farmers' wives tended to work only in close proximity to the house and farmyard.

The name we called Mr Brown, was 'Brown Cow'. I'm not sure who came up with the nickname, but it seemed a natural title for a man who kept cows – though we had never seen any cows. They, like Mrs Brown, must have conducted their business closer to home!

We all had good reason to be scared of Brown Cow. He hated us.

The apparent reason for his hate was that we trampled through his crops, breaking and bending the stems which made it difficult or impossible to harvest them. With the typical reasoning of eleven-year olds, we could see no wrong in what we were doing. Noel was the one who came closest to an accurate assessment when he said that there were *millions* of plants in the field and that the rare one or two stems that snapped made no difference either way. More significantly, we *tried not* to break the plants because they gave us more cover when they stood tall and undamaged.

For me, the tall stems were a jungle, a magical forest or the legs of some alien creature from another planet. Our playtimes were based on those imaginings. Even then, I had a talent for making up stories, even though most of them had plotlines which were suspiciously similar to Tarzan and Skippy the Bush Kangaroo or Lost in Space! One of our favourite games was to pretend that our plane had crash-landed in a jungle and we had to find our way to safety while avoiding the tigers and lions that followed and would try to eat us. (It was to be much later that I found out that lions and tigers did not share the same continent!) Sometimes, Noel would be one of the tigers, but usually we played our own characters and the marauding beasts were no more than threatening shadows moving through the plant stems.

Noel played an excellent tiger – his ability to creep up on me and Barbara without making any noise was uncanny. His only failing in the role was that when he was about to reach out with his claw-shaped fingers, he made a low growling noise at the same time. Barbara would normally hear it first and let out a blood-curdling scream before running into the greenery. When our imaginary lions and tigers were not played by Noel, he would still give a low growl to indicate that there was one nearby. The cue for us all to run was when Barbara screamed.

Things took on a new slant on a rainy afternoon as we played in the maize, keeping relatively dry as the overhead broad leaves sheltered us. The drips of rain created an extra illusion of wild animals stalking us. We spread out in a wide line and crept forward in crouching positions, signalling to warn each other when we 'saw' a lion. Noel carried a long plant stem that he called his gun. He only had three bullets, he said, so he had to be sparing in how many lions he could shoot. Noel was always the practical one!

I was on the far left of the line, Barbara on the far right and Noel in the middle.

Noel looked across at me and held up two fingers - his signal that he could see two lions. I nodded and gestured that we should veer to the left to circle them. Before we could signal to Barbara, she let out a shocked scream and lunged forward into the crop. It was a long scream, so it partly drowned out another sound at first. The sound was a man's roaring voice.

Noel and I ran into the depths of the green stems, taking our own routes. I was aware that, this time, there really was something to run from.

In a few seconds, I came to a halt in a disorientated panic. Barbara's screams had been overpowered by the man's voice 'GETOUTOFMYFIELD!'

My brain broke it down into understandable language and I knew that Brown Cow had finally had enough. He had never run after us and shouted before. Instead, he had always waited near the gate and lectured any of us who emerged from the depths of the crop. I stood in a state of high alert, trying to determine the direction of the shouting. It seemed to be going further away from me. Barbara's screams stopped and all I could hear were Brown Cow's angry shouts that, I hoped, were reducing in volume.

I continued to creep around through the stems until I spotted a telltale streak of orange – Noel's sweater. He saw me at the same time and we clustered together quickly.

'Where's Barbara?' he whispered.

'I don't know' I whispered back.

All the shouting had stopped and we hardly dared to breathe too heavily in case we were heard.

Noel whispered that we should follow our tracks back to where we had first seen Brown Cow and, from there, follow Barbara's tracks. It sounded like a good idea, though our previous running around earlier that afternoon had left plenty of confusing footprints in the soil, so that particular plan was soon thwarted.

We relaxed into the thought that Brown Cow had gone and Noel soon turned the whole episode into a game where Barbara had been captured by vicious natives and we had to make attempts to rescue her. I let myself be led into the spirit of this game – suggesting different avenues we could incorporate into it. With the resilience of youth, we soon forgot about Barbara and threw ourselves into our new game – a game that meant we could swear more colourfully as there was no girl present. Noel was a practised swearer! His home life was peppered with swearwords – especially when his father came home drunk. Even his mother could be heard to use the foulest of words when they quarrelled. I was brought up with much more gentility. My elderly parents were chapel-goers who frowned upon bad language, though I'm sure my two older brothers were fluent in the subject. They were seventeen and nineteen and I was referred to as the 'little accident' – a term I did not understand at that time.

My contribution to swearing was limited to 'Pwrs' and 'Diawl' – which meant 'scrote' and 'devil' and were respectable markers of how street-wise I was. I threw in the odd 'bloody' for effect, but I was careful not to use it too often for fear of letting my guard down at home. (It strikes me as amusing now, that the only Welsh words I remember are the swearwords!)

Meanwhile, Noel and I fought cannibals and shot deer in typical Boys Own fashion.

We were sitting down at our imaginary campfire (which in our plot, was soon to be the target of a cannibal attack), when we spotted a colour which was not part of the undergrowth. We must have seen it at the same time as we both rose to our feet ready to flee, when a small voice said 'Hywel?'

We turned around and saw that it was Barbara, crouched into the smallest imaginable size she could manage. Despite the bright colour of her clothing, she had kept herself hidden among the plant stems. It was a talent we had not noticed when we had played Hide and Seek, but now that I think back, it had been there all the time.

We went to her as she got to her feet.

'Did he catch you?' Noel asked.

'No' she said, shaking her head 'I ran too fast for him'.

'I think he's gone now' I said.

'What happened?' asked Noel.

'I just ran and ran. I could hear him behind me. I thought he was going to catch me. I dodged from side to side and when I got far enough ahead, I hid down in the plants and didn't move' she explained.

'Well, well, said Will to the wall' said Noel. It was his current catchphrase when he was presented with a notable situation. I had heard others say it, but not as often as Noel. Sometimes he chanted out the whole saying which ended with 'But the wall said nothing to Will'. It sometimes got irritating.

'He could have caught you on the floor' he added 'then he would have just killed you.'

The killing part was probably an exaggeration on Noel's behalf, but Barbara's eyes stretched to large circles and her mouth formed an 'o'. Even I glanced around nervously.

From then on, we developed a code. Whenever one of us saw or heard Brown Cow, we shouted 'SPY!' as loudly as we could and then ran in different directions while he plundered behind us like a bull that had been stung by a bee. Having an insight into how much he hated us was a help to us as we escaped his wild charges. It became much more than a challenge; it became fun. Our previous imagined adventures faded into insignificance once we had a real live bogey-man to outwit!

We did not see Brown Cow every day, but nevertheless, we kept a lookout for him. The threat of attack was always present and added an extra thrill to our games.

We normally met up every afternoon outside Moses Evans's shop opposite the Baptist chapel. The shop seems like something from another planet when I remember it – an ordinary little end-of-terrace house that had a small shop in the front room. Moses only sold sweets and cigarettes, so he was a regular magnet for children and for men on their way home from work.

Noel and Barbara were usually sitting on the stone wall of the chapel by the time I got there – they apparently had more freedom than I did. My mother insisted that I carried out my chores of sweeping the garden path and other boring activities after breakfast. Then I had to sit down and read aloud from the Bible before lunch (which we called 'dinner'). She rarely listened to me, but I can see that it was her clever way of ensuring that I was actually reading rather than sitting and daydreaming!

Once I met up with the others, I had an important role to play. We went into Moses's shop so that I could buy sweets. I was the only one of the three us who had pocket money! Inside the shop looked just like something out of a Harry Potter film – presumably JK Rowling (whom, I hear, spent part of her childhood in Wales) also remembers the traditional set up of the sweet shop!

There were rows of clear glass jars which were filled with different varieties of confectionery – all with tantalising names and tempting colours.

Moses looked ancient to us, though he was probably no more than sixty. Here was our proof that being old was not necessarily a guarantee of wisdom. He wore a slightly moth eaten cardigan and had a distinctive smell about him – not dirty like Noel, but somehow musty, like an old chair or pair of curtains.

We trooped in through his front door and turned left into the room he used as a shop. It would have been called a parlour in my parents' house. A bell above the door signalled to him when there were customers in the shop. Moses was a slow mover with an obvious limp in one leg; he sometimes used a walking stick and we could hear the irregular tap of the stick on the lino as he walked down the passageway to the shop. We all called him Moses – an unusual practice in those times – every other adult had to be addressed as Mr, Mrs or Miss something. Even Noel's mother and father (who were considered slap-dash in their parenting skills) insisted that adults were treated with respect and not called by their Christian names.

When we went in, one of us would yell 'Shop!' just in case Moses had not heard the bell. In our case, this was just a formality that we followed because everyone else did it. Our little trio preferred it if Moses did *not* hear us coming, but it would have been considered suspicious behaviour on our behalf if we had walked in silently. We had some scruples! We would never have dreamed of going in very quietly, without activating the bell, filling our pockets and sneaking out again. Ringing the bell and calling 'Shop!' was our way of giving Moses a fair chance. It was our responsibility to ensure that we were not caught!

While we were waiting for Moses to shuffle down the passageway, I would turn around and stand in the open doorway, while Noel and Barbara selected a packet or two of Love Hearts or a Milky Bar to stow away in their pockets. As soon as Moses appeared, I would cough to alert the other two. Moses must have thought that Llanefa was constantly in the grip of some childhood coughing disease as most children used the same ruse, I believe.

Once he was in the shop with us, I would choose whatever cheap sweets were available (they had to be cheap - Penny Packets or a Bazooka Joe Bubble Gum - to ensure my pocket money lasted the whole week. If I had blown it all on an Aero or something equally extravagant on the first day, we would have had no legitimate excuse to go into Moses's shop). If my choice entailed Moses having to turn his back on us to climb the small wooden step ladder to get a jar off the top shelf, Noel sometimes had a chance for second pickings.

Now that I employ a full-time accountant to sort out my finances and have cause to think about such things, I wonder if Moses ever filled in an income tax form and put 'thieving little bastards' under his 'Legitimate Losses' column!

Once we had left the shop, we would amble down the road, past the last council house and on to the lane that led to Brown Cow's cornfield. We had usually finished our sweets long before we got there and had passed the Bazooka Joe cartoon strip round so that we could all read it. Noel would normally announce the caption on each Love Heart before he popped it into his mouth and then sing the first bar of 'Yummy, yummy, yummy, I've got love in my tummy' as he walked along (though he rarely sang 'love' but would improvise with his own word choice such as 'sweets' or 'gum' or whatever else he thought of) – that, too, could get irritating.

By the time we got to the gateway of the cornfield, we had satisfied our sweet craving and were ready for adventures in make-believe land. Brown Cow had put a chain and padlock on the gate, but we simply climbed over it in less than a few seconds. In minutes we were immersed in another dimension, playing characters that could do anything, fight off all evil and still be home in time for tea. This was the way we spent our days.

One Wednesday, I jogged down to the Baptist chapel to find Barbara sitting on the wall by herself. That was highly unusual. Although I sometimes missed a day because I had to go with my parents to visit someone, Noel was always free to spend his days as he wished.

Barbara was swinging her legs back and forth on the wall and singing something under her breath. I looked across at Moses's shop, expecting to see Noel coming out.

'Where's Noel?' I asked.

Barbara shrugged.

'Ill maybe?' I suggested.

'Dunno,' she said.

We waited for a while, but once we realised that he was not going to turn up, we set off for the field on our own. Neither of us had the courage to go into Moses's shop without him. It was a strange situation for us. Noel was the lynchpin of our trio. We played half-heartedly, then set off for home while playing a silly word game as we walked.

The next day, Barabara and I met up by the chapel and, with the absence of Noel, set off towards the cornfield straight away.

We had just passed the last council house when we heard a shout of 'Oi!' behind us.

We turned and saw Noel trying to catch us up on his bike. This was even more unusual. Although all three of us had bikes – mine was new while the other two had battered hand-me-downs – we never brought the bikes down to the cornfield as we had to leave them outside the gate and alert Brown Cow to the fact that we were there.

As he got closer I could see that Noel had a black eye and a long cut at the side of his mouth. Noel had always been injury prone. The teachers in school would often ask him what had caused his injuries and he would normally answer with a brief, 'Fighting, miss.' which ended the conversation. As Noel only had two sisters – one of thirteen or fourteen and the other only seven – I often wondered who he fought with outside school hours.

He caught up with us and climbed awkwardly off the bike.

'You've got a black eye,' said Barbara, as if there was any possibility that Noel was unaware of the fact.

Once off the bike, it was obvious that Noel had much more than his facial injuries. He walked with a limp and a slightly sideways, crab-like gait.

'What have you done?' I asked.

'Old man gave me a hiding' he said 'I stood on his glasses and broke them. He came back from the Red Cow and gave me a good walloping. He's a whoring bastard and I wish he would die.'

126

I wasn't sure what a whoring bastard was, (and I suppose that Noel probably didn't either), but his wishing a parent dead made me go cold. I was sure that Jesus would hear and that my own parents would die as a punishment to me for listening to Noel say such a terrible thing.

I could see that Noel's face was pale under the bruising and swelling.

'What did your mother say?' asked Barbara.

'She was there. She gave me a slap when I shouted at him to fack off.'

I winced internally. I could not imagine what punishment I would receive if I had sworn at a parent.

But there was more.

'He gave me such a wallop that he knocked me out – bang!' he said 'I sort of woke up straight away I think and my mother was shouting at the old man. That's when he asked me if he had managed to knock some sense into me and I told him to fack off. I was ok though. I could have come down the field yesterday, but I was sick three times in the night and after breakfast so I stayed in.'

This was a huge confession on Noel's part. His admitting to an illness (which he saw as a failing) was rare. Although I now understand that Noel was probably suffering from concussion, we attributed the vomiting to something that we all had from time to time. In the Eagle comics that we read, our heroes such as Dan Dare, never threw up after they had been knocked out – they just groaned for a few seconds, then continued blowing up bridges and rescuing prisoners!

We continued on to the cornfield, pausing only to hide the bike in a thick bramble hedgerow on the way. Noel slowed us down because of his limp and we both made a conscious decision to walk more slowly after he coughed a few times and pressed his hand to his side from the resulting pain.

Once we were in our leafy refuge, we sat down and played silly word games – making up new words for existing ones and

127

hooting with laughter when they came out sounding rude. Noel again had to press his side when he laughed.

Barbara looked at his face and said 'That's the best bruise you've ever had!'

Noel glowed with pride.

'I've got a better one than that' he bragged and pulled up his sweater to show us the reason for his clasping of his side whenever he laughed or coughed.

The size and colour of it impressed us both and we peered closely while making appropriate comments.

Soon we were in competition and Barbara suggested that she had had a blacker bruise on her shin from when she had fallen off her bike. I lied that I had once had a bruise the size of a dinner plate on my back after falling off the garden gate while swinging on it.

This was Noel's territory and he told us about the colourful bruises he had suffered on various parts of his body. Then we went further when I showed them the scar on my elbow from the time I had caught my arm on a cracked window. Even then, Noel was able to better us by pulling his sweater up over his shoulder and showing us an irregular shaped scar running up his arm towards his neck (an exercise that revealed his latest beating in all its glory).

'Old man threw a chisel at me in the Easter holidays. Blade cut me,' he said proudly.

We sat quietly for a while, before Barbara asked the question that partly changed our destiny.

'Can't you escape when he's trying to hit you? Do cartwheels or something to get out of the way?'

Noel looked on in interest, saying nothing, but I could see his mind was working.

However, I was the one who came up with the idea.

128

'Judo!' I said 'Then you can throw him over your shoulder when he's trying to give you a hiding!'

The other two faces lit up!

'Yes!' they said together.

'Like in the Eagle comics!' said Noel.

'I've got some Mandy comics at home. I'll find the ones with the good Judo throws in them,' offered Barbara.

'Well, well, said Will to the wall!' Noel commented.

Impatient to start training, Barbara and I practised some moves as we thought they should be done, while Noel offered criticism and advice from a sitting position on the ground. Not used to being in physical contact with each other, I was slightly unnerved by how soft Barbara's skin was and the way her body gave when I clasped her waist to pull her backwards over my extended leg. I later prodded my own waist and discovered the difference; I was angular and bony. I concluded that girls were softer – like an over-ripe fruit that was in danger of bursting. I stopped imagining any more comparisons in case Jesus was watching me.

We made our way home, exiting the cornfield as carefully as possible, so that we could avoid Brown Cow. It was clear to us that Noel was in no condition to run away.

We got out without incident and walked back to where we had hidden Noel's bike.

'We could go into Moses's shop on the way back' I suggested 'I've got some money.'

Noel looked nauseous for a second.

'Nah' he said 'My old man might be there getting fags and I don't want to see the cont.'

This was a frightening thought to all of us and I promptly dismissed the idea.

When I got home, my mother asked me where I had been playing. She always did this and I gave her the same answer.

'Down by the chapel with the others.'

It wasn't an outright lie, so I felt certain that Jesus would not be taking account of how many lies I was telling, though I never expanded on the answer – just in case I pushed my luck too far. Some instinct told me that I should not tell her the whole truth. The fact that Brown Cow disapproved of us playing in his field was reason enough to keep quiet, but my mother also frowned on my friendship with Noel. His family were 'common' she said. And as for admitting that one of my friends was a girl – that was taking honesty too far. My mother would have probably called her family 'common' too as Barbara's father was no longer in residence and an 'Uncle Selwyn' was the guiding male influence in her home. Barbara called Uncle Selwyn a lodger and I never knew if he was a real uncle or not, but in 1968 Llanefa, the concept of two people living together out of wedlock was the stuff of nightmares and there were many households with resident uncles!

The next week passed as normal for us. Noel gradually stopped limping and holding his side – which was just as well because Brown Cow appeared out of our jungle and chased us again. We split into separate routes and managed to lose him fairly quickly. Again, we didn't find Barbara until we almost fell over her. It was incredible how she could make herself invisible!

Once we were certain that Brown Cow had gone, we crept out of the field and sprinted down the road.

The next day, when we got to the field, there were deep tyre marks on the ground and the grass on either side of the gateway was flattened. The gate was still padlocked and the crop still stood tall, waving gently like a calm sea. We hesitated a moment, checking that there was no activity in the field by listening intently. As we gazed ground-wards, Noel pointed to the side of the gate. There was a balloon-like object on the floor; an off-white, wrinkled balloon that had obviously deflated.

'Look. A Dewrex,' he said.

We looked around, but could only see the balloon.

'That's a balloon,' said Barbara.

'No it's not,' argued Noel 'It's a Dewrex. My cousin told me about them.'

We both must have looked bemused.

'You know,' he said, 'men put them on to stop them getting a girl in trouble.'

This was news to us. We looked again with more interest.

Noel picked up a stick and poked at it.

'The man puts his co...' he hesitated before looking at Barbara '...his thing... into one of those before he puts it into the woman's thing. It fits on tight and stops the white stuff coming out and making a baby. Spunk, it's called. My cousin said.'

I had a brief moment of feeling very strange. The ring of the Dewrex looked so big! I couldn't imagine that anyone had a penis so big that it would fill that ring and its wrinkled extension. It gave me a funny sensation in the base of my spine.

But, before I could speculate any further, we were both distracted by Barbara bursting into tears and wailing into her hands. Noel and I glanced at each other in confusion. That's girls for you, his expression seemed to indicate.

Barbara quickly climbed over the gate and we followed. She was still sobbing and hiccupping. Every time we thought she had stopped, she would start again. Noel and I were completely bemused, but also unaware of how to deal with it. We would never have considered giving her a hug or stroking her arm. Dan Dare never did that kind of thing!

'Stop crying, Bar,' said Noel 'it's just a Dewrex.'

That set her off on an even louder bout of crying and we looked around nervously in case Brown Cow had heard and was sneaking up on us.

'What's the matter?' Noel asked impatiently.

'I've got into trouble,' she blurted out before yodelling some more.

Noel and I were even more confused by then. We both knew what 'getting into trouble' meant if you were a girl. Expecting a baby. Noel had sisters and I expect he heard the usual order barked out to them by his parents 'Don't you bring trouble home here!'

My own brothers often received the same advice when my parents thought I wasn't listening.

We didn't even know the word 'pregnant' then.

Barbara pulled herself together.

'Uncle Selwyn put his.... thing... in... my rude and all the white stuff came out' she said in a bubbling, increasingly louder tone 'He didn't have a Dewdex... balloon thing. That means I must be in trouble.'

Whatever else she said was drowned in a gurgling, wailing sound. We both knew what a girl's 'rude' was – though I had never seen one. And, thanks to Noel's impromptu lesson, I also knew more about the workings of sex.

'Well, well said Will to the wall,' said Noel 'but the wall didn't say anything to Will.'

Her sobs subsided into sad, sharp intakes of breath.

'My cousin said, you can do it once and it doesn't get the girl in trouble,' said Noel reassuringly 'but if you do it again, then it makes a baby.'

Barbara wailed out loud again

'He does it every Friday when Mam is at the shop' she said (or something similar – it was difficult to make out what she was saying).

'Well, well, said Will,' said Noel, clearly out of his depth.

Barbara's tears had unblocked some kind of release valve and she blurted out more information in between sobs. How Uncle Selwyn said that she was a good girl and that he was very fond of her; that he said that her mother was unkind and would give her away to a children's home if she found out; how he sometimes

132

tried to put his thing in her mouth, but she had heaved. This last bit of information was particularly bizarre to us. We could not imagine why anyone would want to do such a thing! What if it tasted of pee? Noel said as much!

Barbara calmed down eventually and was able to respond to our bemused questions (though most of the questions came from Noel – he was like a mathematician who had just discovered the secret of pi).

Then we sat quietly for a few minutes, each digesting the information in some disbelief. I had even gone as far as to wonder how Barbara would come to the cornfield to play if she had a baby in a pram with her. I considered whether or not we could hide the pram in the hedge and carry the baby over the gate and lay it on the ground while we played. I'm sure today's youth are far more informed by the time they are potty trained!

Eventually the silence was broken by Noel in his own eureka moment.

'You can't be in trouble!' he said 'You've got to have bazookas to get into trouble. And you haven't got any bazookas.'

He patted his own chest to make the point.

'I *almost* have,' Barbara responded, patting her own chest, but looking slightly more hopeful.

'And you haven't got a big belly,' added Noel.

That was true, but I remembered the soft feel of Barbara's waist while we had been practising our Judo throws. Was that what it would feel like if she was 'in trouble'?

'I hide on Fridays,' she said 'Sometimes, I crawl between the settee and the wall and stay there until Mam gets back. Once, I hid in the wardrobe in my bedroom, but he found me. He wasn't cross, though.'

It was years later that I remembered the connection between the talent Barbara had for making herself hidden and the need for such an action in her day-to-day life. In 1968, however, we accepted everything at face value and soon put the unpleasant thoughts away. We resumed our normal games and Judo practice. We became even more inventive in our imagined playtime situations.

The next time I even thought of Barbara's plight was when we saw another 'Dewrex' at the side of the lane. I tried not to look at it for fear of attracting her attention and setting off the hysteria we had witnessed in the cornfield. We all sauntered by, taking great pains to ignore it, though I'm sure we all, especially Barbara, had seen it.

During our dramatised games in the cornfield, the 'bad men' were always cannibals or murderers or alien beings. None of us considered that a paedophile would rate an equal place on our 'Public Enemy' list. In the real world, Brown Cow was the most frightening adult we knew. Even Noel's father ranked lower by virtue of the fact that he was quite an ordinary man when he was not drunk. (Perversely, we thought of Moses as a 'bad man' rather than the victim of our petty thieving!)

No-one mentioned the possibility of Barbara's being in trouble after her lachrymose confession. To our childish way of thinking, if she didn't have a baby fairly instantly, then it was not going to happen! She, too, seemed to have put the worry behind her and our primary concern was dodging Brown Cow who was appearing more often and shouting louder than ever.

Noel managed to escape further severe beatings, but bore the marks of less serious cruelty on a weekly basis. He considered this a shame as he had wanted to try out a Judo throw, he said.

The weather became warmer and highlighted Noel's smelly clothes which were rarely washed. We acclimatised to it – just as long as we didn't get too close to his feet – they were just too ripe!

The plants grew taller, thickened out and became a sickly yellow-green that signalled their approaching maturity. In the warm spell that followed, they became even more mysterious and magical in my eyes. The heat haze made them swim in and out of focus and had a hypnotic effect on me. The overall result was to send me into a trance-like state and, had I been unlucky enough to be the one nearest to Brown Cow when he exploded through the crop on that fateful day, I would have been caught in seconds. But, luckily for me, my torpor broke one Sunday morning as I went to chapel (and subsequent Sunday School) with my parents. One of their acquaintances, Ifor, who lived in the row of council houses at the top of the lane to Llwyncelyn Farm, stopped for a pre-service chat outside the opened giant chapel doors that reeked of furniture polish, mothballs and Sunday Best clothes. (I would always think of it as the smell of Godliness!).

In mid conversation, he turned to me and said 'That's a good hiding place you've got down there, boy. I see you and your friends every afternoon.'

My mother's head jerked sharply towards me and I felt alarm pulsing through my body.

I smiled politely and he continued his previous conversational gambit with my parents.

Later, my mother asked me where he had seen us playing and I told her that it was down behind the council houses.

'We start off by the chapel then end up on the lane by the council houses,' I said.

It was an explanation that seemed to satisfy her and she responded with the token parental mantra – 'Don't get up to any trouble.'

It sharpened my senses enough to be more aware of my surroundings when we played in the cornfield. It had never before occurred to me that someone watched us as we came and went from our playground. My new-found sense of alertness may have helped me avoid Barbara's fate; that's what I sometimes think these days. What happened to Barbara was bad enough, but had it been me instead there would have been very different repercussions if it had all come out into the open – I realised that only after my last visit back to Llanefa.

The last time we played in the cornfield, we had devised a new adventure. In one of our comics, we had read about the hero digging a hole and covering it with branches so that they could trap a lion. Noel suggested that we could trap wild natives in the hole instead. We began digging, but without shovels, the best we could achieve was a dent of about two feet square and four or five inches deep. Nevertheless, in our imagination, it was six feet deep and we gathered old plant stems to cover it.

We were fully engrossed in the game when I caught sight of a movement in the depths of the crop – a hint of brown tweed that was dangerously near to me.

'SPY!' I yelled and ran into the corn.

Barbara screamed and I was vaguely aware of our collective wild gallop into the yellowy-green forest. I can still remember the silence, broken only by my panting and the thup-thup of feet pounding the ground. Plants swished past me until I considered it safe to stop. I held my breath and tried to determine if I could hear anyone. The silence was unnerving.

Suddenly, Barbara burst out of the crop, her face distorted into features that I would not have recognised as someone I knew. Close behind her was Brown Cow. His face was purple and contorted into an expression of hate.

Barbara passed me and I spun around and ran with her for a few seconds before outstripping her stride and veering off on my own. I ran for what felt like hundreds of yards before I was forced to stop with my sides aching from a stitch. I stood and panted, trying to listen again. I could hear a faint whoosh-whoosh of stems. It didn't sound close by.

My breathing began to slow down and my ears strained harder to hear any sound.

There was one single scream from Barbara, then nothing.

I don't know how long I stayed there. It felt like an hour, but was probably no more than twenty minutes, but the waiting ended when Noel appeared, his eyes large and his face white. An old bruise on his eyebrow stood out in contrast to the paleness of his skin.

'Has he gone?' I whispered.

'Dunno,' he said.

We crept through the corn, heads swivelling side to side – all our practice at avoiding cannibals coming into use.

There was no sound at all. Every few strides we stopped and listened. All I could hear was the sound of my blood pounding through my ears.

Noel began to relax, but I was still on the alert and not ready to resume our game until we had found Barbara.

'We have to look down on the ground,' I said quietly to him 'She always crouches down to hide.'

Noel happily accepted this as a new game and we went forward in a line with a few yards between us – just as we did when we were tracking lions.

We could have been going around in circles for all I knew; the density of the crop was almost at its peak. It was only when we suddenly emerged out of it and found ourselves facing a hedge that we knew we had been moving away from the gate entrance. We turned left and followed the hedge around until we could see the chimney tops of the council houses in the distance, before going back under the leaves again.

We edged forward in a crouched position again, gradually moving further apart so that we could cover more area. Suddenly Noel stopped and lifted a hand to me. I looked and saw him point to his left. I peered in the same direction. There was definitely a hint of an unnatural colour that could have been Barbara's clothes. We both turned in that direction.

We saw it was tweed at around the same time.

Brown Cow was lying on his back, eyes staring sightlessly upwards. His face was as purple as if it had been painted. His flat cap lay beside him but the stick remained clasped in his hand.

We pulled backwards, expecting him to leap up and chase us, but he continued to lie there motionless. It started to scare me and I wanted to turn and run – anywhere, but out of the range of those blank eyes. Noel sniffed and lifted the bottom of his sweater to wipe his nose. I think he may have been crying.

Somewhere beside me, I heard the sound of a sob. We both swung round and saw Barbara curled into a ball on the ground.

'Bar!' said Noel.

She looked up with tear-blurred eyes.

'He caught me,' she said.

We looked back at Brown Cow.

'Did you kill him?' asked Noel in little more than a whisper.

Barbara started crying more loudly.

Noel turned to the figure on the floor 'Mr Brown?' he said tentatively. There was no response. We didn't want to touch him. Not because we thought he was dead, but because we were still afraid that it was some kind of trick. Didn't we read that kind of thing all the time in the Eagle? The victim (usually a villain) would pretend to be dead or unconscious, but the moment our hero went near them – pow!

'He grabbed me from behind and put his hand on my rude,' said Barbara in a small voice 'I did a Judo throw on him. He fell over and then he sat up and looked at me. Then he sort of snored and just fell back again.' She started crying once more.

Noel and I were lost for words for a few seconds. In all the killing we had done in our imagination and through our reading of various comics, we had no idea how to deal with a real death.

'We can't tell anyone,' said Noel, recovering his practical side once more.

We all nodded. We had no concept that we had done anything wrong, but the threat of being sent to a children's home was always present in our minds as a consequence of being involved in anything major. (Even my own parents had used this threat following my occasional bouts of what they called 'un-Godliness').

'You didn't kill him, Bar,' said Noel, 'if he got up after he fell. Maybe he's just been knocked out.'

We all looked at Brown Cow again. His face had become an even stranger shade of purple – like a bruise, but also like a plum that had grown mildew under its skin. The colour of the side of his face was an even deeper shade - not the colour of a human being. But his eyes were the strangest of all. I had never seen eyes that did not focus. Even more unsettling was the fact that they didn't seem as wet and glossy as real eyes. They reminded me of the woodwork around the doorway in Moses's shop. In the past, someone had obviously rubbed against the paint before it had dried and it had a matt quality to it. Brown Cow's eyes were matt.

'We have to get out of here.' said Noel.

We clustered together immediately.

'And we've got to swear to God that we won't tell anyone,' he reminded.

Barbara and I nodded vigorously. We put our hands together palms up and said, solemnly in unison, 'I swear to God. Mother's life.'

We made our way to the gateway, glancing nervously over our shoulders in case it had been a trick and Brown Cow was behind us. When we climbed over the gate, I suddenly remembered Ifor who had seen us from his council house. My childlike mind could not total up the implications, but I knew that it could bring all sorts of trouble for us.

'What if someone sees us now?' I asked. I was afraid to say that Ifor had spoken to me outside the chapel. It would have made me sound like a Judas. Neither of the other two had been challenged as to where they played (as far as I knew) and I was reluctant to confess to the one avenue that may have led us to being discovered.

'Nah.' said Noel 'Anyway, we can play here on the lane, can't we?'

That seemed like a reasonable assumption, but nevertheless we hurried down the lane towards the town. We stopped when we got to the chapel and sat on the stone wall with our backs to the metal railings.

We were a quiet bunch. Every topic that Noel raised tailed off into silence.

Eventually, Noel said 'He would have killed you, Bar.'

She came close to crying again, but fought the impulse so as not to attract attention in full view of anyone who went into Moses's shop – not that there were any customers that we noticed.

When we considered it to be late enough, we each set off for home (with a reminder from Noel to tell no-one). I fretted all evening and left half my supper; my mother put her hand on my forehead to see if I had a raised temperature.

It was the following day that everyone said that Brown Cow had died of a heart attack. I suppose this was assumption at that stage, but a post mortem confirmed it later, I heard. ('See! I said it wasn't you that killed him!' Noel had told Barbara triumphantly, when he heard this.)

The dramatic setting of Brown Cow's death made it a hot topic in Llanefa. Most people died at home or in hospital, unless they suffered some kind of accident. My mother responded in typical Llanefa fashion and was whipped into a frenzy of cake-making to take to the bereaved Mrs Brown. I sat around listlessly and got in her way.

'Don't you want to go outside to play?' she suggested 'It's too nice a day for you to be stuck indoors. You can help me take these other cakes down to Ifor's wife later.'

I froze in my tracks – Ifor's wife? What if he was there and questioned me again in view of the news about Brown Cow? But my mother provided the answer for me.

'Poor Ifor is very ill in hospital with a stroke,' she said 'It happened last night. Make sure you say a prayer for him tonight.'

I nodded, though had every intention of adding a codicil to that prayer 'Please, God, help Ifor to get better, but don't let him get me into trouble about Brown Cow's field.'

In the event, I managed to get out of delivering the cakes with my mother. It felt too close to the scene of the crime for me and I feigned a stomach ache instead. I took some comics out of the stack in my room and sat on the settee to read them while she put the cakes in a wicker basket and covered them with tea-towels.

After that day, I only met up with Barbara and Noel a few times and we never again went to the cornfield. The summer holidays were almost at an end and my mother took me to Siop y Graig to get my new school uniform and the assorted other items that she had on a list from the Grammar School. It also rained quite heavily and this dissuaded me from making an effort to go out.

Once I started at the Grammar School, I hardly ever saw Barbara or Noel, apart from the odd morning when they were waiting for the school bus that took the Secondary Modern pupils on their seven mile journey out of town. I made a new set of friends – ones that my parents approved of – and gradually forgot the episode in the cornfield (although I occasionally had nightmares that relived it).

Noel got in with a rough crowd of friends and I sometimes saw him smoking while waiting for the bus. Some days he had bruises and black eyes, but I never found out if they had been caused by his father or someone else. Barbara stayed pretty much the same as she had been before but, because she was a girl, I was unwilling to show anyone that I had been friends with her. Sometimes, I wondered if her Uncle Selwyn was still around and doing those terrible things to her. It made me shudder to think of it as I got into my teenage years.

Llwyncelyn Farm was sold and the new owner got planning permission to build a housing development on the old cornfield. I was recently intrigued to see that Llwyncelyn doesn't even exist as a farm anymore. There is a Llwyncelyn Drive which is partly recognisable as the lane we walked down to get to the cornfield, but the open countryside has been eaten up by houses, cul-de-sacs and crescents. There is even a by-pass that cuts off that part of Llanefa. As a child who was force-fed religion, I would have considered that to be some kind of sign, but I escaped the clutches of religion a long time ago!

I was a high-achiever in school and went on to University. My parents were disappointed that I chose teaching as a career; they had hoped for some clergy based vocation. Both died within six months of each other while I was teaching in my first school in Cardiff. It was probably a blessing that they were not around to suffer any more disappointments from me. (I dread to think what they would have thought if they had been able to read any of my books!) They would never have lived with my one-time appearance as a guest on Question Time when my response to an opinion about religious sects was published and heatedly discussed in the national press for a short while!

My two brothers stayed close to Llanefa; both are deacons in the chapel and neither has much to do with me these days. We swap Christmas cards as a token gesture, but they are reluctant to have any more contact than necessary with me. Even when my first book became such a success, they didn't mention it apart from a single line of congratulations on a Christmas card. When my third book was banned, on religious grounds, for a while in Sweden, (an action that had exactly the opposite effect on sales!) that warranted *two* lines in a Christmas card so I suppose I can count that as an improvement!

There was nothing to tie me to Llanefa and I moved further and further away, gave up teaching and eventually settled in Ferring, just outside Brighton. It's near enough to my London publisher. I love the sea and I'm happy there. During the intervening years, I fell in love several times, had break ups, drank too much, made stupid mistakes, had one-night stands, smoked too much (still do!) and lived my life like many other people do. For the last few years I have slipped into gentle, happy, domesticity. It happens to even the most rebellious of us! Jan and I have even talked about getting married next year.

The letter from Llanefa came through my publisher.

It was from Janet Morris who had been in Llanefa Grammar School at the same time that I was there (though I didn't remember her). She was now Secretary of a local charity and support group. The group arranged counselling and support to those families who had lost children or who had sick children in need of constant care. The whole idea had been spawned by an incident that I barely remembered from my Grammar school days. Another class had gone on a trip which had ended in tragedy when one of the girls had fallen into the sea and drowned. In those days, the family had to grieve alone and had somehow come to terms with what had happened. Over the years, no doubt many other tragedies happened too and the support group was born. They were holding a charitable auction in the Poacher's Rest, Llanefa where various services were offered to the highest bidder. Janet had asked if I would be interested in attending and maybe 'selling' an appearance in my next book to the highest bidder (she had added that the 'appearance' needed to have the person acting as a 'wholesome character' only – presumably, she has read my books and baulked at the thought of a Llanefa pillar of society starring as the devil incarnate or possessed priest!).

The Poacher's Rest had offered to install a hand-carved bench in their restaurant. The bench was to bear the inscription To The Memory Of Carol Jenkins - the girl who had drowned some forty years before.

I get a lot of similar requests, but I thought – Llanefa, why the hell not? It was time to deal with my fear of the place. I wrote back saying I would be happy to attend. The same day, I booked two nights at the Poacher's Rest before I could change my mind. I used the name Hywel Jones for the booking – it seemed more natural. We decided that I would go on my own while Jan stayed at home with the excuse of looking after the two cats. It can get boring, being a well known author's partner, I'm told – a bit like being invisible! Besides, Jan has been with me to some very prestigious events and places - a small town like Llanefa just did not have the necessary appeal!

I drove down to Llanefa on the Friday, the day before the auction. It had been many years since I had last been there for my mother's funeral and I truly expected to see the place as it had been then. I followed the by-pass and managed to miss it altogether and had to turn around to go back into town. There was a new one-way system (new to me, anyway) and there was even a small McDonalds where the petrol station used to be.

I found the Poacher's Rest (which had been called The Half Moon when I lived there) and parked in their purpose made, secure car park. The landlord was called Owen Bell and he had moved to Llanefa from Coventry. His wife booked me in and showed me to my room.

Inside the room, I could have been anywhere in the UK. I don't know what I expected, but it proved how my upbringing had turned Llanefa into a place to be feared. I looked out of the window and saw the castle and standing stones on the two hills in the distance – the only clues to my location. I opened the window as far as it would go so that I could look further on to the town. Groups of people walked by and I heard their accents – Essex, Bristol, Norfolk – hardly a Welsh accent to be heard. I didn't know if they were residents or tourists taking advantage of the Whitsun break. It seemed to me then, that my ghosts had left Llanefa and I was just another passer-by amongst my fellow travellers. I began to regret coming. What on earth was I going to do until Sunday morning?

I sent Jan a text message and received one back before setting out for a walk. I started off like a stranger in a new town, but gradually, the roads became familiar by their shape (if not their modernised buildings) and I found myself standing outside my parents' old house. It had obviously received many makeovers in the intervening years; an extension to one side doubled its floor space, making it an imposing sight. The house and I faced each other and I thought about how both of us had changed and grown. I don't know how long I stayed there, but an anxious face at the window reminded me that I had no business to be staring at someone else's house. In the 21st century, that kind of thing was apt to make people nervous – even if it was in Llanefa!

I moved off and headed down towards Moses's shop and the chapel. Moses's house had reverted to being just a house; a smartly painted end-of-terrace with terracotta pots in the front garden. The Baptist chapel was gone and in its place were two large houses – one with a Porsche parked half in and out of a huge garage.

The road we had taken to get to Llwyncelyn Farm was gone too. A dead end with a small park and children's playground blocked the way. I doubled back and found that the only way through was by means of a pedestrian underpass from a supermarket car park. I could hear the by-pass traffic revving overhead as I walked through the tunnel. The other end emerged at the top of the old lane (which was now called Llwyncelyn Drive). I stopped. I had seen enough. I had subconsciously wanted to re-visit my childhood, but the scene before me was the backdrop from someone else's life and I had no interest in it.

I went back to the Poacher's Rest and did some work on my laptop and watched the TV in my room (switching to the Welsh language channel just to see if I could still understand it – I couldn't!). I went back down, had a meal in the restaurant and, later, a drink in the bar while chatting to the staff before going to bed – just like any visit to the multitude of towns I had been to while promoting my books in the early days.

The next day, I had one more pilgrimage to make. That was a walk to the old Grammar School – now a comprehensive. It was mostly unrecognisable. The spacious grounds, with its decorative magnolia trees, had been invaded by ugly new buildings which were probably additional classrooms. Only the clock tower, above the building that I recognised as the gym and cloakroom, gave any indication that it was the same place that I had known.

The one place I had no intention of going to was my parents' grave. I remembered my parents in my head and not through an inscribed stone on a piece of ground that someone had designated as holy. I had not been there since the final funeral.

I again went back to the Poacher's Rest where a carload of guests was causing some excitement. A girl-band called the Tribells were unloading their equipment. They, too, had been asked to make an appearance and were offering to include the highest bidder's name in the title of their new album. The lead singer, an attractive girl called Tara, had lived in Llanefa until she was fifteen and had thought it good publicity to come back for the charity auction. They were an entertaining lot and I spent much of the day talking to them in between their rehearsals. We swapped funny stories about places we had stayed and the weird people we had met and been stalked by.

By the evening we were ready for the auction and I changed into smarter clothes for the occasion (Sunday best, my mind suggested).

The organiser, Janet, came to introduce herself to me. She was a tall, thin woman who had been known as Coch in school because of her bright red hair, she said. I made noises that suggested I remembered her, but the reality was that I had not seen a single face that I recognised so far.

I spent a short time talking to a journalist from the Llanefa Guardian and signed some autographs. I could see that Tara was similarly engaged (though she was more recognisable than I was!)

Once all the talking and thanking was done, the auction got under way. My offer was bought by a man called Tegwyn Prydderch who was apparently a high ranking police officer. His name was familiar to me from my school days, but I did not recognise his face.

While some of the other bidding continued, I made my way outside for a much needed cigarette. A young man and his heavily pregnant wife passed me in the opposite direction. It would be accurate to say that I recognised him instantly. And, I could not help but notice his tortured expression. His eyes flicked away from me as soon as his brain registered who I was. Poor bastard, I thought.

His wife was talking over her shoulder to someone behind.

I looked at the young man 'Remember Popeye!' I said and carried on walking before I could see his reaction.

I stood outside, inhaling the much needed satisfaction from the cigarette when I heard a cheerful voice say, 'Hywel, you old bastard!'

I looked up and saw a fat man walking towards me with the aid of a stick. He was mainly bald but had long greasy-looking hair around the sides of his head.

He held his hand out, 'Don't you remember me? Noel!'

I put on my most welcoming smile and went forward to shake his hand and throw my arm around his shoulders. It was no imposter. Noel smelled almost as bad as he had in the old days. He pulled away slightly. I reminded myself that men didn't hug in Llanefa.

'Of course I remember you!' I lied 'How are you?'

It was a question I wished I had not asked, as Noel launched into the list of ailments that he now suffered – diabetes, high blood pressure, heart murmur, arthritis – along with the failings of the NHS which didn't appear to be able to treat him in a manner he considered that was due to him. (I wondered how much of his failing skeleton could be attributed to the beatings his father had given him?)

I tried to divert him to other subjects, but some innocent word would trigger off a personal health topic and Noel would be back on his soapbox.

In the end I came straight out with it, 'I see they've built all over the old cornfield where we used to play. Brown Cow's land.'

Noel's face cracked into a smile, showing many gaps and blackened teeth 'Brown Cow!' he repeated 'I haven't thought of him for years. Had a heart attack, didn't he? Bang! Gone! Could happen to me with my ticker the way it is. Do you know what they told me in hospital last month...?'

I stopped listening. I noticed that the young man I had seen earlier had come out of the door, but turned back in when he saw me with Noel. I was glad. I regretted having said anything to him.

I was rescued by Janet who asked if I would come and have a word with someone called Karen who was running the Llanefa Motor Neurone Disease Association and had wondered if I would donate a signed book to the raffle they were organising. I went gratefully and spent a little while talking to her and some of her friends. While talking to them and trying to find a polite way of getting away, I felt a pair of arms being flung around me. It was accompanied by a shriek near my ear and followed up by a smacker of a kiss on my cheek.

'Hywel!' the voice shrieked.

I recognised Barbara at once! I hugged her back. I had last seen her at the funeral.

'Look at you!' I said 'You haven't changed a bit! Still looking fabulous!'

She grinned 'Easy to see you make up stories for a living! You don't look so bad yourself – even with the silver fox hair!'

I grinned back, 'I dye it this colour for effect. It's still dark brown really!'

We walked outside where we could talk in peace and have another cigarette. I was relieved to see Barbara lighting up too.

She brought me up to date with her life. She was a chiropodist; she had two grown up children and a grandson. She had been divorced for several years and now lived with a man who had been in prison for VAT fraud. This was groundbreaking stuff for Llanefa! In turn I told her my story, about Jan and our plans to get married.

Eventually, I said 'Do you still think about that thing in the cornfield?'

She glanced nervously to check who might be listening.

'Not really,' she said 'It's one of those unpleasant things that I've tried to forget. And, it wasn't as bad as it seemed at first. Not when I thought about it as an adult.'

'I suppose not...' I said, though I had no idea what she meant by that.

'I mean, he was just chasing us. He had a heart attack. I don't think I was responsible for that...' she added.

'It was unforgiveable, though,' I said 'what he was trying to do to you. You had enough to deal with at home.'

She coloured slightly. 'That twat, Uncle Selwyn! My mother kicked him out! She never found out, though. Thank God! He died a few years later. Stepped out in front of a car.'

'Sounds like there was natural justice for him and Brown Cow.' I said.

She looked questioningly at me.

'You do realise, don't you, that Brown Cow never tried to do anything... improper to me?'

I stared at her, 'But... I always thought...'

'I've thought about it so many times. He saw us as trespassers. All he did was grab the first part of me that he caught hold of. I was hyper-aware of that kind of thing because of what happened at home. Poor Brown Cow! I just stopped and tipped my upper body over and I think gravity did the rest... You remember we had that Judo craze? He just fell over me. He didn't mean me any harm. He wouldn't have... You know what he was like. He wouldn't have touched me like that.'

I must have looked unconvinced.

'You must have known,' she said 'I was not... well... he was... not that way. He was like you.'

I continued to stand there while my cigarette burned through.

'You mean....?' I floundered in disbelief.

'He was gay,' Barbara said 'Don't you remember all those young men who went to work for him? Most of them didn't last long. But the occasional one did...'

'I had no idea!' I gasped.

'You can imagine how that went down here,' she said 'Well, you know from personal experience how prejudiced they are here. Even now, it's still considered a sin with a lot of these idiots!'

I thought of my brothers. Barbara was right. We stood in silence for a minute.

'Anyway,' said Barbara 'this wedding of yours, will you take Jan's name or will he take yours?'

'I can't cope with being Mr de Hooge!' I said 'Can you imagine changing my name to Timothy Hywel de Hooge?'

She laughed and I felt a great love for her because she had stayed in Llanefa and was still able to accept me for who and what I was. A shame my family had not been able to do the same. I finally accepted how much that hurt me. My brothers had not even come to the auction.

We went on to chat about other topics until we realised that there was no more to talk about between us. We had caught up and filled in the gaps in each other's history. It was time to return to real life again. I gave her a hug. My admiration for her had increased tenfold; she was so at ease with herself – despite the trauma of her early life.

The evening passed and I went to my room and called Jan before going to bed. It's what long-term couples do.

The next morning, I was loading the car and preparing to leave when I was aware of someone standing and watching me. I turned around and saw the young man who had been with his pregnant wife the previous night. He was alone.

In my earlier years it would have been different. He was so good looking and obviously unaware of it. He had the look of a farmer's son, too. I felt sorry for him.

'I hope you don't mind...' he said, 'It's just... err... I thought... err'

'Yes?' I said.

'What did you mean about Popeye last night?'

'It was a stupid mistake,' I said 'I shouldn't have said anything.'

He continued to look bemused.

'You know Popeye's catchphrase?' I said 'I Yam What I Yam? I just saw you with your wife and thought of myself when I was younger. My situation then. I am what I am, but I had to get out of Llanefa. I'm glad. I'm happy out of here. Homophobia is still a national disease, but Llanefa has a terminal case of it.'

An image of my brothers passed through my mind.

He looked around to see if anyone else could hear.

'How did you know?' he asked in a low voice 'I've never told anyone or... done anything about it... You won't tell anyone, will you?'

'Call it recognition,' I said. 'Besides, you had that hunted, desperate look about you. Don't think others won't see it too. You won't be the only gay man in Llanefa – it just feels that way. It's up to you if you live a lie, but it's your choice. Beyond that, it's none of my business.'

He looked relieved.

'Thank you,' he said and turned as if to go.

Then he stopped and asked one more question 'Is it difficult when you... come out?' his voice was so low that I could hardly hear him.

'That's up to you,' I said 'Honesty comes more easily to some than others. People should be more accepting now than they were when I was young, but there will always be bigots. Even in the twenty-first century. And you're going to be a father soon. I've never had that to deal with. I'm sure it makes it more complicated.'

'Thank you,' he said, then added 'Have a safe journey home.'

'I will,' I said 'I've got a wedding to plan.'

As I drove out of town and left my childhood behind, I remembered a chat show presenter saying, in jest, that I was the second best best thing to come out of Llanefa - the first thing being the A300! I was relieved to be on that same road! I never intended to go back. I had carried part of Llanefa with me for years in one way or another.

There is a lot of death in my novels - indecent deaths, according to a bad review I once read.

The age-old advice to authors is to 'write what you know', but I would defy anyone to find a connection with Llanefa when they read my books.

But whenever I describe a dead body and think of the shock it creates, I am always overwhelmed with images of colour - the sickly yellow-green of the crop and the blotchy purple of Brown Cow's face.

The Llanefa Triangle.

A newspaper cutting sticks out of a sheaf of papers. Tegwyn pulls it out. It is the front and back cover of the Llanefa Guardian. His photograph appears on the sports section of the back page under the headline 'Tegwyn Wins National Police Championships'. Below that is the story of his triumph in the Veterans Squash Tournament. He had never gained such an honour as a non-veteran player, but nevertheless, he looks pleased as he remembers it.

As he folds the paper up, the front page displays its contents.

'Police Allay Witchcraft Fears' it reads.

He had forgotten about that. He had not been involved in it. In truth, there had been nothing to be involved in, Tegwyn believed. He had nurtured his own theories at the time, but then the story had faded away and Llanefa life had returned to normal.

Hardly anyone in Llanefa knew what Bara's real name was. Even Bara himself had to think about it if he was asked. His parents rarely called him by any name; their reluctance to confuse him clashed with their greater unwillingness to call him by a name which was, basically, an insult.

When he was born, after a long and difficult labour, Bara had seemed like an ordinary baby. Or even extraordinary to his parents, who had been childless for years and had resigned themselves to that situation. His arrival was the cause of great celebration in the Thomas household. That the miracle child was also a boy simply compounded the degree of elation felt by the family. In 1974, it was still more desirable to have a boy than a girl.

As the young Iwan Wyn grew beyond the age at which he should be walking and talking, his mother began to suffer some doubts (which she kept to herself for superstitious reasons). Her fears were partly alleviated when her son suddenly discovered the art of walking, but his vocabulary remained in the territory of babyhood.

By the time he was at primary school, it was obvious to everyone that Iwan was 'not right'. He had been able to communicate by then, but few people were able to understand him.

Much later, experts said he had Learning Difficulties and had called him 'Special Needs'. Everyone else called him Bara.

The origin of the cruel nickname was the old phrase 'In with the bread, out with the buns' to describe someone who was 'half-baked' – Bara being the Welsh word for bread.

'What's your name, bach?' his mother would sometimes test him.

'Bara,' he would say.

'No, not that name. Your real name – in case you get lost and have to ask a policeman to help you come home.'

He would think for a few seconds before blurting out the answer 'Iwanwynthomas.'

By the time he was in his last few years at school, everyone had accepted that Bara would never be any different. His brain told him that he would be at his happiest playing with children of around ten years old, but his parents were not happy with that situation. Bara's mother told him that he was not allowed to play with girls – an order he was happy to comply with. He was only interested in playing with boys. There was nothing he loved more than building mountain-bike ramps and obstacles, making them higher and higher and watching in delight as his young friends courageously flew over them. To his dismay, his mother discouraged him from doing that too. For a while, Bara wandered around where he could see the boys playing, but never went too near.

At around this time, Bara's mother approached a local man known as 'Gil the Ferret'. Gil was a man of few words - a long retired council road worker who had always kept ferrets and a lurcher or two. Bara had shown a curious interest in Gil as he pushed his bike past the house. Bara was particularly intrigued by the ferret-box stacked in the front basket and the pair of reddish brown eyes that peered out. From then on, Bara would accompany Gil as he set off to kill vermin for some farmer or trap rabbits to give his neighbours to cook.

By the time he was twenty years old, Bara could kill rats, trap rabbits, track foxes and badgers, but was often not able to tie his own shoelaces. Gil also taught him to catch fish from the Pwll Efa and the much larger Efa Fawr – a highly illegal occupation as neither possessed a fishing licence and the waterways were fiercely guarded by licensed fishermen and the Water Bailiff! When Gil eventually died, Bara was already in possession of his own lurcher (who slept on his bed) and a pair of ferrets (who, by his mother's decree, slept in a hutch at the furthest point in the garden!).

Bara accepted the death of Gil in his own blank way. Gil was no longer there – that was the end of the matter.

As well as being an excellent catcher of vermin, Bara was built like a wrestler. Llanefa farmers often used him to help them with tasks that involved heavy work – holding cattle to trim their feet or lifting bales into a loft. The pocket money they paid him was dismal, but Bara treated it like a lottery win as he found that he was able to buy his own Mars bars (to which he was addicted).

The way he saw the world meant that Bara was very much a creature of habit – it was the only way he felt truly at ease. His mother had made many rules for him to follow. He was not to play with children (though, in his thirties, he still looked longingly at the boys and their bikes), he was not to hit anyone, he was to wash his hands before he ate anything (or the germs would crawl inside him and kill him, she had said) and there were certain things he was only allowed to do in private. His mother had explained that if he wanted a pee-pee or poo-poo, he had to go to the toilet. If there was no toilet (such as when he was hunting vermin) he had to find a private place where no one could see him. She had added another rule – unless he was going to the toilet or washing himself in the bath, he was not to touch himself on his privates. This was one rule that Bara broke – sometimes he just couldn't help himself. He didn't know why he sometimes felt the need to do it, but his fear of his mother's anger meant that he always made sure he did it in private. Occasionally, she caught him picking his nose or cleaning wax out of his ears and that, too, earned him a telling off. At home, Bara often sat with his huge hands spread out on a table in front of him. That way, he could see them and know that they were not doing anything that would anger his mother!

His parents were ever conscious of the responsibility they had in ensuring that Bara fitted into society. They monitored TV programmes and made sure that he didn't watch anything that contained sex scenes or violence. They had given up with regards to swearing as Bara's contact with farmers had resulted in a huge expansion in his swearing vocabulary! What they didn't realise was that the farmers he worked for often talked among themselves about women and sex scenes they had watched on TV. Bara usually sat and listened in bemused silence. Some of them would bring porn magazines along to the cattle market and cruelly show them to Bara – ('How would you like to find her in your bedroom, Bara?' one of them would say. Bara would close his eyes; the graphic images did no more than frighten him.) If, though, he saw a teenage girl dressed in shorts or tight fitting tee-shirt, occasionally he would get a feeling that something was happening to his body and he needed to go somewhere private to deal with it. The sad fact was that Bara's brain had no idea that his body was thirty-four years old and made him respond to stimuli that would have aroused a thirteen year old boy.

To everyone in Llanefa, Bara was just Bara – harmless, but it was better to leave him alone – just in case.

Bara's dog was called Jess. It was his second Jess - the first having died at a reasonable old age. He had accepted the death of the first Jess in the same way he had accepted the death of Gil the Ferret. His parents had ensured that the first Jess had been neutered so that they would be spared the problem of unwanted puppies. However, the second Jess had not yet been neutered as she was only fifteen months old and had not yet had her first heat – the marker by which the vet measured the maturity and suitability of dogs needing to be neutered. It was unusual, but not rare for a bitch to be so late having her first heat so Bara's mother managed to talk the vet into spaying her as soon as she could get a date arranged. She tried to find a way of explaining to Bara that

Jess would need to go to the vet for an operation, but each time a possible date was planned, Bara had become stubbornly unwilling to let them take the dog away from him (he had been young enough to accept parental orders when the first Jess had been spayed).

Despite his reputation as a vermin exterminator, Bara was an animal lover. Jess was his constant companion and he also took time to stroke the ears of cats he saw sitting on garden walls. Ponies, too, earned themselves a rub on the nose if they appeared friendly, though he was a little more cautious of larger horses. Due to his contact with farmers, Bara was also aware that animals sometimes had to be killed. He had seen cows with broken legs and dogs who had been run over and who had to be put out of their misery. He was aware, too, that dogs who were caught worrying sheep had to be shot. His limited understanding accepted this as normal life.

A few miles away from Bara's home, life had taken a downward turn for Meirion Jones. The financial status of his poorly run farm at the far end of Pwll y Coed was draining away like sand in an egg timer. He blamed the poor profit margin on the fact that his land was higher and less fertile than other, more fortunate, farms owned by those who didn't deserve them. His main philosophy in life was that some people were handed prosperity on a plate and that more deserving individuals, like himself, were made to suffer because of it. Meirion had always been of the opinion that if a quick buck could be made without hard work, then he was your man!

Meiron's animal husbandry left much to be desired. His lambs always looked scrawny and struggled to make the desired weight compared to the others in the autumn mart and his beef cattle had bony protrusions where there should have been plump muscle. The recent decline in his life was, however, down to his wife, Mair. That lazy bitch, he thought, whenever her name popped into his head.

Mair had become absent from their marriage some four months before. The official line was that she had gone to look after an elderly aunt who lived alone up near Aberystwyth. Mair herself had told many people about the sick aunt (though she had not told Meirion until after she had gone). Meirion was certain that the sick aunt's name was Derek James and that he ran a bus company in Aberaeron. It did seem true that Derek was, in fact, not well. By all accounts he had had a stroke and, because he lived alone, needed help about the house. The reason that Meirion did not go to Aberaeron and apply some physical common sense to both was simple. If he went along with the story that Mair was looking after a sick relative, then he was accepting that she was still his wife and all was well in their marriage. Furthermore, if Derek popped his double-deckers, the chances were that Mair would inherit his business (Meirion had found out that Derek had no family) and then he could play his winning hand by divorcing Mair and claiming half the money (which would amount to considerably more than the farm was worth). Meirion hoped that Mair was being very, very nice to Derek!

As well has having sheep and cattle, Meirion had, some years previously, done what the Farmers Union had advised struggling stockmen. He had diversified and become a dog breeder. His ramshackle buildings housed some thirty breeding bitches of different varieties. He changed the breeds occasionally as some film or advert used a particular breed of dog and the ensuing public demand created a niche in the market.

Prior to developing a case of Sick Aunt Syndrome, Mair had been responsible for the day-to-day running of the breeding kennels. She fed the dogs, clipped the coats of the long-haired breeds to prevent them matting and cleaned out the pens. She also filled in the paperwork when applying for Kennel Club Registration and when dealing with the local council. There was little left for Meirion to do, the most important being to arrange a meeting with the dealer who collected the puppies on a weekly or monthly basis and hand over the wriggling bundles in return for cash. It had worked well.

After Mair had left, Meirion had soon encountered some trouble. A whole litter of Westie puppies had gone down with parvovirus – a highly contagious and fatal disease – the result of his negligence in vaccinating the puppies' mother. Meirion tried to isolate the mother and her surrounding kennel mates and told himself that he would have to disinfect the pens – sometime.

The remaining litters of Shih Tzus and King Charles Cavaliers were due to go to the dealer the following day and Meirion met up with him as usual.

'Thought you had some Westies for me,' he had said.

'No, sold them privately,' Meirion said. It was a believable scenario.

A week later, the shit had hit the fan. The London pet shop that had sold the pups had received complaints from their customers to say that the pups had all died of parvovirus. A huge campaign began and was highlighted in the Daily Mail. 'WELSH PUPPY FARMERS' REIGN OF CRUELTY,' said the headline, followed by a blistering report on the numerous puppy farms that regularly supplied the pet shops of London and Manchester.

An action group who called themselves Puppy Vigil descended on Llanefa and nearby localities where it was known that puppy farmers plied their businesses. They were a peaceful group who stood at the end of farm drives holding banners and chanting. They were eventually moved on by the police, but the stigma remained for Meirion and his fellow dog breeders.

As a result of the bad publicity, Meirion earned himself a visit from the council. He normally received a visit every year to ensure that he was complying with the terms of his licence, but this was an unexpected call. He refused to let the council official into the kennels, saying that he needed notice of a visit. The sound of high-pitched barking from different directions alerted the official to the possibility that Meirion had more than his allotted quota of dogs on the premises.

When the council official came back two days later, Meirion had made hasty attempts to clean some of the pens and had bundled a dozen or so bitches into the sheep trailer and driven it to a hidden location on a distant field, where he intended it to stay until after the visit was over. His licence stated that he could only have eighteen breeding bitches at any one time.

Mark, the council official, was no fool and was prepared for Meirion.

'You know you should only have a maximum of eighteen breeding bitches?' he reminded Meirion.

'Yes – the other ones you can see are stud dogs. I can have as many of those as I want,' said Meirion, telling the truth for once.

'What about the ones in the other building?' said Mark, gesturing over his shoulder.

'No dogs there,' said Meirion 'These are the lot.'

Mark looked at him with distaste.

'We've checked with the Kennel Club,' he said 'and you have registered twenty-four litters from different mothers in the last six months. If you want to increase your bitch quota, you need to re-apply to us.'

'Umm... that must have been... umm,' said Meirion 'The wife's away now with a relative who's very poorly. She deals with all that.'

'So, you're happy for me to look in that building?' said Mark.

Meirion winced.

'You can have a quick look if you want,' he eventually said, grudgingly.

Mark went and opened the door of the empty shed. The evidence of the recent presence of dogs was clear. Piles of faeces (some of which had a furry growth), filthy food bowls and urine soaked wood shavings lay around on the floor.

'I appreciate that you've got to earn a living, but this is what we're going to do,' said Mark 'I'll come back in two weeks time and I expect to see these buildings cleaned up. I'll also want to see your Puppy Sales Record and Record of Bitches Owned. If you've got more than eighteen, you've got a chance to find homes for them. You know what a scene this Puppy Vigil lot have caused. If you don't comply with council rules, we'll have no choice other than to revoke your licence.'

Meirion said nothing – though he later informed his fellow drinkers at the Red Cow that he had told the council man to fuck off and stick his Puppy Record up his arse – he was basically a coward who tried to find the easiest route out of trouble.

After Mark had left his premises, Meirion was left with a problem. He couldn't afford to have his licence revoked – the dogs paid better dividends than the cattle and sheep put together. It was obvious to him that he was going to have to do some cleaning up to satisfy the council for their next visit. He looked around in dismay and, for a brief moment, saw it as an outsider would have done. He sat down and lit a cigarette until he had some plan worked out in his mind. Firstly, he was going to have to get rid of some of the bitches – the Jack Russells for a start, they were the lowest earners – then anything high maintenance like the Maltese whose long white coats attracted knots and shit and whose hysterical yip-yip-yip was enough to drive him up the fucking wall! Secondly, he was going to have to get something unusual – a real money spinner – what that something was remained a mystery to him at that point. Thirdly, he was going to need help to start the clean-up operation – and it had to be cheap.

He went indoors and looked up the phone numbers of some other puppy farmers who were known to him. Within an hour, he was delighted with himself. He rubber his hands together – he had sold four Jack Russells, three Maltese, a Shih Tzu and all the bloody Westies to three other breeders.

Early the next day, he put the dogs in the back of his van and delivered them to the pre-arranged buyers at what he told them was an indecently low price. On the way home, as he drove through town, he passed the retarded boy and his lurcher who were walking towards Castle Woods (even though he was thirty-four, everyone thought of Bara as a 'boy'). Meirion remembered that Bara was often used as cheap labour by local farmers – his mind seized this piece of information as a gift from the gods.

Meirion knew where Bara's parents lived, so he turned his van around and made his way to their house. Bara's mother was happy for him to do some clearing up for Meirion, she said, providing that he was given plenty of tea and *absolutely no* alcohol.

Did she think he was running a fucking holiday camp, he thought, but he nodded gravely all the same! He would no more give Bara alcohol than he would give him a three-course cooked dinner! He arranged to pick Bara up the next day and he drove home with the feeling that he was making progress.

As he had two litters of Cavalier King Charles puppies at home, he set about ringing up the dealer to arrange a date for collecting them in a few weeks' time. It was bad news! The dealer wanted nothing to do with him following the parvovirus fiasco into which he had also been dragged.

Undaunted, Meirion phoned around until he eventually made an agreement with another dealer called Malcolm who lived near Bristol. Malcolm told him that he made regular pick-ups at Cross Hands near the end of the M4 – a bit of an inconvenience for Meirion, but also a chance to get a cooked dinner at the services before coming home (Meirion's culinary skills did not stretch as far as making cooked dinners).

'If you hear of anything unusual, I'm in the market for it,' he told Malcolm.

Malcolm hummed and tutted to himself before offering to sell him a Dogue de Bordeau. Meirion wasn't sure what they looked like, but he had heard that they could be nasty bastards who could eat him out of house and home, so he told Malcolm that wasn't quite what he'd had in mind.

'The only other thing I can offer you is a pair of wolf-hybrids,' Malcolm said 'No Kennel Club Registration to worry about. Lots of people like wolf-hybrids. They make an unusual pet. These are first generation wolves crossed with a German Shepherd. I've got a dog and a bitch. And the bitch is due in season anytime now. You could be seeing returns in just over three months and I'll be happy to buy any pups off you.'

Meirion was instantly hooked – no paperwork and rarity value! They haggled over the price for a few minutes before coming up with a figure that satisfied them both. He arranged to meet Malcolm and collect the wolves in two days time and rang off, rubbing his hands together in anticipation of his new venture.

That night, down in the Red Cow, the sixth pint of beer prompted him to mention that he was getting a pair of breeding wolves (he thought that 'hybrids', also synonymous with the word 'mongrel' in his mind, sounded far too tame). His beer-pals looked impressed and asked some stupid questions, such as, did he have to feed them fresh blood (no, regular dog food, he had said) and would they try to attack him (no, everyone knew that wolves were timid animals, he said – a fact that Malcolm had trickled into the conversation).

The topic moved on to how the new by-pass was progressing and how much tarmacadam they might have left over for use by local farmers needing to re-surface their driveways and Meirion's wolves were forgotten.

The following day, Meirion picked up Bara and was relieved to see that he had a sandwich box with him – at least he wasn't expected to provide food for him too!

If Bara had been anyone else, he would have found the journey in the van (and being in close proximity to Meirion) very unpleasant. Meiron's former morning routine, that he used to call his 'Triple S' (Shit, Shave and Shampoo) had, since Mair's leaving, been reduced to a 'Single S' (his stubble had become a straggly beard and his hair had become lank with grease as he forgot to buy razors and shower gel). The odour of his unwashed body wafted in waves around the inside of the van. Jess sat down in the foot-well and flicked her eyes nervously in Meirion's direction at intervals.

Once back at the farm, Meirion showed Bara what needed to be done and gave him a wheelbarrow, shovel and yard broom to get started. Meirion's dogs detected the presence of an intruder in the guise of Jess and set up an alarmed barking until Meirion went into the shed and yelled at them to shut up, for fuck's sake!

Bara, as usual, worked as though his life depended on it and had soon made great headway into the job. Meanwhile, Meirion set about strengthening and heightening an existing pen in readiness for the arrival of the wolf-hybrids.

At 12.30 on the dot, Bara emerged from the shed he was working in and stood in confusion in the yard.

'What's the matter?' asked Meirion.

'Time for dinner,' said Bara (though, without a watch, it was a mystery how he knew).

'Come on, then,' said Meirion reluctantly and led the way towards the kitchen.

Bara followed, bringing his sandwich box and Jess with him.

'Is that dog coming in here?' Meirion asked.

Bara nodded. He checked that her feet were clean – the way his mother insisted before she came into the house. Then he removed his own wellington boots and left them in the small hallway.

They went into the kitchen and Meirion put the kettle on. Bara stood in the middle of the room with his hands held away from him and a distressed look on his face.

'Fuck's the matter now?' asked Meirion.

'Wash hands,' said Bara.

'Use the sink over there,' he gestured, rolling his eyes as he turned away.

Bara looked in dismay. The sink was heaped full of dirty dishes and there was an unpleasant smell coming from it. The worktops and draining board were also laden with dirty dishes bearing signs of burnt-on food. The window sill and cooker were covered with greasy pots and saucepans which were coated with the remains of long-ago meals.

Bara was holding his hands even further away from his body. His mother kept their house in an almost sterile condition and Meirion's kitchen was a very long way out of Bara's comfort zone.

'Germs go inside and kill you,' he said solemnly.

Typical, thought Meirion that he had to fucking end up with Llanefa's answer to Howard Hughes!

'You'll have to use the bathroom, then,' he said impatiently – though, in reality that was not a great deal cleaner.

Bara went to the bathroom to wash his hands and examine under his nails, then looked worriedly about him for a towel that seemed clean and eventually settled on a dark coloured one that showed no obvious marks of soiling.

Back in the kitchen, he sat down at a table heaped with cereal boxes, a bag of half-spilt sugar and several cartons of spoiled milk. He cleared himself a small area to place his sandwich box and began to eat. He ate unselfconsciously with a wide open mouth and slurped his tea with enjoyment. Meirion looked at him distastefully and switched on the radio to drown out the sound – if there was one thing he hated, it was a noisy eater!

After lunch, Bara got on with his allotted task and Meirion had to admit that he was an excellent worker.

At the end of the working day, Meirion gave him his fiver (Bara's mother had insisted that he paid no more as too many Mars bars would ruin his teeth – a request that Meirion had been delighted to honour) and drove him home.

The next day, he gave Bara his instructions then left him there while he went to collect the wolf-hybrids. As he knew that he would be away all day, he had told Bara to walk to a neighbouring farm after he had finished his work. Byron, who lived there, would give him a lift home, he said, though he forgot to ask the neighbour if this action would be in order. At the end of the day, Bara and Jess made their way up Meirion's farm drive, along the tarmac road and down the next driveway which was about a mile away. It had started to rain heavily and, when he knocked at the farmhouse door, Sally, the owner recognised him and said 'Bara bach, you're soaked through. Come in.'

Bara removed his boots and checked Jess's feet and entered a clean, wiped down, clutter-free kitchen that was familiar territory to him. The room stretched into an even cleaner sitting down area with neatly stacked magazines and a TV gleaming on a metallic stand. It was home-from-home for Bara.

'Been working for Mei-on,' he said in his thick, raspy voice. 'Lift home.'

Sally's mouth tightened. Her opinion of Meirion was low at the best of times, but she was discovering hatred of him for the first time.

'Where's Meirion, then?' she asked, trying to keep a level tone so as not to alarm Bara.

'Gone to get dogs,' he said, keeping his slow gaze on her.

Sally felt a little uneasy. Bara had a way of looking at people that sometimes made them want to move further away. Sally, like most people, thought of Bara as a boy, but occasionally his giant frame and powerful arms reminded her that his body was that of a man's.

'Ok,' she said 'I'll have to get Byron back here. He can take you home. I'll make you some tea and you can watch telly while I fetch him. He's only repairing a fence in the bottom field.'

Although she didn't think that Bara was dangerous, Sally was reluctant to drive him home and be contained in a vehicle with him. The image of fastening the seat belt as it crossed between her breasts while Bara looked at her with his lazy gaze sounded an alarm in her mind. She gave him a mug of tea, threw on a coat and switched the TV on as she went out through the door.

'I won't be long. You just sit there till I'm back,' she said as she closed the door to the sound of the talking Bulldog on the advert for Churchill Insurance.

Bara loved watching TV. He especially liked watching Crocodile Dundee that his parents had on DVD at home.

'Oh yes, yes yes!' he repeated with the talking dog while he held his mug in one hand and idly stroked Jess with the other.

The adverts came to an end and Bara's education took a new turn.

In her haste to fetch her husband, Sally had forgotten one thing. Their early-rising lifestyle meant they were rarely able to stay up to watch any late-night programmes. To combat this, they

166

often set the kitchen TV to record anything they wanted to watch. When Sally spent an afternoon doing some baking or ironing, she usually put the TV on and watched as much as she could of the recorded programme while she finished her task. It was normal for her to see the programme in three or four sittings as there was always some task outside that took priority before the recording finished.

The previous week, Sally had recorded 'Small Town Legend' – a popular film that had been a hit in the cinemas, but that she had not been able to go and see. The plot, based on US farmers who battled to make a living despite the harsh conditions, centred on a contaminated young man who became a werewolf and ripped apart women and animals before falling in love with one of the farmers' daughters. Sally had managed only to see the first third of the film and the TV automatically picked up at the last watched section. (Sally and Byron watched the large TV in the lounge when they sat down for the evening, so the kitchen TV always maintained its recording status.)

The film resumed on the screen and Bara watched in horror as the young man dropped on to all fours and began his transformation. Further disturbing scenes followed as he killed people and animals. One of his victims had managed to escape and was himself infected – the wolf hairs growing rapidly on his hands. Bara sat with his lower jaw hanging half open and clutched his mug handle tightly. He had never imagined such sights! He wasn't even allowed to see the news at home - not that he wanted to, but his parents had created a mystery around it that held some intrigue for Bara. He closed his eyes when blood spurted from the neck of a deer as the man-wolf continued his rampage. Then all went quiet as a deer hunter came into focus, patently unaware of the danger he was in. The view changed to the man-wolf hidden in the undergrowth, his yellow eyes watching while the hunter wandered nearer.

Suddenly, the kitchen door burst open. Bara leapt to his feet.

'Fuck!' he shouted out.

Sally whipped off her coat 'Did I give you a fright, bach?' she said.

Byron was right behind her.

'I'll take you home now, Bara boy,' he said 'Can't have you walking in this.'

Sally absent-mindedly turned off the TV without ever registering what Bara had been watching and shut the door behind them as they left the kitchen.

The next day, Bara was collected by Meirion as usual. The clean-up was going well and Meirion began to think of other jobs that Bara could do while he was there. Feeding the dogs was a chore to him and he delegated this task to Bara. Jess stayed a cautious distance away while Bara went into the pens and scooped dog food kibble into the grubby dishes. Bara enjoyed the added duty. He managed to give each dog a pat and a rub of the ears as he fed them. He was delighted by the puppies who wanted to crawl up his legs and chew his trousers.

At the end of the row of pens, Bara started to pull back the spring-bolt when he caught sight of the new acquisitions inside. Two pairs of yellow eyes regarded him with caution. Bara stopped. The memory of the film came back into his mind. Man-wolf, his mind said.

Meirion's voice came from outside 'Be careful you don't let those two big ones out. They're not safe to be let out.'

What Meirion had meant was that the two hybrids were unsure of their new surroundings. If they ran out and escaped, he would not be able to catch them and he had visions of his investment disappearing into the Llanefa countryside.

Bara froze. He knew how unsafe they were! Hadn't he seen them on TV?

The bigger of the two took a step backwards while keeping its eyes on Bara. The other one gave a feeble wag of its tail, but stood its ground. Bara filled a scoop of food, opened the pen door a few inches and hurled the contents in the vague direction of the dishes. Most of it went on the floor and he repeated the action. The two hybrids stretched their necks forward to sniff before the smaller of the two went forward and started to eat. Bara quickly bolted the pen gate and hurriedly made his way to the other end of the building.

Meirion was on his way in.

'Did you feed the wolves?' he asked.

Bara nodded and swallowed hard; Meirion's words had confirmed his belief in what the two big dogs were. He was glad that Meirion had imprisoned them. Very soon, they would be shot, Bara supposed, in the very basic way that his mind worked.

He continued his work for Meirion for another week – the transformation making a huge difference to the filthy building and pens. Bara was taken aback to see that the wolves were still imprisoned and even more concerned that they both came forward to greet him when he took their food in. He used a long pole to pull the food dishes towards him so that he could tip the kibble into the dishes without going into the pen. Cleaning them out was an even more hazardous job that required reaching into the pen with a shovel and scraping the faeces and wood shavings towards him while taking care that they did not try to come any closer. When he had to take water to them, he poured it through the metal grid into their bucket. The smaller of the two hybrids tried to lick his hand as his fingers momentarily poked through the metals squares. Bara shuddered and examined his hand for signs of wolf hair growing there, before going to rinse his hands vigorously under the tap in the farmyard.

Unknown to him, the female hybrid had come into season and he interpreted her fierce reaction when the male went near her hindquarters, as the behaviour of a dangerous werewolf. He knew he had only a day or two left to work for Meirion and each day he would ask his mother 'Last day?' when he heard Meirion's van arriving to collect him.

To his relief, when Meirion dropped him off that night, he told his mother 'The job's finished now, bach. I won't need him again. He's a fast worker,' though his main reason was to avoid paying Bara any more money.

Bara soon fell back into his usual routine – hunting vermin, going to the cattle market with some of the farmers – and the memory of Meirion's wolves began to fade.

Life was not quite as easy for Meirion, who was discovering that the female hybrid was having nothing to do with the male despite his interest in her. Eventually, the male became afraid to approach her and Meirion could see that it was unlikely that a mating would take place. Unknown to him, the pair were actually brother and sister and the wolf gene had come to the fore where matters of breeding were concerned. The female was dominant to her brother and would not accept him as a mate. She had, however, set her sights on a golden coloured Cocker Spaniel stud dog that Meirion also owned and gazed longingly at him from her pen.

Meirion was keen for a quick return on his purchase and he worked out that a wolf-hybrid was a wolf-hybrid – regardless of what it was crossed with – and considered the possibility of mating the Cocker Spaniel to the wolf. Chances were that the pups would be large and grey coloured, he thought, and Malcom would take them regardless. The only fact that held him back was the difference in size between the two dogs – would the Spaniel be able to reach his target? He decided to hang on a few more days in case the female wolf-hybrid decided to accept the advances of her present kennel mate when she was nearer to ovulation – he had seen this behaviour in breeding bitches before.

But before he could decide what to do, Meirion had the council visit to contend with. Once again, Mark appeared on his farmyard, armed with a folder and pen.

Meirion was ready for him. He had retrieved a bundle of pedigrees and Puppy Sales Records that Mair had previously put away, had photocopied the Puppy Sales Receipts, painted Tippex over the date and re-inserted a recent date before photocopying again. The pedigrees were no problem to him as he always registered a fictitious extra puppy or two in most litters so that he had plenty of 'spare' pedigrees if the need arose.

170

Mark walked around the kennel building with him and had to concede that conditions were greatly improved – though his main concern was with planning issues rather than animal welfare.

At the end of the building, Mark stopped and looked at the hybrids.

'What are these, then?' he asked.

'German Shepherds,' said Meirion without pausing to draw breath 'Just bought them. Haven't had the paperwork back on them yet.'

'They look like wolves!' said Mark.

Meirion said nothing.

'We had a call from an anonymous member of the public to say that you had a pair of wolves,' he continued 'These are wolves, aren't they?'

Meirion wasn't sure how he stood in relation to keeping wolf-hybrids. Malcom had never mentioned needing a licence, but Meirion was a fast thinker when he saw trouble approaching. He laughed a little too loud and clapped Mark on the shoulder.

'Wolves! Good God, no! I've been teasing Noel in the pub. Telling him I had a pair of wolves just to wind him up. Someone else must have heard me. These are German Shepherds. The colour is unusual – sable, they call it. Look how friendly they are – tails wagging...'

Mark looked. The smaller one was wagging its tail slightly, but both were at the furthest point of the pen with their yellow eyes focused on the stranger.

Mark shrugged. It was nothing to do with him *what* they were. It was true that they *had* received a call from someone and, bearing in mind the bad publicity that had arisen from Meirion's sick puppies, the council could not be seen to be endorsing bad practices. The place had been cleaned up beyond recognition, the paperwork was dubiously acceptable and he saw only eighteen breeding bitches. His mind was already planning his next move when he got back to the office, where a temporary member of staff was making it clear to him that she was available for extra-mural activities. He filled in his form, told Meirion that he would recommend another visit in six months and drove off with his head full of lecherous plans.

With the council problem temporarily out of the way, Meirion concentrated on the wolf-hybrids. He felt the desperation of someone who was about to lose money. He made up his mind to try the Cocker Spaniel male with the female wolf-hybrid. He went into the shed and carefully opened the pen. The larger male was a suspicious creature and stood behind the female. Meirion tried to get the male out to put him in another pen, but the animal was having none of it! Afraid of being taken from his companion, he dodged back and gave a token lift of his lip.

Ok, thought Meirion, if he couldn't get the male out so that he could put the Spaniel in, he would take the female out and put her with the Spaniel. He tried to catch her and drag her out by her scruff, but by then she, too, had become suspicious and was unwilling to be handled.

Trying another tactic, Meirion opened the Spaniel's pen and let him out into the interior alleyway between the pens. He raced up and down, while making a high-pitched excited yelp. When Meirion opened the wolf-hybrid pen the next time, the female hybrid shot out past him in her eagerness to join her chosen mate. Meiron quickly shut the pen door on the male hybrid as he hurled himself against the wire.

The female ran up and down the alleyway, leaping at the Spaniel and attempting to flirt with him while the male wolf-hybrid howled in distress at being separated from his sister.

The Spaniel was a little overcome by his large, boisterous mate-to-be and alternated between play-flirting and running away. Together, they raced back and forth until the Spaniel decided that it was all too rough for him and he backed up against the wall of the shed and showed his teeth. The wolf-hybrid was too enamoured to notice and she threw herself at him in delight. The Spaniel snapped at her and gave a loud warning bark. She stopped, then launched forward again. This time, in panic, the Spaniel flipped himself over backwards and rolled heavily towards the

172

shed door. Meirion, in his usual negligent way, had not shut the door properly and it swung open. In a second, he saw both dogs running through the gap into the farmyard, while he ran out behind them.

'Here!' he shouted 'Come here!'

The Spaniel halted and blinked his eyes – not used to being out in natural daylight. The female wolf-hybrid had decided that the Spaniel was not a dominant enough mate for her and, combined with Meirion's shouting, headed for an open gateway to a field. Meirion's further shouts of 'Come here!' sent her into a gallop and she was out of his sight in a few seconds.

Meirion turned to the disorientated Spaniel and gave him a kick on his rump. He yelped.

'Stupid fucking dog!' he shouted at him before scanning the countryside for any obvious movement.

The male hybrid was howling in long unbroken sessions and although Meirion's instinctive reaction was to go into the shed and tell it to shut fucking up, some kind of inner wisdom suggested that if he wanted to secure his investment he should leave it alone in case its noise would bring the female back.

Ignoring the mournful howls of the male hybrid, he man-handled the Cocker Spaniel back to its pen before going into the house for a cup of tea and a cigarette. As the nicotine surged through his system he perked up at the thought that the female would almost certainly be mated by a dog of *some* description as she wandered the countryside; there were plenty of sheepdogs on the surrounding farms who were free to wander at will. As long as he had wolf-hybrid puppies to sell in the near future, Meirion cared little as to what their parentage was. He decided to leave a bowl of dog food kibble out every night so that the female would return on a regular basis. He had not worked out the final details of how he was going to catch her, but Meirion was a great believer in things working out for themselves.

When Bara went to the cattle market to help out the following week, it was clear to him that Meirion was the cause of some widespread anger. He caught parts of conversation between the farmers.

'I've told him if I see it on my land again, I'll fucking shoot it straight away,' Tom Garth Isaf said to Byron, 'The cattle were terrified. Milk yields right down that night.'

'Is it really a wolf?' asked Dewi Tanyfron 'You know what a bull-shitter Meirion is!'

'I don't care what it is. If it upsets my animals again – bang. Bye-bye doggy, wolfie – whatever he wants to call it.'

'I bet Dai Cwm Efa wishes he'd had a gun with him when he caught it ripping his sheep to pieces!' said another.

'A real waste,' added Tom, 'not only did it kill one sheep, but it did some serious damage to two others. Dai had to put them down. They were both infected.'

Bara never really listened to the farmers' conversations. He found it difficult to follow their talk. But the word 'wolf' had alerted his memory to the terrible scenes he had witnessed on Byron's television. The term 'infected' had also stayed in his mind after seeing the film and learning that this word meant the result of being bitten by a werewolf.

'Mei-on wolf!' he said, his voice thicker and more rasping than usual.

Everyone looked at him.

'Have you seen the wolf?' asked Dewi, remembering that Bara had done some work for Meirion.

'Two wolf!' said Bara 'Bad wolf. I fraid.'

'No need to be scared, Bara boy,' said Byron, pulling a meaningful face at the others 'It's not going to hurt you. It's looking for rabbits to eat. That's all.'

They swiftly changed the subject and no-one noticed Bara checking his fingers to see if there were wolf hairs growing there.

During the following week, as Bara went about his normal routine, Jess came into season. It was not something that Bara had been taught to notice and, combined with his mother's efforts to keep the house spotlessly clean and Jess's own clean habits with regard to washing herself, it did not become noticed by anyone except his mother. The previous contact with Meirion's breeding dogs had triggered Jess's body to produce the necessary hormones in the same way that a pack of wild dogs follow the heat of the alpha female.

Bara's mother hoped that Jess would not be mated by a wandering stray and would have liked her to stay indoors for the relevant three weeks, but was reluctant to bring up the topic with her son as it would have necessitated some embarrassing explanations. Instead, she found jobs for Bara to do at home so that he and Jess would be 'off the road' until the danger time had passed. It had been a good idea, but as the days wore on, it became obvious that Bara was becoming stir-crazy due to his routine being changed.

Once she realised that it was not practical to keep both at home for three weeks, she arranged for his father to take them in the car and drop them off at some secluded spot where Bara could trap vermin, but would not have to walk through Llanefa and attract stray dogs in the process. She admitted that this plan was not perfect as neither of them knew when to expect Bara home, but at least she was halving the risk of having to deal with a litter of mongrels (and, she feared, Bara's insistence that they kept them all).

Bara's father drove him to various woodlands that he told his son were in need of vermin control. Bara's mother always prepared a back-pack for him when he was going to be out in the countryside all day. She put in a sandwich box, Wet Wipes and hand sterilising fluid. To this burden, Bara himself added some digging equipment and the ferret box which he carried by a satchel-style strap over his shoulder. Once he was dropped off with his supplies, both parents had no more than faint twinges of concern about him. Bara was too big for anyone to bother and they felt that his education would prevent him from doing anything illegal or improper. He walked for miles and often bumped into farmers on their tractors while he was out. While some of them didn't feel that they *needed* vermin control, they all knew how important it was to Bara to do his 'duty' and gave him *carte blanche* to continue. Most of the time, no-one saw him and he carried out his daily 'work' as Gil had taught him.

His territory had become more far reaching due to his father's efforts to taxi him away from the confines of Llanefa.

When he found himself at the far end of Pwll y Coed woods one afternoon, he heard a sound that made his blood run cold. A long, mournful 'woooooo-ooooooo' which was replied to by a similar sound from another direction - Meirion's wolf-hybrid was still living rough.

Bara again checked his hands for wolf hairs.

He packed up his supplies and quickly moved on to another location nearer town. He stopped at regular intervals to look behind him while his heart thumped loudly in his chest.

After a few hours, he relaxed and forgot about Meirion's wolf while he tested the ferret at obvious rat-holes in the hedge. He was engrossed in watching the ferret when Jess gave an alarmed bark. He looked up but saw nothing. A moment later he again heard the distant howling from further away. It was a sound that made him put his back against a tree and look around him in fear.

While he was in this high state of alarm, a brown and white shape began to emerge through the woodland towards him. As he stared in frozen shock, the shape came fully into view and revealed itself as a small male terrier. The terrier was on a mission! It had picked up the scent of Jess and was intent on having his way with her. It gathered speed and ran at Jess, leaping the last few feet in his eagerness to get at her. Unfortunately, Jess was not yet receptive and scuttled away with a sharp growl. The terrier was used to rejection and made a determined leap in her direction. The resulting fight was mainly due to Jess making a stand against the marauding mongrel, but in Bara's stimulated imagination, it was an 'infected' dog that had been bitten by a werewolf and was now attacking Jess.

With a loud yell, he jumped at the fighting pair and grabbed the terrier with his huge hands. The terrier tried to turn on his captor, but Bara was in fear of his life in case he was infected by it. He grasped the terrier's front legs with one hand and pulled the dog's jaw and head upwards with one powerful yank of the other hand. It was instant. The terrier never had a chance to make a noise, before it collapsed into a lifeless mass in Bara's hands.

Bara checked Jess and was relieved to find no injuries. Then he examined his own hands for cuts or wolf hairs.

He took a small gardening shovel out of his backpack – the one he used to dig out rat holes – and began to dig a grave for the terrier. He did this because he knew that a dead animal left out on the ground would attract others to come and eat it. He understood that if that happened, other creatures would be infected too. After he had buried the terrier, he began a thorough cleaning of his hands to rid himself of werewolf germs.

It was the beginning of Bara's fight against the werewolf. It had never occurred to him that he should stay at home. Every few days, a straying dog would appear, beckoned by the scent of Jess. He killed each one and buried it.

In the town itself, he saw hardly any wandering dogs. Owners tended to take their dogs for walks on leads and most male dogs were neutered so showed no interest in Jess.

People were beginning to notice how many dogs had gone missing and the subject was a favourite talking point. Others said that their cats had also gone missing (though poor Bara had had nothing to do with that). Bara's mother told him to be careful not to let Jess out of his sight – a statement that made him even more determined to deal with every werewolf he saw.

'Don't let wolf eat Jess,' he agreed.

His mother wasn't sure where he had heard about a wolf, but it was true that some of the farmers were talking about a wolf that was wandering the countryside – melodramatic nonsense in her opinion.

Meirion, meanwhile, had given up on ever getting the female hybrid back and had heard rumours that she had been shot for worrying sheep. He was getting a lot of grief from some of the farmers about it and he eventually decided to sell the male hybrid to whoever would take him. The fucking thing was howling day and night, refusing to eat, but still managing to shit through the eye of a needle, Meirion reflected. It was time to call the whole thing a bad experience and move on. He'd heard that Alpacas were selling well. They ate grass too. No having to shut them in a shed, no shit to clean up and, more importantly, no council on his arse every time he sold one. He was going to forget all about wolves.

But, while Meirion was prepared to forget about wolves, nervous farmers were not quite as dismissive. They harangued him at every opportunity, causing heated discussions at the feed merchants or at the sheep market.

The level of hysteria following the vanishing of so many dogs had also risen to a peak. The Llanefa Guardian ran a feature on the mysterious disappearances and called it the Llanefa Triangle. A short time afterwards, the local TV news channel aired it, though the general public lost credibility in the story when they heard interviewed residents speak of possible witchcraft practices and vivisection conspiracies.

By that time, Jess had long finished her season and Bara saw no more wandering dogs during his 'working' day. He always kept a lookout for any possible dogs that had been infected by the werewolf and checked his hands at regular intervals.

Eventually, both the stray wolf and the missing pets slid off the public radar to be replaced by other topical issues. The female wolf-hybrid had died after eating poisoned rat bait in the garden of a remote cottage. She had gone into hiding in the woods and stayed there while the strychnine attacked her muscles and internal organs. Carrion-eating animals fed off her corpse and themselves died of the same cause. Maggots and flies cleared what was left and, if anyone ever saw the skeletal remains, it would not have been identified as a wolf-hybrid (or even a particularly large dog as bone structure looks much smaller than the complete animal).

Bara continued to be vigilant, but saw nothing that alarmed him.

One day, he saw Sally in the feed merchants while he was helping to stack sugar beet bags.

'Hello, bach,' she said 'Have you finished working for Meirion now? I haven't seen you for a while.'

'Finish,' he said.

'Good,' she replied 'Better for you to work here.'

'Where wolf?' he asked her.

Sally looked blankly at him. Sometimes it was difficult to understand Bara.

'Wolf gone?' he asked again.

Sally realised what he was talking about. Bloody Meirion, she thought, causing terror to the likes of poor Bara...

'Yes, bach. Wolf has gone!' she said 'Forget about him. No more wolf.'

Bara relaxed his posture. The ever-present worry had sometimes given him nightmares. He had leapt awake screaming on a few occasions, though he never remembered what he had been dreaming about. His mother thought she heard him shout 'Man-wolf' when he first woke up, but even she was not certain.

Despite Sally's reassurance that the wolf had gone, Bara's memory would not give him total freedom from worry and he would occasionally forget what she had told him. Those who saw him could probably pinpoint those days as he developed a wary, frightened look and jumped at every sudden noise. However, Bara was Bara and no-one took notice for long.

In the cattle market one week, he was shutting a cow and calf into a pen when he became aware of a commotion nearby. Meirion and Dai Cwm Efa were shouting at each other while standing nose to nose. Dai was furious because Meirion's inadequate fencing had resulted in his cattle breaking into Dai's mature crops, trampling and eating them.

Meirion shouted back that Dai should have fenced his own land more effectively if he wanted to keep animals out. A small, but interested, audience of local farmers had gathered to watch Meirion get his come-uppance.

'I've had a fucking gutsful of you,' shouted Dai 'what with your animals coming onto my land, that slurry you contaminated my stream with and that fucking wolf that killed my sheep...'

'You just think you're better than the rest of us,' bellowed Meirion 'just because you've had good land left to you by your father. We're not all as lucky to have crop-growing land. Some of us have got to slave and work for a living. You've got it too easy, you have...'

'You bastard!' yelled Dai 'What the fuck do you know about hard work! No wonder Mair fucked off and...'

That was as far as he got before Meirion's fat fist shot out and hit the side of Dai's face. In a second, the two were locked in a primitive, clawing, grasping fight. Before any of the others could separate them, they fell on to the floor. Several pairs of hands grabbed hold of Dai and Meirion and tried to pull them apart with loud cried of 'Pack it in!' and 'Come on now, boys.'

They managed to break them up before the Auctioneer made his way over.

'What's going on?' he asked.

Six voices all answered at once that everything was sorted, ok, no problem, bit of a misunderstanding and he went back to his office.

Byron was the voice of reason, 'For fuck's sake, boys, what do you think you're doing? Just get on with your business and stay apart from each other if you're going to behave like wild animals...'

The duelling pair stood panting and red-faced, eyes cast away from each other – each knowing that direct eye contact would probably re-start the fight.

The other watchers started several discussions amongst themselves, each putting forward a different version of how Meirion had hit Dai and how Dai had hit back. Some, who had missed the main event, came forward and asked what had happened while others simply stood and stared in disbelief.

The only one who stared in horror was Bara. He stood at the edge of the farmers, Jess cowering behind his legs. His eyes were locked on both men. Their faces were red and their eyes wild. But more worrying to Bara was the fact that their clothes had become dishevelled in the fight. Meirion's overalls were ripped at the pocket and both men's collars were pulled downwards or to one side revealing the white skin of their chests. It was at this area of their bodies that Bara stared. Both were relatively hairy-chested, though Meirion was much more so than Dai. Meirion's chest hair, as a result of his age, was speckled with grey and it curled, thickly upwards towards his jaw. Dai's was less obvious, but the presence of wolf hair was clear to Bara. Meirion was a werewolf and he had now infected Dai after attacking him.

Bara quickly checked his own fingers and took a few steps back.

He knew what had to be done and where he would need to 'work' from then on. He was an expert at tracking and killing vermin. Occasionally it took a little more effort than usual. He could not have put it into words, but he was aware how long it sometimes took to entice the vermin into the open. He had developed the patience to wait. And, although he could not express himself he knew that he intended to kill all the werewolves in time.

The Perfect Wife.

The transcript of the interview lies in a plastic envelope on its own. This had not been his case; he had simply been involved as a result of geographical logistics.

Tegwyn remembers the girl's face. A combination of innocence and honesty — rare qualities these days, he thinks.

The case had been heard in Cardiff Crown Court. He recalls the obligatory celebration drink he'd had with the investigating team after the case was over. And the feeling of guilt when he later emerged from the pub and saw Glenis and Jack Price waiting for their train back to Llanefa.

My name is Imee, sir.

Yes, I am from Manila. I come to Wales to be Adrian's wife. I see in Internet Cafe that Adrian is forty years old and look for Perfect Wife. I meet him in Manila.

I am eighteen, sir.

They are both dead, sir. They died in the flood many years ago. Then I live with my cousin and his wife. My cousin say I should be married and he was also happy to meet Adrian.

Adrian tell him that I am beautiful and that he want to marry me. My cousin is very poor and cannot pay for my wedding. Adrian say it is ok for us to get married in Wales. I say goodbye to my cousin and his wife and we come to Cardiff. There we get married. The wedding was very small and it was only one other person to write the papers.

No, sir, I do not have the paper. Adrian keep all papers.

I do not know the place name. Adrian say they do special wedding.

We go to Cardiff. We live in Adrian's flat. I learn to make the Shepherd Pie and he teach me many thing about Wales. Soon we move to other flat. I know not the address but is number twenty-eight.

Adrian buy me much clothes. But he think like a man and buy me Skin Clothes!

Pardon me, sir?

Skin Clothes are small clothes like leather short and crop-top. He think we are still in warm Manila! I ask for other clothes and he buy them for me. He say I cannot go to buy them because Cardiff shop do not understand me.

Adrian have much, much friends. They come to play cards in his flat. I make them the Toasty Sandwich and bring them beer. I am Perfect Wife, Adrian say.

Then he tell me about old Wales custom when new bride is shared with husband's friends. He say I must follow custom because I am Perfect Wife. His friends will give him gifts of money, it is part of the custom, he say. I think now, maybe this is not so.

No, sir, I not share with Adrian's friends. I say I am unhappy to do Wales custom. Adrian is a little angry, but then say it is ok.

Adrian's parents, sir? One time, we come to see them. They live here. Adrian teach me how to say 'Llanefa'. It is small town with small mind, he say. I show respect to Adrian's parents like Perfect Wife should do. Adrian's mother very angry with him. She not say why but I can see it is so. Adrian's father not angry, but kind to me.

When Adrian go to bathroom, they ask me how I meet him and I tell them about Internet Cafe. I tell them also about my cousin who is kind to me when my parents drown. Adrian's mother ask where we get married. I tell her – place in Cardiff – Adrian have the papers. She also ask how old am I. She look very angry when I tell her. I try to show more respect but she not willing to talk to me more. I tell her I can make the Yorkshire Pud and that Adrian like my food. She ask me what religion am I. I don't know what to answer. I am afraid to make her more angry.

Adrian's father make us tea and give us very sweet cake to eat. I am trying to eat it all but I am not liking it. He say I must like curry more so I smile and bow my head in respect for him. He wink his eye at me. I think he is very kind old man.

When I go to bathroom, I hear much shouting.

All of them, sir.

I walk half way down the steps and hear them. I was afraid it was my fault so I stay on the steps. There is carpet on the steps and they cannot hear my feet.

What they shout, sir? I hear them shouting about a person called Maria. I do not know who is Maria. Adrian's mother say, *How can you do this to us? Now we will never see the children.* I do not know what children she talk about. She also say that he has been in Sham Ceremony. I think that mean the special wedding we have. I think maybe she is angry because she did not see wedding.

Adrian's mother is shouting that this cannot be so. There was no nullment – I think it was that word she say - no nullment from Maria. I am confused because she talk too fast and loud.

She then tell Adrian he would not get a penny from her. I do not know why Adrian want a penny. I know he have much money in his pocket. The shouting is more loud and Adrian's father say that it illegal. I am very afraid so I open the door and walk outside very quietly. I am standing in the garden and it is beautiful. There are flowers on the wall and hanging by the door. The petals are not large like in Manila but the colour is just the same. I want to go back to Manila when I see it. I know it is bad wife to say that...

Some boys walk by. They stare at me. Then they walk away and come back with more boys and stare. One of them is shouting to someone else and then they run away. I can hear them shout more. I stay outside the door and hear the shouting still inside the house. Everywhere inside and outside, there is shouting! Adrian's mother is shouting the most.

Then the boys come back. They have man and dog with them. The boys are telling the man to talk to me. The man looks very strange and he is staring at me. The boys are laughing and saying, *Ask her!*

No, sir, I did not know what they mean.

The man look at me and step forward a little.

The door opens behind me and Adrian come out. The same time, the strange man say, *Wanna fuck?* to me then make noise like animal and I am scared. Adrian hold my arm and pull me to gate. He look at strange man and say, *How much money you have? Do you want to have her?* Adrian very angry and the boys all run away. The strange man start to cry then he go away too with dog following him. Adrian's father come outside. He is shouting at Adrian, *You treat that girl properly! You hear me? Or I...* He not say what he do.

Then Adrian pull me through gate and round to where car is. He push me into car and he drive away from there.

I am afraid to speak to him. A Perfect Wife must show respect and not make her husband angry.

We go back to Cardiff, to Adrian's flat.

No, sir, he did not say why he was angry.

No, sir, I did not ask him who is Maria.

Yes, sir, he talk to me about the strange man. He say we can get lots more money if I can be nice to strange men. He say it cost many, many peso – excuse me, sir, I mean pounds – to bring me to Wales and we must pay more if I want to stay. I am crying because I want to stay. I am missing my cousin too, but I give great shame to my family if I go back without husband.

Adrian say I can be Working Girl and still be Perfect Wife. It just the same as custom of sharing new wife with friends he say. I say I not sure if it is right, but he say I will be ok and because I am Perfect Wife he will be very satisfied with me.

In Manila, is very important to make husband happy and have good things to make perfect house. Adrian say it is my duty to help bring money to our house. I show my respect to him.

Then, sir?

Very soon he take me in car to strange road in Cardiff when it is dark. I get out and he tell me to walk from traffic light to newsagent and sometimes stand by wall. I must look pretty and not wear a coat. I am cold because it is not like Manila. Adrian drive by many times to watch me. I see woman from India come out of newsagent with garbage bags. I smile and hope to talk but she wave her hand and say, *Go away from here.* I not know why she angry with me.

Then Mister in car stop to talk to me. He say, *Are you lonely?*

Adrian come back and speak quietly to him by car window. The Mister nod his head then Adrian go. I get in car with Mister and he drive to parking lot and stop in the place where no other cars are.

Yes, sir, he talk to me. He ask if I am cold and say I am pretty.

He take his trousers loose. He is fat man and his belly hide his man-parts. He put his hand on my leg and say he want hand-job. I know what this mean and I try to do it but the belly is so big I cannot get my hand inside the trousers.

He say, *Do you know what to do?* and sound a little angry.

I bow my head with respect and try with other hand.

I am feeling sick because the man has bad smell, but I know I must do it.

Then he tell me to take crop-top off because he want to see my titties. I take it off and then he push car seat more back. I can reach him then, but when I put hand on him, he is finished. No, sir, not change mind. Finished - jizz on my hand and arm. He get tissue box from back seat and give one to me and take some for him. I use tissue to wipe the jizz but I am crying so I use it to wipe my face also.

The Mister drive me back to the road, sir. Adrian waiting there and speak to man again. Mister give him money and I get out of car. Three more times this happen with other Misters. Some drive the car when I get in and some get out of car and come with me to alley by newsagent where it is dark. I must do hand-job for all of them.

Adrian bring his car and tell me to get in and we go home. He is satisfied with me and say I am Really Perfect Wife. Then he ask me to tell him what I do to the Misters.

After that, sir? He want to have sex with me. I am ashamed but know I must obey my husband.

Every night Adrian take me to the road and I am Working Girl for many hours.

About three weeks, sir, before I stop going to the road.

Adrian said so, sir. Because I took a Mister to the alley and he was not able to make the jizz come. Mister shouted at me. I was doing it wrong, he say. Then I try and try but, no. Then the Mister hit my face and then the jizz come. After, he tell Adrian he have friends who like to correct woman. So Adrian tell me we do it at our flat after that.

I was happy to go away from the cold street, sir.

No, sir, I did not know what 'correct' mean.

It was next time I found out.

Adrian bring Mister to our flat and we go in room where he keep computer. Adrian have put small bed in there. He say I must have sex with Special Misters. They pay much money and I am Excellent Wife, he say. I am unhappy, but I am obedient.

The first Mister come and try to have sex with me but cannot. His man-part is too soft. Then he get angry and say I am bad woman who must be punished. I am afraid. Mister take off belt and hit me with it. I am yelling and saying stop. I try to run to door but Mister hold me by my arm and throw me on bed. He hit me again and I see his man-part is very hard and he jump on me and have sex with me. It is very quick and I am glad.

No, sir, he did not have rubber. Adrian make me take pill because we have not got money to have babies yet.

Then I know what 'correct' mean. And I know Special Misters want to hurt me. Some bring knife and start to cut me and some are tying a rope around my neck and hands. I am afraid, but Adrian is happy. We will soon have enough money for me to stay in Wales and have babies, he say. One Mister come back many time. He is very bad man. He have many knifes with him. He put knifes on bed by my side and pick up different knife to put against my neck while he is having sex with me. Some are very big knifes; the handles have decoration.

Later, Adrian tell me he is putting video camera in room so that he can watch Mister having sex with me. This is because he want to see that I am safe, he say. I do not understand because he cannot watch it until after the Mister has gone. I think maybe he is telling me untruth because he have friends who call and they watch DVD while they play cards. I am not permitted to go in room when they are playing cards and watching DVD. He tell me to put the Toasty Sandwich and beer on tray outside door for them. His friends are also taking DVD with them when they go home.

After, Adrian tell me I have email from my cousin. He let me read the email. He is ok and his wife is going to have a baby. They have four children when I leave Manila. He ask if I am ok and happy. He say they will name new baby, Imee, if she is baby girl.

It make me cry and Adrian say my cousin is bad man for making me cry and he will not let him send more emails. I cry more until I see Adrian is angry with me. I try to be better wife and forget about my cousin.

Yes, sir, I believe Adrian when he say that it is ok to be Working Girl and Perfect Wife. I understand it is different ways in many countries.

The Special Misters come back many times, sir, and I let them hurt me.

No, sir, it was not much hurt after several times. I am pretending I am dreaming. Sometimes I am thinking of the flowers in Manila and the little children playing in the street. When

Misters have finished, I wash the jizz and blood away and then I can be Perfect Wife again.

Last night, sir? The bad man Special Mister came back with his knifes. He put them all round my body. He take out thin belt from pocket and tie it round my neck. Then he use all knifes, one, two, three, four and all of them, to cut small holes in my side, my arm, my leg and then he try to cut hole in my throat. I am very, very afraid and I try to get away from him. When I fight and move he get more happy and the sex was finished soon. I am crying and crying. Mister very kind after and say I am now good girl after I am punished. I go to wash the blood and jizz away, but I hide one knife under the bed.

I don't know why I take knife, sir. I just do it. I am afraid of the Special Misters.

When he go away, Adrian come to get video. He put it on machine. Then he say he want to have sex with me while video is on. I am very unhappy and I am crying again.

He make me lie down and take my clothes off. Then he take much of his clothes off and start to have sex with me on small bed in computer room. I am hurting where the Special Mister cut me. I ask Adrian to stop but he hold his hands around my neck and squeeze. I cannot breathe. I am very afraid and I am trying to get away.

I put my hand under the bed and touch knife. I pick it up and push blade into side of Adrian's neck. He scream and let go of me. I take knife out and push it into his belly. He scream some more. His blood is running over me. It feel like the jizz of the Misters. It make me feel sick and dirty. I push knife in him some more.

Then I know I have done a bad thing, sir, and I look at Adrian and try to stop the blood. He is making a noise like water running out of bathtub. Then he is quiet and there is blood all over. He is lying there. He is very still. He had not much clothes on. He looks just like ordinary Mister.

Thank you, ma'am, but is ok. I am happy to answer question he ask me.

Yes, sir, I know it is I who have kill him, but I am not thinking I will kill him when I hide knife. I am only putting knife in him when he is hurting me. *Then* I am wanting to hurt him. My family will have great shame now. They will not let me go back to them again...

Pardon me, sir?

I wash the blood off my skin. I am crying and crying. Adrian is lying on the bed. His eyes are looking at me but he cannot see. I am afraid to look at him. I put clothes on and go to next door flat. I knock on door but no-one answer. I try another door and I am still crying. A woman open door. She is holding can of beer. I cry and say I need help. I say I have done bad thing. Woman look at me and say, *Fuck off, slut,* and close door. I try to knock the door again. This time a man open the door and he shout something at me. I do not understand what he say. He shut door very hard.

I know only one place to go – here, to Adrian's father. He will help me.

I walk outside to road and hold my hand out when cars drive by. Some people stop and shout at me. One man ask if I want to keep him company and I walk away from him.

One car stop and I see man and woman in there.

The woman say *Where are you going?* and I say *M4 West* like I have hear Adrian say.

They drive me to busy road where there are no houses. When they stop, the woman say *We can't take you any further. You can hitch lift from here.*

I walk at side of busy road with my hand out to show I want a car to stop.

How long, sir? Some hours maybe... Then a car stop and a woman is driving. She say, *You should not be walking on motorway. Where are you going?*

I say, *M4 West. Llanefa.*

She laugh and say, *This is the M4 West! Llanefa, did you say? My sister lives there!*

Then she look at me and say, *Are you ok?*

I am crying again and I see blood on my clothes.

Excuse me, sir?

The blood come from hole in my arm.

I nod my head and try to say, *My husband try to hurt me*, but the words are hard to say while I am crying.

She say for me to get in car. I sit beside her and she drive away. She ask me many questions if I am hurt and if I want to go to hospital and if I want to call police. I say only that I must go to Llanefa and I am crying some more.

Later we are driving on road which is not highway and the woman say, *What is the address?*

I look at her and feel stupid. I know not the address, only that there are flowers hanging by the garden door.

What are the names of the people? the woman ask. Her voice is very kind.

It is Adrian's mother and father, I say.

The woman say nothing.

Adrian Price, I say.

We can go to my sister's house until we can find address you need, she say, *you can have some tea and we try to work it out.*

I nod my head.

Woman take out cell phone and call her sister. She speak in different language. I think she speak Wales.

Yes, sir, she take me to sister's house. They are very kind to me. Woman say her name is Jenny . I do not understand name of sister so I cannot speak it. They speak together and they say to me maybe it is house of Glenis and Jack I am looking for. I am not knowing the name of Adrian's mother and father.

Then Jenny say I have much blood on my clothes and ask if I am ok. I say I am ok but Adrian is dead. It make me cry when I say this.

192

Jenny and sister not speak for a minute. Then sister leave room and Jenny say to me that we must speak to police.

Yes, sir, then I wait with them until you come to sister's house and take me here. I am very unhappy and I am wanting to see my cousin and I am wanting to be in Manila.

Pardon me, sir?

Yes, I understand that I must stay here because of what I do tonight.

I know I am not Perfect Wife anymore, sir.

The Family Man.

Tegwyn picks up the folder that contains his last murder case before retiring.

It still doesn't ring true with him. Yet, the case sailed effortlessly through court and the defendant paid the appropriate price. Tegwyn has always had his doubts about this one. A classic case of some secrets never seeing the light of day, he thinks.

A tragic case, too. A family destroyed, the farm running to financial ruin and their children suffering in a way that could never be put right. Especially the girl - her father's favourite – now running wild, getting drunk and taking drugs.

Tegwyn can empathise with the bond between father and daughter.

He thanks an unknown deity that his own daughter never had to deal with such trauma.

It was Mike the builder who kicked things off. He'd been building a retaining wall at Tanyfron Farm because the sharply sloping grass bank behind the milking parlour had been gradually creeping down across the tarmac lane. He had been faintly aware of the smell of a dead animal that had increased in its intensity as the warmest early May on record transformed the hilly landscape into a blaze of buttercups and lush pasture.

He was quite used to bad smells; every farmer in the Efa Valley had been spreading slurry for weeks, though he had to concede that slurry smelled a damn sight better than dead animal!

Mike was on the Llanefa Show Committee and was in charge of organising some of the events for the week-long July festival that preceded it. His mind was on the Car Treasure Hunt that he was planning and he was trying to work out how to include the new retaining wall as part of the route. It would be a shame if the

Treasure Hunters missed his 'Mike Davies. Builder' plaque, together with his phone number, positioned on the wall!

He'd stopped for a cup of tea and a Welsh cake in his van. Working alone warranted more tea breaks in his opinion. His casual helper, Daz, had upped and left him to it a few weeks earlier and Mike was yet to find a replacement. Daz, like most of his casual help, had been a drifter and when he simply didn't turn up for work one morning, Mike had cursed to anyone who would listen about the lack of reliability of the younger generation.

The Treasure Hunt route began to take shape in his mind. There were some details to finalise; for instance, which route to take from Tanyfron to the ruins of Llanefa Castle and from there to the standing stones on the Pwll y Coed road.

At the lowest end of Tanyfron's farmyard stood a fifteen–foot high slurry store. An underground pipe drained the effluent from the milking parlour and adjoining yard into the base of the slurry store. When it became near to full, its contents would be suctioned by means of a large, flexed pipe into the slurry spreader and taken out on to the fields. Staring across at the slurry store, Mike thought it wouldn't be a bad idea to climb up the fixed ladder at the side and take a look across the countryside. The extra height might give him ideas for treasure-hunt landmarks. The Tanyfron family of Dewi, Gwen and the three children had taken the opportunity to go out until milking time as Llanefa School had an inset day. In any case, he thought, he was sure they wouldn't mind...

Decision made, he climbed the metal rungs and stood on the mini-platform at the top of the slurry tank. The smell of dead animal immediately worsened and Mike put his hand over his nose. As he did so, his eyes flicked downwards into the tank and there he saw the arm and back of a man half submerged in the slurry.

Recognition of the shirt that Daz often wore hit Mike around the same time as the sound of the flies buzzing in celebration over their feast.

Mike instantly did two things. The first was to make a half choked noise which sounded a bit like 'Fuck!' and the second was to hurl the partly digested Welsh Cake into the sorry mess.

* * *

Mike sat in the interview room at Llanefa Police Station, where a hastily set up Incident Room had pushed all routine business into the tiny front office.

'Just give me an idea when he last turned up for work,' DCI Tegwyn Prydderch said, running out of patience with the answers he had been given so far.

'I dunno what date, like. 'Bout three weeks ago, maybe...'

Tegwyn looked over his glasses at him 'And you didn't ask around why he just... vanished?'

'He was just casual,' said Mike 'They come and go. They don't give me notice or anything. He was probably on benefits. Not that I know that...' he added hastily.

Tegwyn sighed, 'I don't care about benefits. This is now a murder case. That's why I asked you back here. I really need a few more answers from you.'

Mike's eyes became like fried eggs.

'Murder!' he gasped 'I thought he'd just climbed up there and fallen in...'

Tegwyn was old school. He never showed a full hand until he had to.

'It certainly looked like that at first,' Tegwyn agreed 'but the fact that his bicycle was in there with him tends to suggest otherwise.'

He waited while Mike opened and closed his mouth several times.

'So, Mike, who do you think would have wanted to kill him? Who did he upset? Hmm..?'

Mike had a sudden, frightening vision of himself as a defendant standing in the dock. It was enough to loosen his tongue.

'Well, I don't know about *killing* him, but Dewi Tanyfron wouldn't have gone out of his way to buy him a pint!'

'Oh?' said Tegwyn 'And why was that?'

'Well, he was, you know... er... Daz was messing about with Gwen. Dewi's wife.'

'Messing about?'

'Have I got to spell it out? Shagging her!'

'And you know this for certain?'

'Yeah. Everyone knows. When Dewi was in the cattle mart or something, I used to leave Daz there. Apparently, she used to drop him off at Efa Country Park later on. That's where he used to leave his bike when he met me in the mornings. Saved me a bit of a loop around from my house.

Daz sometimes used to cycle down to the farm on his days off if Dewi and the children were out. When he just didn't turn up for work, I thought things had got too hot for him to handle and he'd moved on. Bloody Gwen nearly drove me up the wall "Where's Daz today, Mike?" all the bloody time and getting more wound up every time she asked...'

* * *

By the following Monday, it was all round Llanefa sheep mart that Dewi Tanyfron had been 'helping police' with regards to the murder of Darren Jones. Since the livestock market had been moved out of the town, there were fewer distractions to tempt the farmers away once their business was done. At one end of the long, modern building a cafeteria lured most of the wellington-boot and waterproof-trouser clad vendors into its welcoming fog of bacon, chips and the chance to sit down.

Everyone 'knew' something different. 'Old Jones' Sgubor Las said he'd once seen Daz and Gwen in her car at Castle Woods car park. Though some may have felt a twinge of concern that Old

Jones had been spying on the pair, most recognised his description of the sex act they were carrying out as having come straight from the late night porn channel!

Tom Garth Isaf said that if he'd known that Gwen was such a go-er he would have had a shot at it himself. A statement that caused great hilarity when it resulted in one of the Brecon sheep dealers expressing the opinion that Tom was not capable of shagging his way out of a wet paper bag! The only one looking on in bemused silence was Bara, who had his lurcher tied under the table – a fact that everyone accepted as normal if they expected to use the cheap labour that Bara provided.

After much discussion, the only thing they were all in agreement with was that Dewi must have covered his tracks pretty well as he had been released on bail pending further enquiries.

*　*　*

Dewi walked up the stairs more like an 80 year old than a 42 year old. It was 2am and he knew he needed to try and get some sleep. The milking would need to be done at the usual time whether or not he had slept. Gwen had gone up earlier and he had been unable to face being in the same bed as her. Every night they both pretended to be asleep just to avoid talking – and rowing – about what had happened. There was no spare bedroom he could use and conceding defeat by sleeping on the sofa was not the image he was trying to maintain. Trying to present a united front was hard even if it was only for the children's sake.

Trudging across the landing, he heard 'Dad?' coming from Carwen's room.

He went to the door. Carwen was lying in bed with the light on.

'What's the matter, bach?' he asked (knowing well enough what had kept her awake and hoping that she had not heard the finer details about her mother). The only ones getting any sleep were the eleven year old twin boys, their age giving them immunity against stress-based insomnia and whose snores could be heard from the landing.

'You ok, Dad?' Carwen asked.

'I'm fine, bach,' he lied.

Looking at her in the half light, although she was only fourteen, he could see what she would look like as an adult - a younger, more beautiful version of her mother. It made something hurt inside him. Carwen was a sensitive girl and a favourite of Dewi's if he'd been forced to admit it. She had always said she wanted to be a chemist. Was bright enough too - and conscientious with her school work. Dewi often heard her helping her friend, Catrin, with her homework over the phone.

'What do you think will happen, Dad?' she whispered.

He sat on the side of her bed.

'I don't know, bach, but the truth will come out in the end. I didn't do it. I never hurt no-one. Don't bex, the police will find the murderer before he hurts anyone else. That's guaranteed.'

Dewi thought Carwen had sighed in relief, but when he looked again, he saw that she was crying. He realised, with a pang of sadness, that she had reached an age where she no longer believed all her parents said. It was time to have a longer talk with her.

* * *

DS Lewis changed the tape again while Tegwyn Prydderch looked on. It had been a long interview interspersed with several cups of coffee (black for him due to his life-long aversion to milk) and, despite the high that the extra caffeine had given him, Tegwyn had a feeling that something was not quite right. Of course, he was delighted that Dewi had come in and confessed to the murder of Darren Jones – a 'cough' was the ultimate aim in all crime investigations – but, in this case, he was sure that Dewi was hiding something. In his long experience, that 'something' was usually the evidence that came back and bit him on the arse when the case came to court.

He thought it through for a moment. It had been fairly straightforward; the body of a man had been discovered drowned in an open-topped slurry tank; the deceased had been having an affair with the farmer's wife; the farmer himself had denied all knowledge during his first interview, but today had come in and given himself up. A DCI's dream! But... what about the spanner?

His Scenes of Crime Officers had been knee deep in cow shit inside the slurry tank (the lowest level it could be drained to, much to their disgust) looking for evidence when they had found a heavy duty spanner. The original post mortem results had shown a head injury. When asked, Dewi had been vague on the subject. Further into the interview he became certain that he *had* been carrying a spanner and that he probably *had* hit Daz on the head with it.

Then, during the interview, Tegwyn was called out to be given a message that the pathologist had decided that the head injury had almost certainly been sustained in the fall rather than by the spanner. Furthermore, forensic opinion was that the spanner had been in the tank for some time before the murder and was not relevant to the enquiry.

Tegwyn rubbed his eyes behind his glasses.

'Ok,' he said 'Just run through it one more time for me.'

Dewi had been crying and he wiped his arm over his eyes and runny nose.

'How many more times? He was messing about with my wife. I shoved him in the tank. That's it!' He started crying again.

Tegwyn sighed 'Tell me again when you found out about the affair...'

'I came back to the farm to get something. I don't remember when it was. I heard voices in the milking parlour and looked in the window and ...' he sobbed, 'they were at it in there. Half naked. Both of them.'

'And you didn't confront them? No-one could have blamed you for going in there and getting angry...' Tegwyn suggested.

'I didn't know what to do. I just had to get away from there.'

'But, you were angry then?'

'I was... gutted...'

'It's strange,' said Tegwyn 'when they were in there, how they didn't hear your vehicle coming back?'

Dewi stopped sniffing but didn't say anything.

'I don't think,' suggested Tegwyn 'that you actually saw them or caught them in there. I think you were guessing at the fact that they were having an affair.'

'They were in there. Hardly any clothes on.'

Tegwyn flicked through his notes, 'Anyway, moving on to the day you pushed him in the tank, where was Gwen that day?'

'I can't remember. Tesco's maybe. Daz turned up on his bike, gave some excuse about having left his MP3 there. He had a look around then said maybe Gwen had put it away safe. I told him Gwen was out. I didn't encourage him to stay. He was about to go and I... just saw a way out.'

'Just explain it to us again,' prompted DS Lewis.

'Last year, my best man, Daniel, got divorced. They had a farm over in Cae Du. Been in the family for generations. She went off with another bloke. Good riddance! But, the bitch of it was, Daniel had to sell the farm to pay her out. Not only that but she took the two girls with her. He never saw them. He worked in the feed merchant's for a while. He started drinking and lost his job. They found him dead in his own vomit a few months ago. One of the girls, Catrin, is in the same class as Carwen. It's finished her. The poor kid will never get over it. I could see us – me – ending up the same, just because of that... bastard.'

'So, tell me again exactly how you tricked him to go up the ladder of the slurry tank.'

'I just asked him to shimmy up and untangle Wyn's kite from the top of the steps – said it was in my way – something like that. He said, ok, went up the steps. When he was up there he shouted down to say there wasn't a kite there. I said, yes there is, you have to lean over to see it. He said it definitely wasn't there so I climbed up behind him and pointed to under the platform. He leaned right over and I shoved him in. He didn't go right under straight away. He was shouting and struggling. The tank was nearly full then - it was before we started spreading the slurry. Then I went down and carried his bike up and threw it in. It was one of those very lightweight ones... it took a little longer to sink...' He began sobbing again.

'And the spanner?' asked Tegwyn when Dewi had regained some control.

'I think I had the spanner in my hand when I first went up. I wanted to hit him. I can't remember if I did for certain.'

'This is the bit I can't get my head round,' said Tegwyn 'One minute you say you hit him, then you say you're not sure. A couple of hours ago, you'd even forgotten you had it!'

Dewi sat up and visibly pulled himself together.

'Look,' he said 'I've never even hurt anyone before. This has just been... There are parts of it I just can't get right in my head. I've been having bad nightmares... It's got all mixed up with real life...'

Tegwyn sighed. That's all he needed. Evidence of mental instability would knock the case sideways. And, as this was probably his last serious case before retirement. Tegwyn intended to go out in a blaze of glory – his record of no unsolved serious crimes intact!

Then Dewi restored his faith in the justice system.

'The only thing I can tell you for certain is that I killed him. For what he was doing to our family. I knew what I was doing. You don't need to look any further. I've told you it all – word for word as it happened.'

He laid his head on his arms on the table and closed his eyes. He felt some relief. There were some parts he wasn't sure about – the fucking spanner for instance, where the hell had that come from? Not that it made any difference to the end result. Some lies had to be told. His children were worth it.

And he had told it word for word. Just the way Carwen had told him she had done it – from the discovery of the affair to the killing of Daz - as he sat on the side of her bed the previous night.

Heatwave.
Tegwyn's Story.

The view from the Pwll y Coed road as it spilled down to Llanefa was one that tourists cherished. The vantage point from the lay-by at the bend just before the town was said (by Dai the Post, whose expertise on most matters was rarely disputed!) to be more photographed than Niagara Falls. The castle ruins on one hill and standing stones on the opposite rise gave the entire area a mythical air.

The summer of 1976 enhanced the view of Llanefa by virtue of its record-breaking weather and only the most miserable of individuals could fail to be uplifted by its sight.

Tegwyn Prydderch was one of those individuals. As he cycled from Efa Fawr Farm towards the town on an errand, the only cloud present was his own personal black one that hovered closely above him in the only way that an almost-sixteen year old boy can be immersed in misery. The occasional car overtook him, some of the drivers beeping their horns as they recognised him. His classmate, Eifion Thomas, was a passenger in one and it was the only occasion that Tegwyn managed a smile in response to the passers-by.

Tegwyn felt the sweat running between his shoulder blades - the result of the last uphill stretch before the sweep down to town. He started to freewheel down the hill, letting the artificially created breeze take the worse of the sweat away.

Out of the corner of his eye he could see the Grammar School perched on the hillside just above the town. It only served to make him more miserable. There was less than a fortnight to go before the 'O' Level results came out – the day after his birthday.

He was expected to do well. He was quietly confident that he *had* done well. The headmaster had spoken to him and his parents at the Parents' Evening the previous January.

'Have you thought about staying on for 'A' Levels?' he had asked 'Then, maybe university..?'

'Oh, Mr Morris,' his mother had said, half laughing, 'our sort don't go to university! Tegwyn has *got* a future. A great chance that we didn't have at his age.'

Tegwyn had sighed. Farming! Some future, in his opinion! His parents farmed the higher ground above Pwll y Coed. A small dairy herd ran alongside two dozen beef cattle. The bitter truth was that his parents and grandparents (and probably generations before that) were farmers. It was a good living in their view – and an honourable occupation – one of only a few in their estimation. And being an only son made Tegwyn that most valued part of the legacy – an heir to pass the farm on to.

Hardly a day went by without him having to unravel some problem that involved being kicked, trampled or shat upon by a Friesan cow (or worse still, a Charolais, his father's latest venture, who outweighed the dairy cattle by several hundred pounds and who seemed to delight in challenging him in new ways at every opportunity). His hatred of cows intensified every time he washed their filthy, hairy udders before milking (and got a shit-encrusted tail wrapped around his head for his troubles). The bulging udders had created in him a hatred of milk and where it came from - a hatred that would stay with him all his life. His younger sister, Sian, called him a sissy, but then she rarely got kicked, trampled or shat upon herself!

He supposed that dealing with a Friesan herd in the ideal surroundings of a fully equipped herringbone-shaped milking parlour was slightly better than his father's effective but somewhat primitive set-up. Tom Lloyd had such facilities at Efa Fawr Farm. That name was another reason for Tegwyn to feel miserable as he cycled past the petrol station and its rows of Land Rovers for sale in descending order of age.

Tegwyn had been nominated by his father to do some 'summer work' for Tom Lloyd. Once the morning milking was done, he was expected to cycle over to Efa Fawr and help Tom with his work until after evening milking. Alwyn Prydderch was no fool. He knew that Tom was a leading light as far as farming in the Efa Valley was concerned. Sending his son there was a double edged sword – not only was the boy able to earn some pocket money but he was *also* able to pick up the best farming tips and modern methods to bring home with him.

Tegwyn appreciated the ease with which his work could be done at Efa Fawr, but in his heart, he knew that he wasn't a farmer.

'You're not built like a farmer yet!' Tom had laughed at him as he had failed to lift a bale of hay high enough up the stack during haymaking. Tegwyn didn't want to *ever* be built like a farmer – his lean, tall body was just fine as far as he was concerned. In his daydreams, he saw himself studying politics or law and living in Cardiff where the smell of silage and manure would never permeate his hair and his clothes.

But Tom Lloyd had a little more than the best in modern farming methods. Tom had a daughter. And that, Tegwyn thought, was Problem Number Three (if you counted not going to university and being forced into farming as Problems Number One and Two).

Maggie was nearly two years older than Tegwyn, but she had only recently completed her 'O' Levels, having been 'held back' a year after a long hospitalisation to correct a spinal defect when she was fifteen. She had been in his class during the past year and it was clear that she was not expected to pass many subjects. However, it was hoped that she would gain the necessary passes to become a State Enrolled Nurse at Carmarthen Hospital.

Maggie was a sturdily built girl with breasts like loaves of bread. Her dark, mischievous eyes gave her a flirty look – not that many of the boys in Tegwyn's class looked at her eyes! It was evident that Maggie had missed out on the usual teenage activities with her peers. However, since moving down a class, she had made a new set of younger friends who saw her as the fount of all knowledge in matters of boyfriends and sex.

Raging hormones with unresolved issues ran amok in Maggie's body until they came to focus on Tegwyn. Like most teenage boys, Tegwyn welcomed being a target for female attention.

He had been bagging grain at Efa Fawr Farm one afternoon when Maggie appeared in the doorway of the barn with a glass of ginger beer for him. She wore shorts that were called Hot Pants and a Tee shirt that struggled to contain the legendary breasts. He had put down his shovel and taken the cool glass from her. The side of the glass was wet and, when he had taken it from her, she casually wiped her palm across the front of her Tee shirt in a diagonal movement. Three things happened immediately – the wet stripes from her fingers gave a transparency to part of the material, revealing a hint of a lace edged bra, a nipple popped out in response to the coldness and Tegwyn felt a movement deep inside his groin. He quickly looked away and mentally willed the offending organ to go back to sleep. He half turned away and drank the ginger beer, though it seemed to stick in his throat. Maggie, though, was keen to talk. About how Ffion's brother was learning to drive and had scraped the side of his father's new car against the gatepost; about why Miss Bowen wouldn't let anyone park their bikes in the teachers' bay, and about a dozen other topics, of which Tegwyn heard only random words, while the blood drained from his brain to his nether regions. He wondered if he was going to faint until Maggie abruptly stopped her chatter and went back to wherever she had come from.

The next day, she appeared again, this time in a pair of flared jeans and a lightweight shirt – much to Tegwyn's relief.

By the end of the week, his body had given up the battle and his sleep was disturbed by dreams in which Maggie opened her shirt and leaned herself against him. He woke every night with the familiar wetness on his legs and the even more familiar embarrassment in his mind as he tried to hide the evidence prior to his mother changing the bedclothes.

One Saturday, Tegwyn had been left to re-stack straw bales in the large calf shed so that the space was better utilised. Tom and his wife had gone shopping, but Maggie had been left at home to do the ironing. It was not long before she appeared in the doorway with yet another glass of ginger beer. (Tegwyn had come to the conclusion that he would never again look at a glass of ginger beer without getting an erection!) This time, Maggie dispensed quickly with the small talk and soon she uttered the unthinkable question.

'Have you ever done it?'

Tegwyn's head felt as though it was going to explode. In the time it took his heart to beat twice, he had explored the possible answers he could give, but the best he could come up with was 'Errrr...'

'You know, with a girl. Done it,' she repeated.

By then, Tegwyn's brain had decided that it couldn't deal with the question and passed the buck to his groin instead.

'Well... err... not exactly... just,' he stuttered, trying to herd up the different straying parts of his body that were now entirely out of his control. If he had been honest, he could have told her that the nearest he had come to 'doing it' was feeling up Rhian while he was snogging her at the back of Llanefa hall after the weekly disco. For some reason, he had never found the courage to try anything more advanced.

'I have,' she said, 'I can show you how.'

At that point, Tegwyn's body had become one throbbing mass of hormones and he was grateful for the upright bale of straw in front of him that hid most of his lower body.

She came towards him while undoing her shirt buttons. The magnificent breasts sat like two puppies at a Dogs' Home – both vying for attention. Tegwyn swallowed hard. She leaned forward and undid his fly and belt. He tried not to pull backwards, but she sensed his reluctance and put her hand under her bra and yanked it upwards, releasing the puppies to bounce joyfully in random directions. She unzipped her jeans and opened them. He could see low cut panties and the suggestion of pubic hair. He gulped again.

'Don't be shy,' she said, 'you'll like it.'

Tegwyn was *already* liking it! Although half of him (the top half) was giving him reasons why this was wrong – the main one being, what if her parents came back?

It was years before the term 'multi-tasking' was to be invented, but it was what Maggie did by grabbing his hand in one of hers and delving into his underpants with the other. She grasped his penis at around the same time she pushed his hand down into her panties where he felt the familiar-but-different texture of her pubic hair. It was too much for him and his body convulsed into an orgasm which splattered semen over her hand and belly. Even in his ecstasy, he was aware of a shame invading his mind.

In a business-like manner, she wiped it off with the bottom of her shirt, corralled the breasts into her bra and fastened the shirt buttons back up.

'I told you you'd like it,' was all she said while he gave in to his to embarrassment and tried to put his clothes back in order. To his relief and bemusement, she turned and went back to the house.

By the next day, he had been ready for a replay. But, in age-old fashion of women who knew what they were doing, Maggie did not come to see him and he had cycled home burning up with lust.

The next time, he did a little better and Maggie seemed happy about it – if that's what her writhing and gasping meant while he had wriggled his fingers cluelessly inside her!

Soon after, Maggie appeared when they were alone and announced, 'We'll do it all the way today. I've got a Frenchy.'

The thought pushed Tegwyn into a panic. He had no idea how to put a French Letter on! As if she had read his mind, she said, 'Don't worry, I'll show you how to do it.'

She did, indeed, show him how to do it and with skilful stopping and starting, she eventually gave Tegwyn his first experience of full sexual intercourse – an activity that he took to with great enthusiasm and success!

After they had finished, he flopped back onto the hay bales that Maggie had chosen as the prime location. Once he had got over his combined delirium and delight, his mind went back to normal-thinking mode and he wondered what he should do with the French Letter? Did boys just go home with it still on? He didn't think so as he had seen plenty of them discarded in lonely gateways that had been used by courting couples in cars. However, he had not been sure and he didn't feel able to ask Maggie as, by then, he considered himself to be a Man of the World and didn't need to ask advice.

Maggie, however, had answered the question for him.

'Don't leave that here in case my father sees it,' she had said, gesturing vaguely towards his groin, 'Wrap it up and throw it away somewhere on your way home.'

While he considered how to do this, Maggie had produced a tissue and handed it to him. As she leaned towards him, she let out a shriek. Tegwyn had nearly fainted and had fully expected to see her father looming over them!

With that dreadful fear dispelled, his only emotion was that of shame at the way Maggie stared at his naked lap with its wrinkled, soggy contents. He felt himself shrink even further.

Instead, Maggie had peered more closely at his groin, 'Has it split?' she asked in horror.

Tegwyn had no inkling of what it was supposed to look like, but he could see that there was a small tear along the side of the French Letter.

'Shit!' she nearly shouted and had leapt to her feet and got dressed.

'I'd better not be pregnant,' she warned him as she finished dressing and fled the scene.

As she had gone before he could ask any questions, Tegwyn was left with his mind full of unanswered dilemmas. He wrapped the hated French Letter up in the tissue and pushed it into his pocket with the intention of throwing it into the hedge on his cycle route home.

The sinking feeling he had harboured since Maggie's hasty exit intensified when, just after milking, while he was washing down the yard (a job that had to be carried out, despite the drought), Tom's sheepdog came up to him and markedly pushed his nose against Tegwyn's pocket as if trying to point out to everyone what had happened. Once he had been sure that Tom was not looking, Tegwyn had given the dog a sharp slap across its muzzle, but it had later seemed like an omen to his sensitive mind.

He had not seen Maggie for a week after that, though he felt his eyes pulled towards the house a thousand times a day. The Lloyds and the Prydderchs had noticed the sick-calf look in his eyes and had mistaken it for love. In truth, they had both been happy with the situation. Tom had no other children to pass his farm on to and the Prydderchs were doubly happy that, not only would Tegwyn have a sustainable future in farming, but that he would have *two* tracts of land to farm. With the possible purchase of a five acre field that lay between them, the combined acreage would create the biggest farm in the area! Both families were already thinking ahead with regards to a possible wedding in three years' time!

When Maggie next spoke to Tegwyn, it had been in hateful tones.

'I'm late!' she had snarled at him.

'But...' he had failed to bring any comment or hope to the conversation.

'If I'm pregnant, we'll have to get married,' she warned him.

'Perhaps you could... err...' he had ventured.

'Kill it, you mean?' she said, accusingly before walking away.

Many years later, Tegwyn had found this amusing. The rest of Britain had been cohabiting in a daring fashion - though as a prelude to getting married in many instances – but in Llanefa the unspoken law was – you got a girl pregnant, you married her!

And so began the misery that coated every waking moment in Tegwyn's life (and even his sleep, as dreams of crying babies and hundreds of hungry cows invaded his subconscious).

An even stranger thing happened to him when he thought about pregnancy and its associated symptoms. He had seen a woman giving birth in an educational film in school. It had been particularly distasteful to him (as was the probable intention of screening it to twenty hormone-fuelled teenagers!). But the more he thought about it, the more he dwelt on Maggie's magnificent breasts and the realisation that they would become engorged with milk. In other words – udders! In Tegwyn's mind, the connection between the hated udders he washed twice a day and the ample bosom that he had only recently worshipped, became so strong that he found himself almost gagging whenever he saw a large breasted woman. And there were plenty of them being displayed in the on-going heatwave! Even seeing large brassieres hanging on washing lines were enough to make him turn his eyes away.

His hatred of milk intensified to such a degree that he had to drink his tea without it.

Meanwhile, as he cycled into the car park of the Llanefa Veterinary surgery, there was little he could think of to lift his mood.

He leaned the bike against the wall and went into the surgery waiting room. Gillian, the wife of one of the three Llanefa vets, was sweeping up some dog hair clippings. She, at least, thought Tegwyn gratefully, was a thin woman with no breasts to speak of.

'Shw'mai, bach,' she said over her shoulder 'Come to get Tom Lloyd's mastitis tubes, have you?'

He nodded. The small penicillin tubes were a common remedy. The fine plastic nozzles were normally inserted into the cow's teat through the natural opening and the contents squeezed in twice a day until the condition improved. Udders again! The irony of the situation had not escaped Tegwyn's notice.

'Those special hoof-trimmers he ordered have come in, too,' Gillian remarked 'You might as well take them with you.'

With Gillian's help, he tied the hoof trimmers to the cross-bar and hitched the box of mastitis tubes under his arm before getting ready to set off in the heat of the day.

'Do you want a glass of ginger beer before you go?' asked Gillian – a question that almost had Tegwyn leaping out through the door before she had finished speaking!

'No thanks,' he said, though his throat was as dry as sandpaper.

He pushed the bike for a few feet before swinging his leg over the seat and setting off. It was then that he discovered a practical difficulty. The long metal arms of the hoof trimmer protruded downwards slightly and jabbed him painfully on the leg each time his knee came up with the pedal. He thought about the return journey and the long walk ahead of him if he was unable to pedal. The hoof trimmers were too awkward to carry in combination with the box of mastitis remedy, so, as he passed the petrol station on his way out of Llanefa, he stopped for a moment.

To the left of him was a minor junction that led to some scattered properties and a dead end for cars. However, a rutted path, used by horse riders and farmers accessing fields on tractors, joined the end of the tarmac road and cut across the landscape. The path came out at the top of a hill that ran towards Efa Fawr Farm. Tegwyn considered whether he wanted to push his bike the longer route on the regular road or suffer a bit more discomfort pushing it along the bumpy path and then free-wheeling down to Efa Fawr Farm having cut a mile and a half off his journey.

Checking his watch, he could see that it was half past two. Milking was at four. The shorter journey would probably take him an hour. He swung to the left hand road and chose the route that would change his life.

* * *

Tony Morgan loved cars. All his life it was as if he had been genetically programmed to look under axles and tinker with points. It was his dream to own three particular vehicles - a vintage car, a rally car and a real classic like a Bentley. The fact that it was not likely to happen did not cross his mind, or, if it did, the reality did not trouble him for long. His mind whirred with brake horsepower, turbo engines and go-faster stripes. He was a frequent buyer of cars – cheap ones that needed his magic touch to get them running long enough to sell on. His wife bore it all in typical laid-back fashion. She had forgotten what colour Tony's hands really were; so often were they smeared in oil that refused to come off with normal washing. By the time one oil mark had been removed, several others had congregated round his knuckles and nail beds to replace it.

'It's only a bit of oil,' she would tell people, 'It's not dirt or anything.' Though she made him keep his hands in his pockets if they were going to a funeral or to see the bank manager.

Tony's job with the Electricty Board placed him amongst a group of men who only partly shared his passion. Most had heard what he had to say on numerous occasions, so it was a novelty for Tony to have a fresh audience. For the past week, Tony had been reading the electricity meters in the Llanefa area – a boring rota for most, but a treat for Tony as he noted the cars parked in various drives and farmyards. It took him slightly longer than most if he spotted a new species and was able to chat to the owner.

'Is she a twin-cam?' he would ask, or 'How do you find her road-holding?' and, very often before the owner was aware of his own actions, the bonnet would be open and Tony would be waxing lyrical at the treasure that lay beneath.

On the same day that Tegwyn cycled into Llanefa to pick up Tom Lloyd's supplies at the vet's, Tony was reading meters nearby. He had a brand new R registration Ford Escort car. Unmarked as yet by the South Wales Electricity Board logo, Tony felt as though it was his own as he put it through its paces. They usually took a Morris Marina van to read the meters, but the last driver of the van had run it into the back of a tractor, hence Tony had the unexpected treat of using the car that the bosses would normally use to make site visits.

He had eaten his lunch-time sandwiches in the car and put the radio on. It was a fine radio and he could not resist the urge to explore the various channels while he chewed at tomato sandwiches that he did not taste. His perfect working day so far was compounded by the radio presenter playing Johnny Cash's car-building song, 'One Piece At A Time' followed by his favourite oldie, 'Born To Be Wild'. He turned to his list of properties left to visit. Not too many. With a bit of luck he could be back at the Carmarthen depot to finish before four o'clock and be able to pop in to one of the garages on the way home. He always liked to check out cars for sale.

He wrapped up his sandwich papers (being careful to shake all the crumbs off them – in his opinion it would have been sacrilege to spill crumbs in a new car) and packed everything away while humming Born To Be Wild under his breath.

He started the engine.

'Come on, Bessie bach,' he said lovingly as the car purred into life and eased into the road as if on a bed of air.

He ticked off the places as he visited them. Some, he marked with an 'E' which meant there was no-one home and the electricity bill would have to be estimated at Head Office. He had made good progress by the time he turned up the same lane that Tegwyn had taken shortly before him.

The best part of that day, for Tony, was testing the car's abilities up the steep hill and while negotiating two awkward hairpin bends on the approach to the first property. He made a mental note of the car's failings so that he could pass them on to others while discussing the merits of Ford Escorts (which he was able to do at length when talking on the driveways of the elderly male occupiers of the first two cottages). After reading the first few meters, the road eased into a steady uphill that narrowed between the gangly trees. He passed a tall, thin boy pushing a bike and considered offering him a lift, but realised that there was nowhere to stow the bike – a shame, as he could have demonstrated the car's qualities at first hand, he thought! The last cottage lay a good distance away from any of the others. Tony saw, on his list, that it was called 'Sri Lanka', though he was certain it had been called Pen y Bryn in previous years when an old couple had lived there.

He turned right into the driveway and down the short hill into the frontage of the smallholding. He could see some goats paddocked to the left of the house, but he only noticed them because, parked between the paddock and the house, and half under a rickety shelter, was an old Rolls Royce. Tony's pulse quickened. A Roller! If a hundred naked women had marched past him at that moment, he would probably not have seen them - which was possibly the reason he also failed to notice a large pool of blood on the floor by the right hand side of the car.

He made his biggest mistake of the day when he pulled up abruptly, close to the front of the house without turning the Escort around to face outwards. The car's nose faced sharply downhill towards the house – a position which would need rectifying when it was time to leave. He got out of the car and went to the front door, praying that there would be someone in so that he could ask questions about the Roller. There was no answer. Still hopeful that someone would be around seeing to livestock, Tony walked around to where the Rolls Royce stood. He noticed (happily at that stage) that a pair of legs protruded somewhere near the back axle of the car. The possibility that someone was actually *working* on the car was like manna from heaven to Tony. He quickened his step before registering that they were a *woman's* legs (clad in some kind of gypsy-style skirt) around the same instant that he noticed the large pool of blood a few feet away.

'Fucking hell!' he said, before taking a greater stride towards it.

Before he got to see who the legs belonged to, there was a yell behind him. He turned round to see a man in sodden multi coloured trousers and long straggly hair standing between him and the Ford Escort.

'Lucifer!' the man shouted and threw a metal bucket at him. Tony ducked, but not before the bucket had caught him on the knee.

'Ow! What's the matter with you? I'm only here to...' Tony abandoned the rest of his words as the man lunged towards him.

Tony turned and ran in the direction of the legs while the man began to run after him before coming to a halt and announcing loudly, 'The days of Lammas are upon us.'

Tony stopped and turned to take stock of the situation. The man was obviously a nutcase.

He continued to face the man to see if he was going to run for him again, but out of the corner of his eye, he could see the woman lying on the floor. A woman with a great deal wrong with her. The fact that she was dead was obvious to him even without taking his eyes off the man, but there was something else wrong with her. When it finally registered in his brain, he had to force himself *not* to look. The woman had no head.

'Oh fuck! Oh fuck!' Tony said in a tone close to sobbing 'Don't come any closer. Please don't kill me. Please don't...'

The man was standing and staring at him as if he had momentarily forgotten what he was doing. He looked down at his feet and muttered.

Tony saw his chance and ran around the back of the house in the hope that he could circle all the way round to the front where his car was parked.

He climbed over a stone wall and the low trellises that supported various plants by the back door, checking all the while that the man was not following him. His pulse thumped in his ears as he rounded the other side of the house and saw his car where he had left it. There was no sign of the man.

He stepped forward cautiously, checking in front and behind him every second. He rummaged in his pocket for the car keys, thanking his lucky stars that he had not locked it – no-one locked cars in Llanefa!

He glanced around to see if the man was in view. He could not see him anywhere. That fact made Tony more nervous, but, nevertheless, he sprinted for the car.

He had reached the car and opened the driver's door when he was aware of the man coming behind him, having obviously followed his route around the back of the house. Tony rammed the keys into the ignition and turned them. In his panic, he over-keyed the engine and it coughed an outraged refusal. He quickly turned the key back and did it again. The engine fired instantly.

'Come on, Bessie, come on, Bessie!' he shrieked as he whacked the gear into reverse ready for a direct exit from the property.

He let the clutch out and floored the pedal. The car lurched backwards up the hill for a few yards before finding it too steep and the engine stalled.

'Fucking bitch!' he yelled before simultaneously putting the gear in neutral and trying to fire the ignition again. The smell of too much fuel flooding the carburettor hit his nostrils as he tried in vain a second time. He quickly gathered his wits and turned the key back again. The engine began running, but before he could do anything else, the driver's door opened and the man with the long hair brought a blood-stained axe down onto Tony's arm and shoulder. The car free-wheeled forwards a few yards where it came to a halt against the stone wall directly in front of the house.

'Spawn of Lucifer!' the man shouted, running to catch up before staggering backwards to lift his axe again.

Tony had been wailing in pain, but threw himself over to the passenger seat as the axe came down on to the driver's seat. He could feel his blood running like a tap under his armpit. The arm flopped uselessly by his side. Tony had a brief moment of being surprised how the pain and his surroundings seemed to be fading.

The man gave another war-cry, giving Tony a well needed wake-up call which propelled him even further on to the passenger side. A rush of adrenalin helped him to open that door with his left hand before sliding out, face first, on to the driveway.

The last thing he thought before fainting was that making such a mess in a brand new car was unforgivable.

* * *

Tegwyn huffed and puffed up the hill, his right arm ached from holding the box of mastitis tubes under his arm. He tried to rest it, and his arm, on the bike seat, but every so often it would slip off to the side. At least it had taken his mind off the twin babies that he was now convinced grew in Maggie's belly!

He pressed on, ignoring the sweat that poured off him. His long legs gave him some advantage as he progressed up the hill. Only one car passed him, going up the hill and he looked on in envy as it left him behind effortlessly. At some point near the end of the hill, he thought he heard shouting – in farming communities, a sound that usually preceded the stampede of a flock of sheep or herd of cattle being driven from one grazing area to another. He kept a vigilant eye on the road so that he could get out of the way quickly if such an activity happened.

He came out into sunshine where the straggly trees ended and he could almost see the end of the tarmac road where it joined the grass track. On his right was a property called Sri Lanka. He stopped for a quick breather. He remembered Dai the Post's son, Glanmor, who was in his class at school, saying that his father had told him that the people living in Sri Lanka were hippies. More to the point, in Glanmor's opinion, was the fact that they sometimes took drugs *and walked around naked!*

His father had actually seen them, according to Glanmor. Everyone knew they were weird because they kept goats – an unquestionable waste of time in the view of Llanefa farmers! Some of the goats were used for milking and some were shorn and their hair used in weaving. Tegwyn had an idea that he had seen the people in town on market days – a long haired, thin couple who had a dreamy look about them and who often drove an old, multi-coloured camper van.

Curiosity turned Tegwyn's head down in the direction of Sri Lanka's drive where he saw a white car with its passenger door open and the engine running. No naked people, he noted. Glanmor had probably made it up. But Tegwyn had another good look just in case he had missed anything.

He heard shouting – a wild noise that awoke the first feelings of alarm in him. He realised that he could see someone lying on the floor beside the car. Was the person *trapped*, he wondered?

Dropping the box of tubes on the floor, he straddled the bike and freewheeled down the drive.

The sight was one of many that would stay with him for a long time. He could see a man lying on the floor surrounded by sheets of paper that were stained and splashed with blood. He dropped the bike and squatted by the man.

'Are you all right?' he said, though the absurdity of the question would occur to him later. The man was, most definitely, not all right. His right arm was partially severed near the shoulder and his clothes glistened with the wetness and volume of his blood.

'Waaaah... uuuh,' said Tony, his face turned mostly against the floor.

Tegwyn gently tried to look at his injuries. Tony's vague noises became louder. Tegwyn saw with alarm that the blood was flowing quite freely. He had seen some bad injuries on the rugby field, but this was far more serious.

'I'm going to press here,' he warned before putting the palm of his hand against Tony's shoulder. Tony increased the volume of his moaning, but the blood still flowed from under Tegwyn's fingers. His panic abated a little. He remembered a heifer of his father's that had caught her front leg on a wire fence. The blood had spurted out in a pulsating arc until they had tied the top of the leg. Tegwyn pulled his Tee shirt off, bundled it up into a roll and pressed it against the wound. The blood continued to seep through. Tony still moaned and seemed to be only semi-conscious, uttering words that made no sense.

Tegwyn jumped to his feet to reach his bike. He tried to untie the string that held the hoof trimmer to the crossbar. His hands shook and he had to have many attempts before it came loose. He crossed back to Tony in one stride and bundled up the Tee shirt again. He rolled him on to his left hand side, supporting him with his knees and tried to tie the pad around the wound. The word 'torniquet' came into his mind from something he had heard in school. He wrapped the string round the top of the padded arm and tied it as Tony slumped into another near-faint. Tegwyn partially got up and dragged Tony's top half closer to the car in an attempt to lift his upper body against the sill of the Escort. Something about elevating the wound was registering in his brain. Despite his sensitive nature, Tegwyn was used to blood and injury – it was a common occurrence in farming life.

Tony came round again.

'Mas of here...' he mumbled.

'We'll get out of here in a minute,' Tegwyn said, though the phrase was an automatic reaction to Tony's words.

Once he had managed to prop Tony up, he added 'Don't move. I'm going to phone for an ambulance.'

Tony came to life 'Noooooo!' he wailed 'Out. Head.'

'It's ok. I can't see any cuts on your head,' Tegwyn reassured him, 'Don't worry, I'll be straight out.'

He momentarily ignored Tony's agitated noises and looked around.

He suddenly became aware that the distressed shouting was still going on and that it was not coming from Tony. There was also a banging noise that competed with the car engine noise beside him. It briefly occurred to him how strange it was that there was no-one else in sight despite the injured man's need for help.

A flash of understanding hit him. All his life he had heard of freak agricultural accidents – people who had been drawn into machinery and lost limbs – even their lives. An urgency came into his movements. There had been an accident here. Someone else was injured and sounded as though he was trapped further away!

So, instead of running to the house to use a phone, he sprinted to the left hand side of the Rolls Royce. As he ran, he briefly registered a person's face under the old car, but in the few strides it took him to stop, he had reached the back of the Rolls and witnessed a hideous sight.

He saw a long haired man on his knees. The man's clothes were splattered in blood and tissue. The sweet smell of raw, chopped liver entered Tegwyn's nostrils and he felt his stomach lurch. The man was chopping a person's body into huge chunks. Tegwyn knew it had been a person only by the remains of clothing that clung to the bone and muscle on the floor.

'Out Lucifer!' the man shouted in a saddened, desperate voice, before looking up and spotting Tegwyn.

Tegwyn turned and started to run back the way he had come, but the man had leapt to his feet and lunged to the shorter route past the other side of the car and came to a halt in front of him.

Tegwyn skidded to a stop just out of reaching distance and ran back towards the butchered body. The man stood where he was, panting and reeking of blood. He still had the axe in his hand.

Tegwyn tried not to look at the scene near his feet. He suddenly remembered that he had seen someone under the car. He leapt backwards. Was it someone hiding? Or another axe-wielding murderer? He felt his feet slide on something slimy and he backed away even further, putting more distance between himself and the exit to the driveway.

The long-haired man was studying the axe closely.

Is this a dagger which I see before me, Tegwyn's mind offered him - the subconscious result of English Literature revising months earlier.

Tegwyn took the chance to see who was hiding under the car.

'You. Under the car?' he said 'Are you ok? Can you help me?'

No-one answered.

He kept an eye on the man and half bent down to see who was there – half expecting the person to leap out.

He took another few steps backwards to give himself a better view without bending too low. He was eternally grateful that he had done so and given himself more distance from the sight. In less than a second, he saw that the 'person' consisted of a detached head. That time, his stomach did more than lurch and he felt an unpleasant upward movement. He stopped himself in time. He couldn't afford to be distracted by being sick. He had to see what the man was doing.

There was another bout of loud moaning from Tony – who Tegwyn had almost forgotten about. The long-haired man had also appeared to have forgotten Tony, but the moans made him turn his head in that direction. Then he turned and walked towards the sound. 'NOOOOOOO!' Tegwyn shouted and took a few steps towards them.

It was not an act of heroism, Tegwyn said later, just an instinctive reaction at the thought of the badly injured Tony being hacked to death before him.

The long-haired man looked back at him then kept going until he reached the Escort. When he stood and looked down at Tony, he muttered something and made the sign of the cross. Tegwyn held his breath.

The long-haired man fell to his knees and shouted, 'And the devil was sent back to his lair of fire!'

He still held the axe while he said this.

Tegwyn wondered why he was not attempting to attack the man on the ground. But, taking advantage of the apparent change of heart, he glanced around towards the back door of the house. Could he risk going in there and using the phone? Was there a phone? Glanmor had called these people hippies. Did hippies have phones? He glanced upwards to see if any obvious cables gave him an answer. He couldn't see any. And what if he went in there and the man came in after him? He didn't know the layout of the house – he could easily become trapped in there – his eyes flicked downwards to remind him what could happen to him if that occurred.

He quickly looked behind him towards the wooded fields that fell downwards into a valley. If he ran that way, he would eventually reach the Pwll y Coed road that he had rejected for his return journey. But the land that surrounded Sri Lanka was poor and uncultivated. The dense woodland would have no obvious way through and, with the injured man still lying by the car, Tegwyn was afraid to leave him at the mercy of his bleeding – or worse!

He saw that the long-haired man was drawing a mark in the ground with the axe – an uneven circle around the car. It was a gesture that made Tegwyn's heart beat even faster. It looked like some kind of sacrificial act.

'NO!' he shouted.

The man looked at him and started to walk towards him; the axe hung loosely from one hand. Tegwyn began to panic. He looked in all directions for somewhere to run. There was nowhere.

'STOP!' he yelled at the man.

To his surprise, the man stopped.

Now what, Tegwyn thought? But while he was thinking, the man got to his knees and began chanting something in a language that Tegwyn did not understand. At the same time, he made shapes in the air with his hands. *The axe lay on the floor by his knees.*

Tegwyn began to move slowly. He had no intention of going near the man, but if he could get out on to the road...

Tony's moaning brought him up short. What was he thinking! There was no way he could leave the injured man here while he cycled for help. He tried to picture how far away the next property was. What if he got there and found no-one home? And the next? Could he risk cycling all the way down to Llanefa? A fast descent, but would it be fast enough?

The long-haired man had leaned forward until his face was touching the floor. His eyes focussed on the underneath of the Rolls and his chanting suddenly stopped. He let out a cry.

'Zelda!' he said 'You have embraced the devil!' and he began to cry the saddest noise that Tegwyn would ever hear. It made his skin feel cold despite the heat of the day.

'Zelda, my love! Why, why...?' and he broke into racking sobs.

It shattered the inertia for Tegwyn. He glanced at the back of the house and quickly headed that way in a replica of Tony's previous escape route. He could still hear the man crying – his animal noises interspersed with chanted foreign words.

Tegwyn climbed over the small wall and the trellises and emerged at the other side of the house where he could see the white car, but not the long-haired man and the Rolls Royce. He could still hear the chanting and crying coming from the hippy.

He made his way slowly to the white car. The engine was still running.

Tegwyn crept around the back of the car, trying to keep the open passenger door as a visual shield between him and the long-haired man. Tony was in more or less the same position as he had left him. The blood was still running from his arm but not as quickly. The flesh on the lower side of the wound had taken on a greyish colour. Tegwyn wondered, much later on, whether his 'torniquet' was to blame for the fate that befell Tony, but at that moment, he only thought about how quickly he could get him into the car.

'Out. Quick!' said Tony in a weak voice.

'You've got to try to get up,' Tegwyn said, 'Got to get you in the car. Quick!'

'In the car,' Tony repeated and started to struggle ineffectively – an action which made him moan again.

'Sssh!' said Tegwyn 'Try not to make a noise.'

He checked that he could still hear the chanting coming from the long-haired man.

226

'Hold on to me with this arm,' Tegwyn ordered, while clasping the man around his ribs and pulling upwards.

The words 'You're not built like a farmer yet!' passed through his subconscious while he hauled Tony upwards and felt something give inside his lower back.

'Push with your feet!' he commanded and with one last haul, managed to get Tony on to the passenger seat, though his feet still hung out on the driveway.

'Go!' said Tony urgently.

'Ok, ok...' said Tegwyn before he saw Tony's eyes – large and panic-stricken peering over his shoulder.

Too late, Tegwyn made the association with what he had said and glanced sideways to see the long-haired man walking briskly towards the car door. Before he could think of reacting, the man had kicked the car door and it bounced against Tegwyn's body as he bent over Tony in his seat. The force of the door knocked Tegwyn backwards and he slid along the side of the car and on to the floor. The long-haired man pulled the door wide open again and looked in at Tony while he gripped the handle of the axe so hard that his knuckles stood out as white spots in the bloodstained setting of his hands. Tegwyn braced his own hands against the floor in readiness to propel himself up and away, when his hand came to rest on something metal. The hoof trimmers!

In an instant, he was on his feet and swinging his arm with its new-found weapon just as the long-haired man began to lift the axe.

With as much strength as he possessed, Tegwyn hit the man across his shoulder and part of his face with the hoof trimmers and heard the unmistakeable crack of bone. The man dropped the axe and fell to the floor. The force of the blow bounced the hoof trimmers backwards and hit Tegwyn in the face, cutting a slice in his cheek. Adrenalin cancelled out his pain. Tegwyn jumped backwards and quickly hooked the axe towards him with his foot.

'Quick, quick!' Tony said in a slightly louder voice 'Oh fuck, quick!'

The long-haired man was half sitting up and holding the side of his head with his good arm, while the other hung at a very unnatural angle at his side. Blood ran from his face and mixed with the liberal coating of gore on the rest of his body. Tegwyn was suddenly aware of the slow, warm drip of blood down the side of his own face and how it ran down his bare shoulder. Tony, meanwhile, had developed a second wind and was struggling to lift his feet into the front of the car. Tegwyn tried to help him, but kept his head turned to watch the long-haired man who was getting less mobile by the second. Tegwyn slammed the passenger door shut once Tony had got both feet out of the way, and ran around towards the back of the car, still keeping the long-haired man in his line of vision. He stopped and, as a second thought, grabbed the axe and hoof trimmers from the floor and continued to run round to the driver's side. He opened the back door and unceremoniously flung the blood stained tools into the back seat before opening the driver's door and jumping in.

He leaned over and pushed all the locks down, then wound up the driver's window.

Like all farmers' sons, Tegwyn had been driving since he was twelve. The workings of the huge tractor held no mystery for him and, although he was not legally allowed to drive on a public road he had moved his father's car to different locations on the farmyard and fields on several occasions. However, all those practice runs were done without any stress and he had never sat behind the wheel of anything as new as the Ford Escort. He realised that he would have to turn the car around. He pressed the clutch and tried to find the reverse gear. Each time he tried, the car started to push forward, pressing the wall it rested against.

'Other way,' said Tony weakly. He was slumped sideways in the seat.

Tegwyn checked to see if the long-haired man was on his feet. He couldn't see him, but that didn't mean anything. He *needed* to see him! He tried the reverse gear again and the car lurched backwards. He stopped by putting his foot on the brake and the car promptly stalled. From his new position, he could see the hippy on his knees with his head leaning forward almost touching the floor.

Tegwyn started the car again, his nerves causing him to push hard against the accelerator pedal and a high revving noise filled the car interior.

'Steady on the juice,' said Tony breathlessly 'And ride the clutch.'

With sporadic advice from a progressively weakening Tony, Tegwyn managed to turn the car around and began to lurch up the drive, veering wide to avoid the long-haired man who, he saw, was lying in the foetal position on the floor. He watched him so intently that a sudden crunching noise made him jump.

'Fuck!' said Tony in mild alarm.

It was his bike, Tegwyn realised. He had driven over some part of it.

He took the car up the short drive in quick lurching movements while Tony moaned at each judder. At the top of the drive, he stalled the car again while trying to turn left. He kept a look-out in the rear view mirror as he re-started the engine, but, once again, he could not see the long-haired man. He told himself that it was because of the angle of the car, but nevertheless his pulse increased until he got going again.

And, in second gear, he descended the hill towards the town. As he passed the scattered cottages towards the bottom of the hill, he considered stopping to use a phone, but the possibility of finding no-one home and wasting time, pushed him onwards. Tony slumped completely beside him and Tegwyn could not get a response from him.

At the junction on the bottom of the hill, he barely checked the road for traffic and lurched the car across the road and into the garage forecourt before stalling at an angle blocking an exit from the petrol pumps.

Tegwyn leapt out of the car and ran for the small shop area where the cashier was stationed. He narrowly missed being hit by a car with a faulty exhaust pipe as it was being driven towards the service bay.

There was a man in the shop, paying for petrol, and he drew back in alarm as Tegwyn burst through the open doorway shouting 'Quick! Phone an ambulance. A man's been attacked.'

Even the cashier took a step away from the counter.

Later, Tegwyn realised what a frightening sight he must have been – a bleeding gash on his cheek, bare-chested and coated with blood (both his own and whatever gore had come off the others.)

The cashier recognised his face, though could not recall his name, and recovered sufficiently to dial '999'. Tegwyn ran back to the car and shouted at Tony. He made weak movements, but did not seem fully conscious. The cashier and a mechanic appeared beside Tegwyn and tried to look at Tony's wound. The mechanic recognised Tony and called his name loudly while gently prodding his uninjured arm. A small crowd gathered to look and offer advice. The owner of the car with the faulty exhaust realised that his vehicle would be in the way of the ambulance and moved it to the furthest corner of the forecourt.

Tony was not a religious man, but he suddenly had a vision of his own god – a vision that helped elevate his blood pressure and stopped his condition from deteriorating while his blood drained away. The noise of the car with the faulty exhaust pipe had entered Tony's consciousness as the sound of a rally car. Not just any rally car, but the RS1600 that his hero, Roger Clark, drove. His breathing became less shallow and the blood left in his system was circulated slightly more efficiently. He opened his eyes and focused beyond his band of helpers. There, he saw Roger Clark, dressed in his rallying gear, emerging from the legendary RS1600. Tony tried to say something, but that was too much effort. Instead, he watched while Roger made his way over towards him and stood behind the other people.

'Bit low on oil,' Roger said, 'you need a top-up'.

Tony tried to turn his head so that the other faces were blanked out, but the boy kept getting in the way. His agitation became more intense and he tried to tell them to move away.

230

The loud siren of the ambulance drowned out all else and, from then on, things began to happen quickly. The crew soon had Tony wearing an oxygen mask and carried him to the ambulance. Tegwyn was also ordered into the back where he was given a pad to hold against his face. Very soon they were travelling at an urgent speed towards Carmarthen hospital. Tony was taken swiftly away and Tegwyn was tended to by the doctors while a policeman waited nearby to question him.

Tegwyn heard the rest of the story much later and found out that the long-haired man was eventually brought to the same hospital and was treated for a fractured cheekbone and skull, concussion and a broken collarbone. It seemed that he had been high on drugs when he had killed his common-law wife with an axe having believed her to have been possessed by the devil.

Tegwyn himself had his cheek stitched – a procedure that made him faint, much to his embarrassment.

In the ensuing days, Tegwyn's life became full of questions – mostly aimed at him from the police, from his family and from the constant stream of visitors to their home.

The policeman who had taken a statement from him had filled in the gaps that Tegwyn had been unaware of and told him what to expect in terms of giving evidence at the inquest and, later on, at a murder trial. Just before leaving, he had asked Tegwyn what he wanted to do when he left school. Before he could answer, his mother had volunteered the information that Tegwyn would take over the farm.

'Shame,' said the policeman 'We can always do with boys like you in the Force'.

Tegwyn also heard that Tony's arm had to be amputated; a fact that surfaced in his mind over the following years, when he wondered if it had been his fault.

Amongst the visitors to his home, was Tony's wife. She brought with her the unexpected gift of a bike – a second hand Raleigh – as a thank-you to him for having saved Tony's life. That also played on his mind in later years.

Having got used to the visitors and having to repeat his story dozens of times, Tegwyn was beginning to enjoy the attention until, at the end of the first week, his mother glanced out of the window and announced, 'I see that Tom has come to see you.'

His alarm was instant. Even more so when he saw that Maggie was with him.

They all sat around drinking tea and eating cake for a while before Alwyn asked Tom to come and see the Charolais bull he had hired.

Tegwyn's mother started to take the tea things away, leaving the two teenagers together.

'Is it true, what they said about those hippies?' Maggie asked 'That they were all naked?'

'No... no-one was naked,' he replied, already feeling flustered.

'Glanmor said he saw them once. Walking around with nothing on except wellingtons,' she added.

Maggie was keen to talk about such matters, but Tegwyn wanted to take the opportunity to ask about more important issues while they had the chance of being alone.

He glanced towards the doorway that his mother had gone through.

He lowered his voice, 'Have you told your father?'

Maggie looked blank.

Tegwyn cast his eyes towards her midriff in a meaningful glance.

'Oh, that!' she said, 'I was only late for four days. It happens sometimes. I had a bit of a fright, though!'

Tegwyn felt as though he was fainting again.

'So it's... all ok?' he double checked.

'Yes, everything's fine,' she answered, 'Were you scared?'

'Yes,' he confessed, 'I thought your father would have killed me!'

'No, not that! At the hippies' place. Were you scared?'

Her total dismissal of the pregnancy issue angered him. He had gone through agonies that she could have dispelled. He stared at her and saw her as a new person – a selfish, immature girl with no scruples. He wondered how he had ever found her desirable.

'No, I wasn't that scared,' he lied, 'even when I saw the woman's head under the car. With all the blood and stuff all over it.'

Maggie blanched and he felt a satisfaction bloom through his body. He wanted to make her suffer the way she had tortured him.

It did the trick and she made a face of revulsion and got up.

Tegwyn's mother came back in.

'You going already?' she asked.

'Yes, if dad's ready,' she said, not even looking at Tegwyn and making her way to the door.

Tegwyn went to visit Tony in hospital, at Tony's request, and was shocked by how weak he looked. He also tried not to look at the obviously bandaged stump where his right arm had been.

'If it hadn't been for you and Roger, I would have died,' he said.

Tegwyn just shrugged. He had heard from Tony's wife about the vision of Roger Clark that had invigorated Tony while he lapsed into unconsciousness on the forecourt.

For the next two years, Tegwyn stayed in touch with Tony and saw him lapse into depression as he failed to resume his former activities of driving and tinkering with cars. He was given a prosthetic arm, but in the 70s, they were hardly more sophisticated than the World War II version. Eventually, Tony and his wife moved away from Llanefa and, apart from a regular Christmas card, Tegwyn lost contact with them for a few years.

The next he heard of Tony was to be a decade later. He had finally given in to his depression and had taken an overdose. His wife had found him dead, in the driver's seat of her car in the garage of their new home. Tegwyn went to the funeral and again asked himself about the tourniquet, though he was careful not to ask anyone else. By then, Tegwyn had a great many experiences of life and playing things close to his chest was his particular strength.

Meanwhile, back in the heatwave of 1976, Tegwyn re-assessed his life while waiting for his 'O' Level results. The stitches in his cheek had resulted in the doctor telling him to stay away from cattle until it was fully healed; advice he was very happy to follow! He wandered down to the milking parlour daily and watched as his sister carried out his milking chores with more capability than he ever had. She had a way with the cattle that calmed them and what she lacked, at fourteen, in strength she gained in her ability to deal with a recalcitrant animal.

Even in backward Llanefa, it was becoming accepted that women were equal to men and Tegwyn admitted to himself that Sian was far more suited to taking over the farm than he was.

The evening before his birthday, and while his father was in a good mood, Tegwyn decided to reveal his decision. He had seen at first-hand how fragile life could be. His life seemed to be an even more precious gift to him and he was determined to use it in a way that was important.

'Dad,' he said 'I've been thinking. I'd quite like to join the Police Force.'

* * *